IN LEADVILLE

TABOR EVANS

A JOVE BOOK

Copyright © 1979 by Jove Publications, Inc.

All rights reserved. No part of this publication may be reproduced or transmitted in any form or by any means, electronic or mechanical, including photocopy, recording, or any information storage and retrieval system, without permission in writing from the publisher.

Requests for permission to make copies of any part of the work should be mailed to: Permissions, Jove Publications, Inc., 200 Madison Avenue, New York, NY 10016

First Jove edition published November 1979

10 9 8 7 6 5 4 3 2 1

Printed in the United States of America

Jove books are published by Jove Publications, Inc., 200 Madison Avenue, New York, NY 10016

"UNBUTTON YOUR VEST, MARSHAL," SHE SMILED . . .

"If you don't mind, ma'am."

"Of course I don't mind. The room is hot. I want you to be comfortable." She pushed the overhanging roll of hair up from her forehead. "I'm a bit warm myself. And I feel gritty from the train ride today. Don't you?"

"Just a little bit," Longarm replied.

"I didn't take time to do more than sponge off when I got home," she said suddenly. "Perhaps we'd both feel better for a nice bubbly bath. Tell me, Marshal Long, would you like to bathe with me . . . ?"

*Also in the LONGARM series
from Jove Books*

LONGARM
LONGARM ON THE BORDER
LONGARM AND THE AVENGING ANGELS
LONGARM AND THE WENDIGO
LONGARM IN THE INDIAN NATION
LONGARM AND THE LOGGERS
LONGARM AND THE HIGHGRADERS
LONGARM AND THE NESTERS
LONGARM AND THE HATCHET MEN
LONGARM AND THE MOLLY MAGUIRES
LONGARM AND THE TEXAS RANGERS
LONGARM IN LINCOLN COUNTY
LONGARM IN THE SAND HILLS

Chapter 1

For the past half-hour, the train had gradually been losing speed as the engine labored up the final grade to Trout Creek Pass. Now it was barely moving, with the pass just ahead. A man could have walked faster without breathing hard. The couplings between cars creaked in protest as the underpowered little engine entered the final, sweeping curve before it made the pass. It seemed to hesitate, trying to find the reserve of power it needed to pull up that last quarter-mile of grade.

When the engine was partway around the curve, Longarm could see it from the window beside his seat in the last passenger coach of the train. Its mushroom smokestack billowed gouts of black smoke that trickled back, shrouding the first cars in the string of empties, gondolas, and freight cars that were ahead of the mail coach, baggage car, and the two passenger coaches. Only the passenger coaches and the mail coach showed any lights; the rest of the cars were dark.

In front of the engine, the narrow-gauge tracks merged under the moonlight into a single shining line up the last steep slope to the pass.

Longarm looked at his watch and thought, *Another ten minutes, then we'll be on the downgrade and making better time. But it's still a long, cold hour's run before we pull into Leadville.* He fished a cheroot out of his inside coat pocket and a match from his trousers. He lighted the match with a practiced flick of a thumbnail across its head, and puffed the cigar into light.

Got to cut down on these damn things, he thought, a resolution that passed through his mind two or three times a day.

Out of habit, Longarm looked around with the first puff of smoke that rose, to be sure there weren't any ladies sitting close enough to him for the smoke to bother them. There weren't, he knew. There were only two women in the coach—one in a seat far to the front, the other at the very back of the car.

His eyes had regained the night vision they'd lost when the match flared in his face, and he glanced idly out the window. At first, he thought the dark figure he saw clambering out of the last gondola car in the string, just ahead of the mail coach, was a brakeman. It was about time for the crew to get on their brake stations, to stand by the brake wheels after the train topped the pass and started downslope into the Arkansas River valley. Just then, the engineer spared enough steam to give the twin whistle blasts that were a signal to the brakeman, and at the same time, a gap appeared and grew between the gondola and mail coach.

Now, why in hell would they be breaking the string at a place like this? he wondered, puzzled. Association and past experience gave him the answer instantly, even before his question had been fully formed.

Reflex action brought Longarm to his feet, catquick. He moved to the front of the coach as the eyes of the other passengers followed him without curiosity. He stopped before he got to the vestibule door, and pitched his voice just loud enough to be heard over the rumbling of the train.

"Now, you folks just keep quiet and stay in your seats, regardless of what you hear outside," he called. "I'm a U. S. marshal, and I think we've got trouble shaping up. Don't worry about it. I'm on my way to handle it. You people stay put."

From the vestibule, Longarm swung himself over the low railing and reached for the grab-bars that were on the side of the coach. He was pulling himself up the bars to the top when he realized that the two passenger cars had been cut from the string and were coasting to a stop. They'd come to a dead halt for a few moments, he knew, then start rolling backward down the steep grade. Atop the car, he paused long enough to twist the brake wheel around and dog it in place before jumping to the car ahead. The two passenger coaches came to a standstill with a rasping of wheel flanges on the rails.

Winter was coming late to the Rockies this year. Denver had yet to see snow, and even at the nine thousand-foot elevation of Trout Creek Pass, the silver-bright September moon showed no more than a few scattered patches. The thinly covered spots of snowy ground threw back the moon's rays in shimmering auras of ghostly white that silhouetted the sparse bushes and lonely pines growing on the sloping sides of the shallow canyon. Between moonlight and snowglare, it was almost as bright as day.

Longarm could see the mail coach and baggage car clearly; they were no more than a score of feet in front of the pair of stopped passenger coaches. The man clambering over the baggage coach, heading for the brake wheel at its rear, wasn't a brakeman. His wide-brimmed felt hat gave him away. Longarm wasted no time in palavering. He swept out his Colt and snapshotted. The man on the coach crumpled and lay still.

A muffled shot sounded from either the baggage car or the mail coach, as though in echo to the blast of Longarm's .44. A second shot followed the first. The two cars in front of the passenger coaches had been moving so slowly their motion couldn't be noticed, if they'd been moving at all. Now, as though the shots had set them into action, they began rolling slowly back down the grade toward the passenger coaches.

Longarm didn't wait. He dropped over the top of the coach to the grab-rail, and dropped from bar to bar until his bootsoles crunched on the gravel roadbed. Keeping in the shadow of the coaches, he ran to meet the slowly moving cars.

Before he got to them, the yellow lamplight streaming from the open side door of the mail coach was blotted out by a man's figure. "Hank!" the man called. "What in hell's wrong with them brakes?"

Longarm answered the question with a shot. The man in the mail coach pitched out and dropped to the ground. His place was taken by still another, and this one came out shooting.

Lead buzzed through the darkness over Longarm's head as a slug lost itself beyond him. A second shot thudded into the thick wood of the passenger coach, and a third shattered the glass in the vestibule door.

By this time, the two coaches that had been cut from the string ahead of the passenger cars were close enough to give Longarm an accurate shot. He could see the arm and shoulder of the man leaning out of the mail coach, and his shot went just where he aimed it. The bandit reeled back, his gun dropping to the ground from his numbed hand as Longarm's slug broke his shoulder.

He'd accounted for three of the train robbers, but Longarm couldn't be sure that there weren't three more inside the mail coach, or on the other side of the train. The slow-rolling mail and baggage cars hit the passenger coaches with a clang and a jar that he could feel through his bootsoles. He hoped the passengers had listened to his instructions and kept their seats; if they hadn't, some of them were likely sprawled on the floor by now.

All of this passed through Longarm's mind while he was running beside the baggage car toward the open door of the mail coach. He reached the lighted opening and looked inside. The last man he'd shot was still in a heap on the floor of the mail coach, with blood dripping from his shoulder. Beyond him, one of the mail clerks was stretched out flat on the rough boards; Longarm couldn't tell whether the man was dead or just unconscious. The second clerk was struggling to his feet.

"U.S. marshal," Longarm called to him. "You all right?"

"Yeah. Just took a whack on the head from that fellow's gun. Guess I was luckier than Frank." The clerk indicated the limp form of the other clerk. "The fellow that jumped out first shot him. Twice. Looks like he's done for."

"How many in the bunch?" Longarm asked.

"Three's all I saw. This one here on the floor, and two more. Might've been another one outside, holding their horses,. Usually is, when a coach is robbed."

"Maybe I better take a look."

Longarm levered himself up into the mail coach, and crossed to the opposite door. It was already open a foot, and he slid it wider to look out. The upslope on that side was shrouded in broken shadows, and he strained his eyes, trying to penetrate their blackness. From a clump of pine trees fifty yards away, a rider, followed by three loose horses, took off with a scraping of ironshod hooves on rocky soil. The distance was too great and the light too bad for any hope of hitting the fleeing bandit. Longarm could do nothing except stand and watch the man get away.

"You were right," he said over his shoulder to the clerk. "There was another one out there with the horses."

"What about the two that went outside?" the man asked. "I was just coming around when I thought I heard shooting out there."

"You did. I got the other two. Ain't had a chance to see if either one of them is still alive."

"Dirty bastards!" the clerk gritted, rubbing his head, where a trickle of blood was running from a cut. "They must've got wind we was carrying a money shipment to the Leadville smelters, for their paydays."

"Wouldn't take much digging to find that out," Longarm commented dryly. "Surprises me there ain't more trains stuck up in places where crooks know there's money moving on schedule."

9

A groan came from the outlaw on the floor. He stirred and tried to sit up. Longarm took out his handcuffs and snapped them around the man's wrists. The wound in his shoulder was still bleeding, but the outlaw was still in shock from the impact of the .44 slug, and hadn't begun to hurt yet.

"You keep an eye on him," Longarm told the clerk after he'd patted the outlaw down to make sure he didn't have a second gun tucked away. "I better go see what's happening outside."

Longarm had to walk upslope a few yards to check on the man who'd fallen out of the coach. He was lying where he'd landed, and when Longarm felt for a pulse, there wasn't any. He turned back to check on the one who'd drawn his first fire, and who'd fallen on top of the coach. The impact of the baggage and mail coaches hitting the passenger cars had dislodged him from the top of the baggage coach. His body was draped limply across the coupling, where it had landed when the rolling cars hit. He was dead, too.

From the top of Trout Creek Pass, the locomotive whistled eerily. Longarm looked up the tracks. The long string of gondolas and freight cars was backing down the tracks. Even at the distance that still separated him from the engine, Longarm could see the heads of the brakeman and fireman, silhouetted against the flare that showed from the firebox now and then. Both of them were looking along the tracks at the four cars that had been cut loose by the bandits.

It would still be a few minutes before the returning train got to the stalled cars, Longarm saw. He swung into the first passenger coach to find the conductor trying to calm the dozen-odd passengers who occupied it. The conductor turned when Longarm came into the car.

"Holdup, wasn't it, Marshal?" he asked Longarm.

"Holdup *try*," Longarm corrected him. "Three of them, and one that was holding the horses. He got away."

The conductor nodded. "I figured that's what was happening. But I knew you were in that other car, and

I decided right quick that the best thing I could do was stay out of your way."

"You turned out to be right. Two of them are dead, the other one's handcuffed in the mail coach."

"What about the clerks?"

"One of them got killed. The other one's all right."

From outside, the engine whistled. The conductor settled his blue uniform cap more firmly on his head.

"Engineer'll be wanting a report from me," he told Longarm. "I better go, Marshal. I'll appreciate it if you'll tell the passengers in the other coach that everything's all right. I've had my hands full in here, no chance to get back there and speak to them."

"I'll take care of it for you," Longarm said. The passengers in the coach were crowding toward the door, streaming past Longarm and the trainman, anxious to get outside and see what had taken place. The conductor shook his head, shrugged, and turned to follow them. Longarm walked through the vestibule to the second coach. There, the half-dozen passengers were still seated, though all of them were craning their necks out through opened windows.

"It's over and done with," Longarm called to them. "Any of you who wants to can go out for a look. Chances are we'll be stopped here a while, till the trainmen get things sorted out."

All of the men, and one of the two woman passengers, started for the vestibule door. Longarm looked at the remaining woman. He'd eyed her off and on since he'd boarded the train at the shabby little Denver, South Park & Pacific depot in Denver, mainly because, of the two female passengers, she was the one most worth watching.

He'd spotted the other woman at once as a Leadville whore going back to work. She had the anxious look that most of the women in that life wore when they were in public, off-duty, and not exercising their charms in an effort to attract trade. Though she didn't have on her professional makeup, her dress as well as her expression gave the whore away. She was overdressed for travel, wearing a satin gown of electric blue and a velvet cape of a slightly darker shade.

In contrast to that woman, the other had the attraction of mystery. She was wrapped in a hip-length sealskin jacket, and wore a toque of the same fur, with a half-veil that came almost to her chin and obscured her features except for a suggestion of full, red lips and an aquiline nose. She had paid no attention to the other passengers waiting on the platform, and had let all of them board first. Then she'd walked with an easy, swinging stride down the aisle to the back of the coach, where she sat down and leaned her head back against the green plush cushion.

And now she remained in her seat. Apparently, she hadn't moved from it since the coach had stopped, and had no interest in going out to join in the excitement that always surrounds a scene of recent violence. Longarm started to say something to her, but, after considering the idea, changed his mind. He looked at her for a moment, trying to guess her age and status. He found that he couldn't, and turned to follow the other passengers out of the car.

He reached the mail coach just as the engine backing down the string of empties ground to a stop. The passengers had formed a little knot around the surviving mail clerk, who was sitting in the open door of the coach, telling the others what had happened.

The clerk saw Longarm and said loudly, "Here's the marshal now. He can tell you a whole lot better than I can what went on. He's the man you got to thank for saving our bacon."

Instantly, the attention of the passengers was diverted to Longarm. Questions flew at him from all directions. He waited, making no answers to any of them, until the spate of words died away in the face of his continued silence.

Then he said, "There's not a whole lot to tell you. From where I was sitting, I could spot what was going on right away. All I did after that was what anybody'd do who'd sworn to uphold the law."

"You sure as hell saved the Leadville banks a pot of cash," the mail clerk said.

"Yes, and maybe saved all of us from being robbed, too," one of the well-tailored men from the passenger coach added.

"Will somebody tell me just what the hell's going on?" the engineer gasped. He was panting, having run from the head of the train.

He saw the conductor, and called out, "Clem, who pulled the damned couplings on these four tail-end cars? I'd like to get my hands on the son of a bitch. We damn near lost this train!"

"Relax, Ed," the conductor said. "The marshal here took care of things. We can pull out for Leadville again just as soon as the boys recouple."

"You mean, just as soon as I get my prisoner fixed up so he won't bleed to death until I can ask him a few questions," Longarm told them, remembering the handcuffed outlaw in the mail coach. "I aim to find out from him who the jasper was that got away."

"Take whatever time you need, Marshal," the conductor said. "We won't be pulling out for a while. We've got the mail clerk's body and the dead outlaws to deal with. We'll put them in the baggage car, where they won't disturb anybody. By the time we get rolling again, we'll be late into Leadville, anyhow. A few minutes more won't make any difference."

"That fellow you shot in the coach is all right," the mail clerk volunteered. "I had a look at him after you left. Took a piece out of the roll towel on the wall, and tied up his shoulder. He won't bleed to death, if that's what's bothering you."

"Thanks," Longarm replied. "If it's all the same to you, though, I'll just ride in the mail coach with you to Leadville, so I can keep my eye on him."

Shaking his head, the clerk said, "Now, Marshal, you know I can't do that, not even if you're a federal lawman. Post office regulations. Unless we've got written authority, nobody except mail clerks rides in that coach, or even gets into it at station stops."

"I'll have to take him in the passenger coach with

me, then. I want to make sure that vinegarroon gets to Denver. I got a hunch this ain't the only train him and his pals have robbed, or tried to. And I want the one that got away."

"Don't worry, I'll guard him," the clerk promised.

"Nothing in your damned rules that says you can't lock him up in that cage where you carry registered mail, is there, Bob?" the conductor asked. "That's tighter'n a lot of jail cells."

Scratching his head, the clerk frowned for a moment, then grinned. "Hell, I'll put a stamp on him, and say the marshal mailed him. Sure, he can go in the cage."

"So you might as well ride the cushions and be comfortable," the conductor told Longarm.

Longarm asked the clerk, "You think your post office rules might bend far enough for me to get in there and help you lock him up? Just so I can set easy, the rest of the trip."

"I guess that wouldn't hurt. All the regulations say is that nobody except us mail clerks and inspectors can ride in the coach, or even come in at a station stop." He looked around at the canyon's moonlit sloping walls. "And this sure ain't a station stop here."

Along the line of empties, the flares of brakemen's torches were moving as the train crew inspected the cars for flat wheels that might have been caused by the emergency stop the engineer had made when he realized his train had been uncoupled. Longarm went into the coach and helped the clerk stow the wounded outlaw into the locked, mesh-enclosed cage used for registered mail. The wounded man made no protest. He was in shock now from the aftereffects of the bullet, speechless and shaking.

"Don't worry now," the mail clerk assured Longarm. "Your man's going to be right here, waiting for you to pick him up, when we pull in at the Leadville station." He indicated the double-barreled shotgun in a rack beside the sorting desk. "And if he starts anything, I've got that to finish an argument with."

Satisfied, Longarm dropped to the ground outside the coach and started walking beside the roadbed to the passenger car. The flares were moving toward the head of the train now. The engineer had returned to his post, and from the intermittent glow now coming from the engine, Longarm judged that the fireman was getting up steam again. He swung aboard the passenger coach and went to his seat. The eyes of the passengers followed him, but none of them spoke. Their shock at having seen the bodies of the mail clerk and the would-be train robbers was almost equal to that of the wounded outlaw.

After a few moments, there was a clanking of couplings as the engineer took up slack, and the train began to creep forward once more. Longarm settled back in his seat and slid a fresh cheroot out of his coat pocket. He frowned as he bit the end off and clamped his strong, even teeth on the cigar. He remembered lighting up just before the robbery began, but couldn't recall smoking the cigar, finishing it, or discarding the butt. He dug a match out of his pants pocket, and was getting ready to flick it into flame when he heard his name called.

"Marshal! Marshal Long!"

It was a woman's voice, and could have come from only one person. Longarm turned. The woman in the veil was leaning forward in her seat, her face turned toward him. She gestured with a white-gloved hand, indicating that she wanted him to join her. Longarm left the match unlighted, and walked the few steps back to her seat.

"I noticed that none of the other passengers bothered to thank you for what you did. I just wanted you to know that at least one of us is grateful to you," she said.

Longarm liked the sound of her voice; it was pitched low, and there was sincerity in its tone. He said, "I didn't do anything that wasn't my regular duty, ma'am. And I don't expect thanks for that."

"Just the same, you probably saved us from being robbed, or even hurt, by those men who tried to hold up the train. It was a very brave thing to do, going out there in the night, and facing three-to-one odds."

"Well, now, I didn't rightly know when I went out that there were three of them," Longarm pointed out.

"Of course you didn't. For all you knew, there might've been four or five, or even more."

"Well, after the bullets started flying, I'll admit that such a thought did pass through my mind. Turns out there were really four of them, only one stayed away from the train, holding their horses for a fast getaway."

"Really? I hadn't heard about that." She noticed that Longarm was holding his cigar and a match, and said, "Light your cigar, if you want to, Marshal Long. The smoke doesn't bother me."

"Thank you," He flicked his thumbnail across the match and puffed the stogie into life. "One thing I'm curious about, ma'am."

"Really? What's that?"

"How you come to know my name. We ain't been introduced somewhere, have we?"

There was a smile in her voice as she told him, "No. I asked the conductor, when he came in with the other passengers. From what he said, you're quite famous."

"If that's so, nobody's ever told me before." Longarm had been growing more and more curious. He'd watched the woman only casually and briefly, at the depot in Denver and on the train later. *She doesn't move like a really young woman would,* he'd thought when she'd boarded and walked down the coach aisle to her seat. *But she doesn't hobble like an old one, either.* Her hands, which might have given him a clue to her age, were hidden by cream-colored kid gloves, and the chill of the autumn air in the depot, and in the unheated coach, had caused her to pull her jacket collar high, hiding her neck and chin.

She said, "I'm being thoughtless, Marshal. And I have an unfair advantage, don't I? I know your name, but you don't know mine. I'm Vivian Montgomery. I live in Leadville. And if you don't mind keeping me company for the rest of the trip, I'd like to hear about some of the things that have happened to you. Things like this holdup tonight. Won't you sit down?"

"Why, I'd enjoy talking with you, Mrs.—Miss—"

"It's Mrs. But I'm a widow. My husband was killed when he tried to keep one of the old gangs of Leadville desperadoes from robbing his smelter, quite a few years ago." As Longarm sat down beside her, she went on, "Perhaps that's why I feel so ashamed that no one even tried to thank you for acting so bravely tonight. If there had been somebody like you in Leadville, upholding the law when the town was so wild, Arthur might still be alive."

"From what I've heard, there wasn't much of any kind of law in Leadville, back then."

"No. There wasn't. But 'back then' hasn't been so very long ago, Marshal. Much less than ten years."

"Oh, I understand that. And even if I wasn't around here then, I've seen enough boom towns to have a pretty good idea just how bad things were, right after the boom began."

"It's not as bad now as it used to be," Mrs. Montgomery said thoughtfully. "But Leadville's still a long way from being tamed. Tell me, Marshal Long, are you going there now because the federal government's going to take a hand in taming it properly?"

"I'm afraid I'll have to disappoint you by saying no, Mrs. Montgomery. If Leadville still needs some more cleaning up, that's a job for Mart Duggan and his men."

"Oh, you're acquainted with Mr. Duggan?"

"We've met up a time or two. Mart Duggan strikes me as the kind of city marshal that can keep a lid on the town, if the folks there really want it clamped down tight."

"Yes," Mrs. Montgomery said thoughtfully. "Yes, I suppose you're right. I sometimes get the feeling that a lot of people in Leadville are secretly proud of the reputation it has for being the wildest, roughest city in Colorado. And I guess it'll be that way until they change their minds."

"It's struck me a lot of times that towns have got to grow up, just like people do." Longarm frowned thoughtfully. "At first, when they're babies, they don't have much aim. Then, when they get older, they get sort of smarty-like, figure it's up to them to show everybody how wild they can be. Then, after a while, they settle down and go about their business the way most grown people have learned to do."

"Well, Leadville still has a lot of growing up to do," she said. "But I didn't mean to keep you so long, Marshal. Really, I spoke to you because I want you to know that someone appreciates the way you handled that outlaw gang."

Longarm knew when he was being dismissed, but he had a nagging hunch that his conversation with Vivian Montgomery wasn't quite finished. He stood up and touched the brim of his hat.

"I'm real grateful for your thanks, ma'am. And Leadville ain't all that big a place. Might be, we'll run into each other again while I'm there."

"Oh, I'm sure we will, Marshal Long," she said.

Longarm wasn't sure, but he thought he could see her lips forming a smile behind her veil.

Chapter 2

Back in his seat, with his hat pushed down over his face and a freshly lit cigar in his mouth, Longarm put Vivian Montgomery out of his mind and slid his six-gun out of its holster. He dug into his coat pocket for fresh shells to replace those he'd fired during the brief gunplay outside the train. He'd have preferred to clean the pistol, but that could wait. Inspecting each cartridge as he inserted it in the cylinder, he replaced the spent loads. Then he holstered the Colt and concentrated on his Leadville assignment. It wasn't one he was looking forward to, and he'd made that plain to Billy Vail when the portly chief marshal had called him into his office earlier that day.

Vail sounded a lot more serious than he usually did when handing Longarm a mission. "It's time you drew a job close to hand, where I can keep an eye on you," he began. "Washington's been on my tail about all the travel vouchers this office has been sending in, and you manage to spend more money than any of my other deputies, when you get away on a case."

"Maybe Washington don't understand how big a territory we've got to cover," Longarm suggested, as he leaned back in the red morocco armchair across the desk from his boss. "Why don't you try sending a map back East, let them pencil-pushers do a little measuring on it?"

"They've got a map," Vail replied curtly. Then, frowning, he asked, "I can't remember whether you've ever drawn an assignment in Leadville."

"Just one, and that was quite a few years back, right before the governor sent the militia in to cool things down during the big strike. I was there for a few days, as I recollect, and didn't do anything except wander around looking, trying to figure out where to start."

"I suppose that's why it slipped my mind," Vail said. "Too many things happened right then for me to keep track of. Well, get ready to go back there. It looks like you'll be staying longer than a day or two, this time."

"Mind telling me a little bit more than that?"

"Just give me time." Vail seemed uncomfortable as he looked across his big, paper-littered desk at Longarm. Finally he said, "You're going to be a bodyguard."

"A nursemaid? Now come on, Billy. You know that ain't a job for a lawman. There's bound to be a better job for me to do than pulling out a handkerchief and telling some rich nabob or politician out of the East when he needs to blow his nose."

Vail smiled. "I don't think you'll need your bandanna where this man's concerned. Judging from his record, he's pretty well able to look out for himself."

"If he's all that good, why does he need a bodyguard?" Longarm demanded.

"Because Washington says he does."

"Then let Washington take care of him. Hell, ain't they got any Pinkertons left, back there? Or has that outfit gone to hell in a handbasket, now that old Alan's putting in all his time writing books, bragging about how good he used to be?"

"All the men Pinkerton's can spare are out of the country right now. They had to send a special force with President Arthur while he's abroad. After what happened to Garfield, everybody back there's skittish as hogs on ice."

"What they need is some kind of special force to

look after the president, then. Not that it's a job I'd envy anybody," Longarm added.

"Or me," Vail agreed. "But it's a job somebody's got to do, and in this case, that somebody happens to be you."

"I guess there's no way I can talk you around, is there?"

"No. I've decided you're the best man to take on this particular job, and that settles it."

"All right." Longarm made no effort to hide his distaste for the assignment. "Who's the high muckety-muck I'm going to nursemaid? Some two-bit senator nobody's ever heard of, except in the state where he got elected?"

"No. I think you'll have heard of this man."

"Well, quit beating around the bush, Billy, and tell me who it is."

Vail leaned forward cospiratorially, and gazed intently at his deputy from under his thick, black eyebrows.

"Ulysses S. Grant."

For a moment, Longarm stared at his chief. "You mean the *real* U. S. Grant? *President* Grant? Or *General* Grant, if you go back a ways further?"

"That's the man."

"You're joshing me, Billy. Come on, now. Who's the real Eastern dude I'm supposed to nursemaid?"

"U. S. Grant," Vail repeated.

"I think you really mean that," Longarm said. He sounded only half-convinced, though.

"I *do* mean it," Vail assured him.

"Why in hell does Grant need me to bodyguard him? There's nobody out gunning for a man like him. Hell, the War's been over for damn near twenty years."

"That's right. But there are men who'll nurse a grudge for *fifty* years. And there's a lot more to it than that." Vail pawed through the piles of paperwork on his desk and came up with a lengthy letter, its pages pinned together. He flipped through it. "Here it is."

He read: "Our informant is of the opinion that the alleged plot is political in nature, though it may also have a connection with the recurring move to demonetize silver—"

"Wait a minute," Longarm interrupted. "What's that twelve-dollar word mean?"

"It means to get back on the gold standard. It was Grant who signed the Mint Bill when he was president, back in '73. Of course, he about-faced a few years later, and signed another bill to make silver money legal again, but people forget about things like that."

"Now, that's really pulling a long bow, Billy. Grant's not the president any more. How in hell could he pull any weight on a deal like putting silver money out of circulation?"

"You ever stop to think he might get elected president again?"

Longarm shrugged. "How could he? He's served two terms."

"Sure. But there's no law that keeps him from running again, and maybe getting elected."

"Funny, I always thought there was."

"No such thing. George Washington started that only-two-terms business, way back when. But there's nothing legal or binding about it. And if you recall, which maybe you don't, Grant damn near got nominated in '80 for a third term."

"I guess I disremembered that. I never was much of a hand for politics, anyhow."

Vail grinned. "Maybe it's just as well. Anyhow, this letter I got in the late mail yesterday is direct form headquarters, and if there's enough stir back in Washington to get them as upset as they are, I've got to do what they say."

"All right. I'll quit arguing. But where does Leadville come into all this?"

"It comes in because that's where Grant's going to stay—at Haw Tabor's house there."

"I thought Silver Dollar was in the Senate, back in Washington, now?"

"He was. For a month. He's not any longer. He's bringing Grant back with him, and the new Mrs. Tabor, the one they call Baby Doe. They'll be traveling on

Tabor's private railroad car, and that means they'll have to switch to Tabor's narrow-gauge car here in Denver. That's where you join up with the party."

"Jesus! Does that mean I'm going to have to get me a stiff shirt and a fancy necktie?"

Vail looked at Longarm, who was wearing his regular city working clothes: a brown tweed suit and vest, a gray flannel shirt with the black string tie that Vails's own regulations prescribed, and stovepipe cavalry boots. He smiled and said, "No. I think you'll be all right wearing just what you've got on. If you had to fight a stiff collar and a four-in-hand, I don't think you'd ever finish getting dressed of a morning, and it takes you long enough to get in here as it is."

Longarm sighed with relief. "Can't say I'd disagree with that, Billy. Well, that helps a little bit, not having to put on some kind of monkey suit. When does this job start?"

Vail leafed through the pages of the letter he still held until he found the paragraph he was looking for. "Let's see, this is Tuesday. Tabor's car is due in Denver Saturday evening. They'll leave for Leadville Sunday morning, so I guess that's when you'll start out. And they'll be in Leadville maybe a week, maybe two. But however long they're here, your job is to stick with Grant every minute, and keep anybody from getting to him. Because if anything happens to him while we're responsible, it'll be my ass, and yours too. You remember that!"

"I ain't likely to forget, after you've made it so clear." Longarm rubbed his chin thoughtfully. "I don't say I'm going to enjoy the job, Billy, but I'll do the best I can. One thing pops into my mind, though."

"What's that?"

"Seeing as it's been a while since I was in Leadville, I'd sort of like to go up there for a day or two and sniff things out a little bit. If there's somebody gunning for Grant, that's the place they're likeliest to make their play."

Vail nodded slowly. "I think that's a good idea. I'll tell my clerk to fix up travel vouchers and expense money. Go on up and stay two or three days, just as long as you're back here to check in with me for anything new that might come in before Tabor gets here with Grant in tow."

During the first stage of his trip to Leadville, while the little DSP&P narrow-gauge was chugging along the South Platte valley, and picking its winding way through the foothills of the South Front Range of the Rockies toward Kenosha Pass, Longarm put a lot of thought to what Vail had said about the reasons for Grant being the target of an assassination plot. The more he thought about it, the more sense it came to make to him. The gunfight with the would-be train robbers drove his assignment out of his mind until all the action had ended.

Now, leaning back against the acrid-smelling plush of his seat, his hatbrim shading his eyes from the glaring carbide lamp that fizzed and sputtered in the ceiling of the passenger coach, he started thinking again.

How in hell can I bodyguard Grant if I don't know what to look for? Vail's letter from Washington said the plot was political, maybe, to keep him from getting to be president again. But then it said money might be at the bottom of it. And on top of that, there's all those old die-hard Southern veterans carrying grudges because the North won the war, and Grant was the chief general. Looks to me like you'll be guarding him from just about everybody, old son. And that won't be easy to do.

Leadville, now. It's silver-mining country, and the silver people figure Grant's against them. Hell's bells, that'd take in everybody that staked a claim and struck a lode, everybody that's got a mine working today, and all the smelter operators, too. And that means just about everybody in Leadville. And politicians. Why, Silver Dollar Tabor himself is up to his bellybutton in politics, and so are most of his friends. Friends are going to be coming here to visit Silver Dollar and Baby Doe, just married, just home from Washington. Why in thunder did Billy Vail pick me out for this damn job?

Well, shit on it. No use borrowing trouble before the job even starts. It's just a job, like any other job. Just eat the apple one bite at a time.

Grinning inwardly, Longarm told himself, *Or, if what I hear about Grant is the truth, don't try to drink the whole bottle in one swallow; just put it away one drink at a time.*

His thinking hadn't eased Longarm's mind, but his final resolution did. He sat up straighter and looked over his shoulder. Vivian Montgomery was gazing out the car window; she might have been alone in the coach for all the attention she was paying to him or any of the other passengers.

It's that damned veil, he thought. *A man keeps wondering what she'd look like with it off, just like he keeps wondering what a woman's going to look like without her clothes on. Forget it, old son, she was just being polite. At least, I guess she was. Anyhow, she ain't got a thing every other woman don't have.*

Though his thinking about the mysterious widow didn't ease Longarm's mind any more than had his analysis of his assignment to guard Grant, just the act of reaching a conclusion about her gave him a feeling of relief. Clearing his mind relaxed him, and he even managed to doze for a few minutes while the train swayed and creaked through the Arkansas River valley, the engineer taking advantage of the level grade and better trackage to put on speed and make up the time lost during the aborted holdup.

Just outside Leadville, where the DSP&P's own tracks connected with the Denver & Rio Grande steel on which the train had been running, the switching stop roused the passengers. They began to fidget nervously; there was much gazing out of windows at the orange glow of the smelter fires that dotted the slopes on either side of the track and extended far ahead. Against the suddenly red night sky, the squared edges of the town's buildings were silhouetted by the furnaces that roared day and night on Carbonate Hill and Iron Hill. When the conductor came through shortly after the switching stop and announced the Leadville station, all except two of the half-dozen passengers jostled into a close knot at the vestibule door and stood waiting for the train to halt.

Longarm and Vivian Montgomery were the exceptions. They kept to their seats and waited calmly for the train to stop. Longarm was in no hurry. He wanted the passengers, small as their numbers were, to get away from the train and out of the depot before he went forward to the mail coach and picked up his prisoner. He glanced over his shoulder at the veiled widow. She was still gazing out the window. Rising, Longarm walked back to her seat.

"I thought maybe you'd dropped off to sleep and didn't hear the conductor when he said we were pulling into Leadville," he explained when she turned her head in his direction. "Didn't want you to miss your stop."

"I think I could get off here in my sleep, and find my way home without any trouble," she said, making no effort to stand up. "There's not much reason for me to be in a hurry. The train's not going anywhere from here, at least not for several hours. These cars will just sit here in the station yard while the engine runs around picking up the loads of ore and amalgamate to haul to Denver."

"I guess you've made the trip a lot, haven't you?"

"More times than I like to think of, Marshal. It's a great deal easier now than it was before the railroads came in. Then, the easiest way to Denver was the wagon road over Mosquito Pass. Instead of a half-day, it took two days in good weather, three when the weather was very bad."

Longarm did a little quick figuring. There hadn't been any Leadville before '78, he'd heard, so Mrs. Montgomery must've been among its very early residents.

She seemed to sense what he was thinking, for she went on, "My late husband built one of the first smelters here, you see. When he died, I took over the business. It's not a big one, like those at the Iron Silver, or the Robert E. Lee, or the other large operations. My smelter handles the ore from a lot of small mines instead of one or two big ones. But it provides a comfortable income."

"That's why you have to go to Denver now and then," Longarm concluded. "Funny, I didn't figure you for a businesswoman."

"I didn't plan to be one, Marshal. It's just one of those things that happen."

"Sure. I can see that. Does you credit, though, having the grit to take over after your man died, and run the business."

"Some of the men in Leadville don't think so. They started trying to buy me out the minute I let it be known I was going to run the smelting operation. And they're still trying."

"All you got to do is keep on saying no," he pointed out.

"Oh, I've learned that. I don't really want to be a businesswoman, but it's the only thing I can see to do. Goodness knows, I don't want to be Leadville's Hetty Green."

"Ma'am?"

Mrs. Montgomery saw that he didn't understand. "Hetty Green's a woman in New York," she explained. "She took over her family's business interests when her father died, and now she's supposed to be making a fortune dealing on the stock exchange as well. Some say she's the richest woman in America."

"I see. Well, I still say I admire your backbone for doing what you think is right."

For the past several moments, the train had steadily been losing speed. Now it came to a dead stop with a muted grinding of brake shoes on steel wheels.

"It seems we've arrived," Mrs. Montgomery said. She hesitated before adding, "I wish I weren't just getting home from this trip, Marshal. I know there won't be anything in my pantry because my cook isn't expecting me. I didn't know exactly when I'd get back. If it weren't for that, I'd invite you to have a late supper with me."

"Well now, that's a real nice thought. But I've got a better one. Why don't you have supper with me, if there's anyplace fit to eat at in Leadville."

"There are several—the Tontine, the Clarendon. And Silver Dollar Tabor's just hired a new French chef for his Grant Hotel. But I wasn't hinting for an invitation, Marshal Long."

"I didn't suspicion so. To tell you the truth, I wasn't much concerned about eating supper till you mentioned it, or I'd've asked you earlier."

"Oh, of course!" she exclaimed. "How could I have forgotten! You have a prisoner in the mail coach, haven't you? You're going to have to look after him."

"Don't let that concern you, ma'am. It won't take me but a minute to haul that owlhoot over to the jail and hand him to Mart Duggan to lock up till I get ready to go back to Denver. That's just what I'd do, even if we weren't going to supper. It won't hold us up but a little while, if you don't mind waiting."

"Of course I don't. But perhaps the best thing would be for me to go home and freshen up. I always feel so gritty with coal cinders after a train ride that I'll enjoy our dinner more if I've taken time to get the dust off my face and hands."

"That'll suit me just fine. But you'd better tell me how to find your house."

"You won't have any trouble at all, Marshal. I live on Carbonate Avenue—that's just a short walk from the depot here. There aren't any numbers on the houses, but mine is a small frame house at the end of the street nearest the business section. It's between two much larger houses—I guess you'd have to call them mansions."

"I'll find you without any trouble a-tall," Longarm assured her. He looked around. The other passengers had left the coach as soon as the train had stopped at the depot. "Well, then, I'll just hand you off the car, and then, in about a half-hour, I'll be knocking at your door."

"I was getting to be afraid I was stuck with this yahoo,"

the mail clerk said to Longarm when he opened the vestibule door of the mail coach. "I thought maybe you'd forgotten he was here."

"Sorry if I held you up," Longarm told the man.

"No harm done, except I looked for you sooner," the clerk said. "It's all right for you to come in, if you want to. The postmaster himself showed up tonight; he usually does, when we run as late as this. I got his permission to let you come in and take your prisoner off my hands."

"This is the end of the line for you, anyhow, ain't it?" Longarm asked, stepping into the coach. The outlaw, he saw, was still locked up in the registered mail cage. He was sitting hunched up in one corner, on the floor, staring sullenly at nothing. He didn't turn his head when Longarm came in.

"Not the end, no," the clerk said. "There's a little bit of mail left, for Climax and Breckenridge and Dillon, that's got to be dropped off when we make the other half of the loop back to Denver. And there'll be the outgoing mail from Leadville, but it won't be brought out until a few minutes beofre the train pulls out, after the crew puts together the Denver-bound freight."

"I had a reason for waiting until the depot was pretty well cleared out," Longarm explained. "If you remember, there was one of the gang got away, the one that was minding their horses. For all I know, he might've cut cross-country and beat us to town here."

"I guess he could've made it in ahead of us, all right," the clerk said thoughtfully. "But I don't see what that's got to do with you wanting the depot clear."

"Simple as ABC. If there's a crowd around when I take this one out, his friend will have cover to jump me from. If I wait till the depot's empty, I can spot him right off. Of course," Longarm went on thoughtfully, "that don't mean he might not decide to wait out in the street. But I figure he'd want to see his partner come out of the car here, because he wouldn't know what kind of odds he was facing if he wasn't watching."

"I guess there's tricks to every trade," the clerk commented. "Me, I wouldn't have thought about all that. Come to think of it, I'm glad I don't have to."

"Well, since you've got other things to do, I'll relieve you of this fellow right now."

Longarm waited while the clerk unlocked the steel-mesh enclosure and went inside. The outlaw still ignored him. Longarm nudged the man with his boot toe.

"All right. On your feet. We're going to take a little walk down the street to the jail. You'll stay there a few days, till I can take you to Denver to stand trial."

"I ain't moving till I get this bullet hole you put in me bandaged up. I try to stir around now, it's going to open up and start bleeding again," the prisoner said defiantly.

"That bandage it's got on it now will hold till the jail doctor can change it," Longarm replied. "It won't hurt you one damn bit to walk the little ways to the jail. Now, move!"

"If you want me to move, you'll have to pick me up and carry me," the man retorted.

"I don't think I'll have to do that," Longarm said, his voice deceptively mild. He reached down and grabbed the chain connecting the handcuffs he'd put on the man earlier, and pulled up. The steel cuffs bit into the outlaw's wrists. To save his wrists, he was forced to lift his arms, and when the motion brought the muscles in his wounded shoulder taut, he let out a sharp yelp of pain.

"All right, all right! That's plenty!" he cried. "Just give me a chance, I'll get up and walk!"

"I sort of figured you would, if I persuaded you a little bit," Longarm said. There was no emotion in his voice. He felt neither hatred nor pity for the man, just the same dislike that all criminals inspired in him.

Making a great show of pain by moving slowly and haltingly, grimacing with every move he made, the outlaw slowly got to his feet. Longarm helped him by keeping the pressure on the handcuffs. When the man was standing, Longarm unlocked the cuff from one wrist and quickly whirled the prisoner around. He grabbed the freed arm, pulled it down and back, and re-locked the handcuffs. Now the outlaw's hands were behind his back.

"I guess you and me better have a little understanding right now," Longarm told him. "You're going to walk alongside of me, when we get out to the street. I'm going to be on the outside, and you're going to be on the inside. I won't be walking too fast, so you just keep even with me. If you break and try to run, don't look for me to play the fool and chase you. I don't run after my prisoners, I shoot 'em. You understand that, now?"

For a moment, the outlaw's eyes locked with Longarm's then the prisoner dropped his head. "Yeah," he replied sullenly. "I understand you. And you're the kind of bastard that'd shoot an unarmed man in the back, so I don't guess I'll give you a chance to take me out."

"Good." Longarm turned to the clerk. "Thanks again for keeping this fellow for me. Maybe we'll run into one another again."

"Maybe we will," the clerk agreed. "And if we do, I sure hope I'm on the same side of the law you are."

Longarm allowed himself a twitch of the lips that could have passed for a smile. He poked the outlaw in the back with a thumb and said, "All right. Let's get moving."

Reluctantly, the outlaw started for the door. Longarm walked behind him through the vestibule, and kept a hand lightly placed on the man's sore arm, as a reminder that any effort to run would bring instant pain. They passed through the vestibule and stepped down from the car to the station platform, then he fell into step with the prisoner, keeping abreast of him, through the depot, and out onto Elm Street.

Leadville had been younger, with fewer mines and smelters, when Longarm had been there before. He wasn't quite prepared for the spectacle he saw when he and his prisoner stepped out of the DSP&P station. On all sides, the sky glowed with a bright nimbus of orange-yellow glare from the smelters that ran around the clock. The glow was brightest from the hills that rose in low humps on the town's northeastern outskirts, but no matter in which direction Longarm looked, the sky was as bright as though the sun were about to rise from all directions at the same time.

Periodically, in a haphazard pattern, an even more dazzling glare would burst out from one or another of the tall, round stacks on the hills whose tops were visible above the geometrical, jagged rooflines of the houses and buildings. One or another of the stacks would erupt in a sudden flash of brilliant yellow, dotted with even more brilliant bursts, like miniature stars. Then, as quickly as it had erupted, the brightness would fade to the stack's more usual orange-tinged hue.

There was no need for street lights in Leadville. The smelters' glow pervaded everywhere, and though the depot clock had indicated that it was almost ten, the houses and buildings that he passed were brightly lit from the sky's glow.

Longarm had remembered the town as a hodgepodge of raw wood buildings and crudely scrawled hand-painted signs. Paint now covered the raw lumber, though the fronts of most of the stores bore rain-streaks in the thick film of fine ash that sifted constantly from the sky and settled down on everything. A faint smell of sulfur hung in the air.

Even at this hour, the street was busy, and when they turned into Pine Street, Longarm got a quick glimpse of the main businesss section a block or two away. He could see that those streets were busier still. Most of the men—there were no women that he could see—who were on the street wore sweat-grimed overalls. They were obviously miners or smelter-workers on their way to or from work. They paid little attention to the handcuffed prisoner; apparently someone being led to the jail was a common occurrence in the neighborhood.

In spite of the years that had passed since Longarm's first and only visit to the town, his retentive mind still held a reasonably accurate picture of its street layout. He marched the handcuffed outlaw along Pine Street until they reached the city hall, which included the marshal's office as well as the city jail. The man had not spoken since his brief flare of rebellion on the train; he walked beside Longarm without protest and without lagging.

Longarm was reasonably sure he'd find Mart Duggan in his office at the jail. He'd met Duggan for the first time on his previous visit to Leadville, and in the years that had passed since then, had seen the city marshal several times when Duggan had visited the federal marshal's offices in Denver on one sort of business or another. Duggan, he recalled, was a night-owl lawman—the kind who preferred to be on active duty during the hours between ten at night and dawn, when crime activity is at its peak—rather than an administration-minded official who enjoys doing paperwork at a desk from nine to five during the day.

Leadville's jail was housed in one of the first brick buildings that had been built when the silver boom took off in '72, and Duggan was in his small, airless office just inside the building's front door. The city marshal looked up when the outer door opened with a creaking of long-unoiled hinges, and when he saw Longarm, his face split in a wide Irish grin, causing his sandy moustache to bristle.

"Well, I'll be damned! Look who's come to give himself up! Longarm, I'm glad to see you. You finally got around to taking up my invitation to come visit me," he said, rising and shoving out a hand that was twice as large as life, and a lot beefier.

Longarm smiled back. "Don't get such ideas about me giving myself up. If you want me in your lockup, you'll have to hogtie me and put me there yourself."

"And don't think I can't do it!" Duggan said, tapping Longarm lightly on the shoulder. Though Duggan was shorter than Longarm, he had shoulders like a bull, and his friendly tap sent Longarm back a step and caused him to bump into the outlaw. "Well, by God! If it ain't Blackie Spencer! I'd rather have him in a cell than you, any day! Where'd you nab him?"

"Just the other side of Trout Creek Pass. Which makes him my prisoner, instead of yours. But I might hand him over, if you've got a charge worse than murder to hold him on."

Duggan shook his head. "No. The worst I can hold him for is robbery. Himself and some of his friends held up the Tam O'Shanter mine's payroll messenger about a month ago. A right clever job, too, I'll have to admit. Two of them made a mock try just outside town, and while the men from the Miners' Guard were chasing after them, the other two jumped on the messenger and grabbed his boodle-bag. But the messenger recognized Blackie here, and the other one, a bad bucko named Riley."

"There were four of them on that job, then?"

Duggan nodded, and Longarm said, "There were four in the bunch that tried to rob the train."

"Likely the same crew," Dugan said. "Too bad you didn't get the other three. They've been busy all around here, not just in Leadville."

"I imagine you'll find two of them in the morgue or the undertaking parlor, or wherever unidentified bodies get taken here."

"Is that right, now? I'll drop in later and see if I know their names. You said there was four. You're not slowing up, are you Longarm, to let one get away from you?"

"It was night, and I didn't have my Winchester. Too much range for the Colt. The one that got away was holding the horses."

"Well, three out of four's a respectable score," Duggan said consolingly. "Especially since I see you left a little mark on Blackie." He indicated the prisoner's shoulder. "What were they trying for? The DSP&P train?"

"Mail coach in particular."

"To be sure, the payrolls. And they'd have made it, too, if yourself hadn't happened to be on hand." Duggan sighed. "Too bad I wasn't there, too. Leadville's gone tame, Longarm. There's not enough to keep me and my men busy these days. I haven't had to knock sense into anybody's head for these past two weeks."

"Things looked lively to me, on the streets, while we were coming from the station."

"Ah, but looks deceive, laddie. Well, I suppose you'll be wanting me to keep Blackie safe for you until you take him back to Denver?"

"I'd appreciate it, Mart. And have your jail doctor fix up his shoulder a little bit, if that's not too much trouble."

"No trouble at all. I told you, it's not like it used to be. We've more empty cells than we know what to do with, these days." He stepped to the door and called, "Flood! Come get a prisoner!"

They waited until the jailer came up the hall, then Longarm took his handcuffs off Spencer.

Duggan said, "You won't object, now, if I have a little talk with this one later on? He might have some information I'd be interested in."

"Long as you're keeping him, it's my treat if you can get anything out of him." Longarm took out his watch and glanced at it. "Mart, I've got to hurry away, but I'll be back to chew the fat with you later tonight."

"About the case you're here on?"

"Something like that."

"And you've got to rush off now, without even having a quick drink with me, because you've got a lady waiting for you? Something like that, isn't it, me lad?"

"You hit the bullseye," Longarm confessed. "But I'll drop in later. If I know you, Mart, you'll be here the rest of the night."

"Here or somewhere along State Street. Just ask around."

"Oh, I won't have any trouble finding you, and I'll take that drink when I find you, too."

Longarm went back out into the fire-shot night. The air was much cooler now, so he buttoned his coat while walking briskly from Pine Street to Harrison. He noticed that most of the stores were still open. He crossed State Street, with its casinos, dance halls and saloons. The chill night air had dried his throat, and the lights behind the saloons' batwings invited him to stop for a long-overdue shot of Maryland rye, but he shook his head. He'd spent more time chinning with Duggan than he'd allowed for, and the hour wasn't getting any earlier.

Lights glowing red in front of the dark houses on Main Street held no lure for Longarm. He went on up the gentle slope to Carbonate Avenue. There was still enough light to see the entire length of the short avenue, and he had no trouble identifying Vivian Montgomery's house from the description she'd given him. What she'd called a modest house, though, looked to him as spacious and elaborate, as bedecked with scrolled woodwork, and having as many stained glass windowpanes as did the taller three-story dwellings on each side, which she'd referred to as mansions.

An aura of perfume greeted him when Mrs. Montgomery opened the door to his knock.

"Do come in, Marshal Long. My wrap's right here in the hall, so we can go at once."

"Hope I didn't keep you waiting too long, Mrs. Montgomery," he apologized. "I got tied up at the jail when I went to drop off that outlaw."

"Oh, I wasn't worried, Marshal. I knew you had business that had to be taken care of."

Longarm stepped inside the wide door with its etched, frosted glass panel. The entry hall was covered with a Brussels rug that extended to within a few inches of the painted baseboards; either the hall had been built to fit the rug, or the rug had been woven to fit the hall. A long, narrow table with a gilt-framed pier glass on the plastered wall above it occupied one side of the hall, and an upholstered mahogany bench stretched along the opposite wall.

"I will confess, though, I'm getting very hungry," Mrs. Montgomery said, picking up the white velvet wrap that was lying on the bench, and holding it out to Longarm. She turned as he lifted the coat to drape it over her shoulders, releasing an even headier puff of her perfume as she lifted her hands to settle the wrap in place.

"I'm about ready to wrap myself around a good meal, too," he said.

Longarm was having trouble keeping himself from staring openly at his dinner companion. She had an ageless face, one that might have belonged to a woman anywhere from twenty-five to fifty, though Longarm placed her age as being in the middle or late thirties.

And old enough and smart enough to know what she wants to do, and got enough spunk to go and do it, and be damned to what anybody else says or thinks, he told himself, studying her face.

Tiny lines, almost invisible in the soft, glowing light that was cast by an amber-shaded ceiling lamp, puckered faintly at the corners of her light gray eyes. The lines were so small that Longarm had to look twice to be sure he was seeing them. Except for a deep circular scar, the diameter of a fingertip, that dimpled the flesh above the inner end of one eyebrow, her complexion was flawless. There were no lines running from her aquiline nose to the corners of her full lips, nor were there any lines visible in the smooth forehead, half-veiled by a puff of dark blonde hair that shaded it. Her lips were generous, the lower extending just far enough beyond the upper to give her the permanent expression of an amused pout. Her chin was long but firm, and the flesh of her neck, above the high collar of her dress, was taut, white, and free from wrinkles.

She'd changed from the clothing she wore on the train. Now she had on a dress of watered silk, cream-colored, with an undertone of light gold that showed in the light when she moved. The lines of the dress were severe; had Longarm been clothes-conscious, he might have identified it as being from Worth. Its only ornament was a large garnet brooch, surrounded by small diamonds, in the front of the neckband. The long sleeves, ending in rows of small buttons that began in midforearm and ran down to the tight wrists, hid her arms, but her hands were smooth and white, though large for a woman.

Looking at Longarm over her shoulder, she asked, "Shall we go? It's just a short walk to Harrison Street. We'll have our choice of the best restaurants there, and we can decide which one we'll choose while we're walking."

Longarm had laid his Stetson on the table while he helped her with her wrap. Now he picked it up and set it in place. "You'd know better than I do about the eating places here in Leadville. Which one do you favor?"

"Sometimes one, sometimes another," she replied. A moment later, after they'd covered the few steps from the porch to the brick sidewalk and were strolling away from Carbonate Avenue, she went on, "I like several of the restaurants about equally well. The new chef at Tabor's Grand Hotel is a Frenchman, if you enjoy that kind of cooking. The Tontine has a lot of French dishes on the menu, too. The Windsor has excellent roast beef, and the Clarendon has made its reputation with its steaks. What kind of food do you enjoy most, Marshal?"

"Well, I got to admit I'm pretty much a meat-and-potatoes man, myself," he confessed. "Oh, sure, there's times when I like a fancy made-up dish, but mostly, I like to see what I'm eating just laid out in front of me without too many fancy fixings."

"I had a feeling you might say that. I suppose our best choice would be the Windsor or the Clarendon, then." She tucked her hand in Longarm's elbow as they reached the corner and turned to cross Harrison Street. "The Windsor's closer and a bit quieter. The Clarendon's food is equally good, but the bar there is right next to the dining salon, and it gets a bit noisy at times. You see, the mine and smelter owners have made the Clarendon bar their unofficial club, and there's seldom a night when there won't be some heated arguments going on in the bar."

"If that Windsor place has got a saloon where I can get them to bring a bottle of good Maryland rye to the table, then let's go there," Longarm said. The idea of a drink was getting more appealing to him by the minute. "And if that other place is as noisy as you say, I reckon I've had about all the disturbance I crave today."

"I'm sure you have. For that matter, so have I, with all the excitement and shooting on the train."

"Funny, ma'am. When I got back to the car we were in after everything had quietened down, you looked just like you hadn't been out of your seat."

"Well, I'll have to confess I hadn't, Marshal. You see, I spent—" she stopped short. After the briefest pause, she added, "I've spent enough time letting myself get upset by things that are happening around me. I've just made up my mind not to pay any attention anymore. But that's all past, isn't it?"

"It is for right now. Even if all of Leadville was to blow up this minute, it still wouldn't stop me from having my supper. You must be getting a mite hungry, too, after I kept you waiting for such a long time."

"I'll admit I have an appetite. I think I'll join you in asking for just plain steak and potatoes."

Longarm had expected a hurried, badly cooked boom-town meal in a restaurant that showed signs of having been hastily thrown together; that was the way he remembered Leadville. He was taken by surprise. The Windsor Hotel's dining room was as well-appointed and hushed, the tablecloths and napkins as snowy white, and the service as quietly assured as their counterparts in the finest restaurants of Denver. The Maryland rye that he sipped from a squat tumbler, while Mrs. Montgomery enjoyed a glass of Amontillado, was as good as that served in the larger and more elaborate Windsor Hotel in Denver. The steaks, surrounded by oven-browned potatoes, were as tender and juicy as any he'd ever enjoyed at the other Windsor.

"Things are a lot different here in Leadville than they were when I was here before," he commented when he and his dinner companion had taken the first edge off their appetites.

They said little after the steaks arrived. Both of them seemed to realize at the same time how hungry they really were. Longarm approved of the way Mrs. Montgomery ate, with a fierce daintiness that showed how much she was enjoying her dinner. He wondered, watching her covertly, if she did everything with the same ladylike gusto.

"How long ago was that, Marshal?" she asked, after taking time to swallow the bite of steak she'd been chewing.

"Oh, back in '78, just before the governor sent in the militia to tame the town down during the big miners' strike."

"Well, Leadville's grown up fast." She paused and shook her head. "I hope it's not like some of the other mining towns in the state that have grown up fast and died even faster than they grew."

"Sounds to me like you've seen that happen, someplace else."

"Just about anybody who's been in Colorado very long has seen that," she replied with a sad smile. She sipped from her wineglass. "I was still in my teens when I came to Colorado, Marshal. It wasn't even officially a territory when I got here."

Longarm did some quick mental figuring. History wasn't his long suit, but as best he could recall, Colorado had been proclaimed a territory in '60 or '61. Vivian Montgomery was a mite older than he'd figured she was, then. She'd be straddling the forty-year mark, give a year or so either way.

"Well, Leadville sure looks healthy to me right now," he said, "and in a lot better shape than it was when I saw it the first time."

"It's certainly a lot easier to live here, from what I've heard of the way things were at first. Though I'm sure it'll never win any contest for being a beautiful town."

"You know, Mrs. Montgomery, I always figured if I had a choice of being ugly or rich, I'd take being rich."

She laughed. "A lot of people would agree with you, I'm sure."

They'd finished their meal by now, and the waiter came to clear the table. Longarm lighted an after-dinner cheroot and reached for the whiskey bottle that had been left sitting at one side of the table while they ate. She put out a hand to stop him.

"If you'd like another drink, we can have it here, but I have some old Maryland rye at home that you might like even better than this," she suggested.

"Now, that's right kind of you to offer, and I'm ready to take you up on it, if you're sure it won't be trouble to you, or keep you up too late."

"You don't know me well yet, Marshal. I don't make offers that I don't want to, or offer to do anything that's an inconvenience to me. I suppose you'd call me selfish in that respect."

"If that's the way of it, then we might as well go."

That was a hell of an expensive dinner, Longarm thought as he settled the check; two dollars apiece for the steaks, and another two for the bottle of claret they'd shared, and a quarter apiece for their drinks. With a tip for the waiter, the whole bill came to nearly ten dollars. But it was the best steak he'd had in a while, and he'd seen a look it was impossible to mistake growing in Mrs. Montgomery's eyes as the meal progressed, so he figured it was worth it. Besides, his expense account could be stretched to cover most of it.

They walked side by side in silence for the first block after leaving the hotel. The streets weren't as busy as they'd been earlier, but behind them, the fires from the smelters on Carbonate Hill and Iron Hill to the northeast, and on the slopes south of town, were still as bright, and the night seemed like a day when the sunshine was veiled by clouds.

"It was a very enjoyable dinner, Marshal Long," Mrs. Montgomery said, after they'd walked wordlessly almost to the beginning of Carbonate Avenue. "I'm grateful to you for rescuing me from my empty house. I looked in the pantry when I first got there, and it was just as I'd thought. The cook hadn't laid in anything for me. She didn't know when I was coming back."

"It was my pleasure to have your company, ma'am," Longarm replied. "I eat by myself most of the time, and it's a treat for me to have a meal with a pretty lady like you."

"I suppose all of us are lonely in one way or another,

aren't we?" she mused aloud. "I'd imagine your job is a lonesome one."

"There are times when it is. Mostly, though, it don't bother me too much."

"And the rest of it? Like the gunfight with the train robbers? Does that bother you?"

"No. Lawbreakers and killers have got to have somebody riding herd on them, and whoever takes on that job has got to be ready to do whatever he's called on to do to keep them in line."

She nodded. "It's a good way to look at it." They'd reached her house now. She took a key from the slit pocket inside her wrap and unlocked the door.

"You'd better let me go ahead of you into the parlor, Marshal. I'll have to light the lamps, or you'll bark your shins on the furniture."

Longarm dropped his hat on the hall table and waited until light glowed from the door of the room adjoining it. He went in. After lighting a single lamp, Mrs. Montgomery had gone to a tall walnut cabinet that stood at one side of the room. She opened its doors and he saw that the cabinet's shelves were loaded with ranks of bottles more numerous than he'd seen at a lot of the small-town saloons he'd been in while on cases.

Running her fingers along the bottles, she selected one, then another. She produced glasses and a silver tray from one of the lower shelves, and brought the liquor to the table that stood in the center of the room.

"I'll have brandy," she said, pouring Longarm's rye.

He took the glass and held it to his nose, recognizing at once the quality of the whiskey.

Mrs. Montgomery poured brandy into a snifter, and raised it to touch Longarm's glass. "To a memorable evening, Marshal Long."

Longarm took half the rye in a single swallow. It was a fine whiskey, smoother than milk, with the afterbite of authority. Mrs. Montgomery held up the rye bottle, and he extended his glass to be topped off. She motioned to a sofa and he followed her to it. She sat down with a flurry of her silk skirt, and he perched on the opposite end of the divan. The wine at dinner and the drinks before it had kept Longarm warm while they'd walked through the night-chilled Leadville streets. Now, in the warm house, he began to feel uncomfortable. He unbuttoned his coat, and started to unbutton the vest beneath it, until the thought struck him that his hostess might think it impolite.

Mrs. Montgomery saw the beginning of his gesture. She smiled. "Unbutton your vest, by all means, Marshal. Perhaps the room *is* a bit warm. The cook comes in every day while I'm gone, to keep the furnace going."

"If you don't mind, ma'am."

"Of course I don't mind. I want you to be comfortable." She pushed the overhanging roll of hair up from her forehead. "I'm a bit warm myself, and I feel gritty from the train ride today, don't you?"

"Just a mite. I was all over the outside of the cars, you know."

"I didn't take time to do more than sponge off when I got home," she said. "Perhaps we'd both feel better for a nice warm bath. Tell me, Marshal Long, would you like to bathe with me?"

Chapter 3

For a moment, Longarm was too taken by surprise to reply. Then he said, "I'll say this for you, Mrs. Montgomery. You've got a way of coming to the point that most ladies I know don't have."

"I told you at dinner, I never make an offer I don't want to."

"So you did. Well, Mrs. Montgomery, I can't think of a thing in the world I'd like better right now than to pop into a bathtub with you, seeing as you've invited me."

"Good. I seldom make a mistake about a man. Bring the tray and come along. I'll go ahead and light the lamps."

Still caught between surprise and anticipation, Longarm obeyed. He picked up the silver tray, finally found its center of balance, and followed Mrs. Montgomery up the stairs. On the landing, he almost dropped the tray when she stopped suddenly and turned to him.

"Don't you think we've reached the stage where we can drop formality?" she asked. "Surely you've got a first name I can call you by? And you don't strike me as being the type of man who has to have my permission to call me Vivian."

"My first name's Custis, Vivian. Except there's so few folks who use it that I don't answer to it real well.

Most of my friends have got a nickname they use—Longarm."

"She smiled. "Scratch a U.S. marshal and find a punster. Well, come on, Longarm. Let's go and get rid of the dust of that miserable train ride we shared today."

They continued up the stairs, to a bedroom where a single lamp, turned low, burned on a dresser. The room was big, but a huge bed dominated it. The bed was turned down, with two pillows plumped at the center of the headboard. Its satin coverlet gleamed silvery against the folds of snowy sheets. The bed and dresser and a single chair were the room's only furnishings. A line of louvered folding doors, closed now, filled most of one wall, hinting at a dressing room and closet behind them. On the opposite side of the room, a single door stood slightly ajar.

Vivian turned up the lamp and said to Longarm. "I'll start the tub filling while we undress."

She went through the already-opened door. Curious, Longarm followed her. Inside the bathroom, he stopped short, staring.

Vivian Montgomery's bathroom was one such as Longarm had never dreamed existed. She'd just turned on the water; it spurted from twin silver faucets into a square, sunken marble tub big enough to accommodate three or four people. The tub was surrounded by a flat coping of marble, perhaps a yard wide. The coping extended to a thick carpet pieced together from fleecy sheepskins. The marble washbasin that was set into a shelf of the same material along one wall had silver faucets that matched those of the tub. The wall opposite the tub was a solid mirror. At the rear of the room, a separate enclosure hid the toilet. Silver bars set into the wall held thick, oversized bath towels. Lamps held by brackets on the end walls shed a clear but subdued light over the room.

After inspecting it from the doorway, Longarm shook his head. "I don't know," he told her. "Most of the places I go to, I'm lucky to find a galvanized washtub to take a bath in. I guess this is going to have to be the finest bath I've ever had."

"I enjoy bathing," Vivian said. She was in the bedroom, standing in front of the dresser, taking the garnet brooch off the neckband of her dress. "You're going to have to help me with the buttons of this dress. They're small and they're in back. I had the devil's own time getting into it."

"If you ain't in all that big a hurry, Vivian, I'd like to get my coat and vest off, first. Then I'll be proud as sin to give you all the help you want."

He pulled a chair up to the bed and dropped his coat, folded once, on the seat. With his back to his companion, Longarm transferred the derringer that was attached to one end of his watch chain into the same pocket that usually held only the watch. He hung the vest over the back of the chair, and unbuckled his gunbelt. Very carefully, he hung the belt over the chair, placing it so the butt of the holstered Colt would be within easy grasp of a hand reaching from the bed.

Vivian Montgomery had stopped her own undressing to watch his preparations. There was respect in her voice when she said, "You're a cautious man, aren't you, Longarm?"

"Sometimes a man in my kind of work stays alive because he's learned how to be careful. Not that I look for anything to happen here in your house, but nobody except a damn fool takes chances when he don't have to."

Longarm sat down on the side of the bed and took off his boots. Barefoot, he padded over to the dresser. His big fingers had trouble with the tiny buttons until he got the knack of slipping them through the equally tiny buttonholes. Vivian, watching him in the mirror, was unbuttoning the long sleeves. She shrugged her shoulders in a twisting turn, and the dress slid to the floor.

"Now it's my turn," she told Longarm. She flicked a corner of his black string necktie and undid the buttons of his shirt until she reached his belt. She undid the belt and the first buttons of his fly, and finished unbuttoning the shirt. With a single sweep of her hands, she pulled his shirt open and down over his shoulders.

Her hands sought Longarm's skin. He felt their warmth as she stroked his chest and ribs, then went around him and pulled him to her. Her face was pressed to his bare chest, her breath gusting warmly. Longarm fumbled at the straps of her shift and pulled them down to her bare shoulders. He rubbed his chin on her shoulders, and the rasping of his day-old beard on Vivian's soft skin brought a shudder of pleasure to her. Her breath was warm on his chest as a gusty sigh escaped her lips.

Longarm was beginning to harden. He fumbled at the knot of her corset laces for several seconds before he gave up the effort to untie it and snapped the lacing with a single twist of his strong hand. The top of the corset yawned open. Vivian released him from her embrace long enough to shrug out of the stiff, clumsy garment. It fell to the floor between them, carrying her shift with it. She pressed her bare breasts to Longarm's chest, and rubbed against him, her shoulders moving from side to side.

Longarm's erection was still growing. He worked his hand between their bodies and his searching fingers found a nipple. He squeezed it gently, and felt it harden and push up erect against his rubbing. Vivian arched her back, bending away from him, her hands on his shoulders now, her big, soft breasts free to his hands, then to his lips.

Longarm's erection grew. He took a hand away from her breasts and started to unbutton his trousers. She stopped him by grasping his wrist.

"No. I want to do that for you. And I like the feeling of your hands on me. Don't stop what you're doing."

Her full, red lips were only inches from his eyes. Their movement, when she spoke, reminded Longarm that as yet there'd been no kisses exchanged between them. He took her chin gently in his hand, and brought his mouth to hers. It opened to his tongue, and they held a long, moist kiss while her hands worked on his trouser buttons and his were squeezing and rubbing her hot breasts. Her nipples grew erect and firm under his caressing fingers.

Longarm felt her pushing his trousers and drawers down over his hips. He was still only partly erect. Her hands found his shaft, lifted it, and she began to rub it over her stomach. He could feel the gentle rasping of her silken bloomers, and released Vivian long enough to pull that last undergarment down to her thighs. In the mirror over the dresser, he could see her back, smoothly white, the deep crease of the backbone at her waist sweeping into the darker, shadowed crease between her white, firmly rounded buttocks.

Vivian brought his growing erection up between them and squeezing herself to his groin, trapped it between their clinging bodies. Longarm grasped her buttocks with both hands and started to lift her from the floor. She pushed away from him.

"No. It's too soon. We'd better go bathe now. It'll be all the better later, if we're not in too much of a hurry now."

Vivian stepped away from him, and Longarm saw her body completely for the first time. Her figure was that of a woman mature but not yet old, a body generous in all ways. Her large breasts, soft but still firm and without a trace of sagging, bulged in a smooth curve down from her satin shoulders. Her stomach was flat, unmarred by rolls of fat, and swept down in a slight curve to a sparse pubic brush, the gold of dark honey, that spread between her plump, swelling, thighs. Her legs were still covered to the knee with silken stockings held up by rosetted silk garters.

She started toward the bathroom, stopping long enough to balance on one foot and then the other while she stripped off the stockings and dropped them. Then she disappeared into the bathroom. Longarm moved to follow her, and found his feet trapped in the clothes, his and hers, mixed in a heap. He kicked free of the tangle and hurried after Vivian. She was in the cubicle that hid the toilet. He waited until she came out, to the accompaniment of a loud, splashing flush, and went in and let his bladder drain.

Vivian was in the tub when he emerged. The water was knee-deep, her feet and calves distorted in its surface ripples. She said, "Come in with me, Longarm. I'll scrub your back, and you can scrub mine. Oh, this hot water feels so good!"

He stepped into the tub and tried to take Vivian in his arms, but she eluded him by sitting down. He lurched forward and almost lost his footing, but managed to keep himself from falling. He jackknifed his legs and sat down, the water coming to mid-chest, warm and relaxing. Vivian stretched out, waving her legs gently and creating a current that blurred the surface of the water, her body a rippling white column beside Longarm's darker-hued skin. He tried to put an arm under her and bring her closer to him, but she slid away, her skin too slippery underwater for him to be able to hold her.

"Let's get the day's grit off before we do anything else," she said, her smile an invitation that took away any sting her words might have caused. "Come on, kneel here by the edge of the tub and I'll scrub your back for you."

Longarm hadn't yet encountered a woman who took such complete charge of things. He didn't know whether to be angry or to go along with the tide. He'd lost his erection in the warm water, and though his mind urged him to grab Vivian and end her stalling, he lacked the urgency that a full erection would have given him. He knelt as she'd suggested.

Vivian opened a jar that stood on the coping beside the tub, and he felt something harsh and gritty being rubbed into his back.

"What in hell is that?" he asked, craning his neck, trying to see what the granules were that she was massaging into his skin.

"Salt. Just plain, coarse salt. It's all I ever use when I bathe. Much better for you than soap."

She'd kept up her rubbing while she talked, and Longarm found the muscles of his back relaxing. He didn't know whether it was the salt or the vigorous massage she was giving him, but it felt good. He leaned forward on the cool marble coping that edged the tub, and let her continue. Soon the grittiness that the salt had caused when it was first applied vanished, and there was only the increasingly gentle pressure of her hands —a pressure so light it became a caress. He felt himself growing hard again. Suddenly, the stroking on his back stopped.

"Slide down into the water," Vivian told him. "And now that you know how, you can salt me as soon as you've rinsed."

"How about my front?" Longarm asked. "You don't plan to let it stay gritty, do you?"

"After you've finished with me," she promised.

She turned over and knelt as he had done, the water's surface lapping at the bottom of her curved buttocks. Longarm poured out a handful of the coarse salt the jar held, and began rubbing it on her back. The hard salt grains soon shriveled and turned into a thin, watery paste, and the combination of warm water, salt, and rubbing seemed to sensitize Longarm's palms and fingers as he stroked Vivian's smooth back. The sensation was one he'd never experienced before. It seemed to magnetize his hands and her flesh, until his palms were tingling and his groin began to twitch as his erection started to return.

His hands swept down her sides, and over the curves of her hips. He felt a roughness on one of them, and looked closely at her hip to find the cause. A patch of rough skin, creased and striated, marred perhaps two square inches of the otherwise perfect texture of her skin. Longarm rubbed more salt in it, trying to smooth the rough spot, but it had no effect.

Vivian turned her head to look over her shoulder at Longarm when he persisted in massaging the scar. A small frown flitted over her face. She turned, still on her knees, and leaned back against the rim of the tub.

"Take some more salt," she told him. "It doesn't work unless you use a lot of it."

Longarm poured fresh salt into his hand, and transferred part of it to the other hand. He began to rub the grains into Vivian's midsection, working slowly up to her breasts. By now, he was a willing participant in this fascinating new byplay. He could feel her flesh warming to a temperature greater than normal, and her skin began to grow pink as he prolonged the rubbing. He massaged her breasts gently, and felt them become firmer under his stroking; her nipples and rosettes turned a darker pink as the rosettes crinkled and the nipples thrust forward eagerly. He worked down her body to her hips, and took fresh salt to rub into her pubic brush, which was just above the surface of the water.

She began to writhe as his stroking continued, and Longarm saw himself getting harder, stiffening under the sensuous effect of the prolonged massage. Vivian saw him becoming erect and, with a twist of her body, slid out of his hands and into the water. She rolled briefly, moving her shoulders and hips to rinse the salt off them, then stood up and said, "Now. Lean on the tub and I'll finish rubbing you."

Longarm knelt, facing her, and leaned back as she had, against the tub's rim. Vivian looked at him and shook her head.

"From the looks of those scars, I'd guess you've had more than your share of narrow scrapes." With a fingertip, she traced a jagged knife scar that ran across Longarm's shoulder, then put a finger on a bullet wound. It's funny," she said. "I didn't notice any scars on your back when I was rubbing it."

"I never was one to turn my back on trouble," he replied. "I'd rather meet it face-on, if I've got to meet it at all."

Longarm was taller than Vivian, and when he knelt on the bottom of the tub, the water came only partway up his thighs. Vivian began rubbing the salt into his chest and shoulder, then down his belly. She didn't spend as much time on his torso as she had when rubbing his back. Her eyes kept turning to his massive erection, which stood out just above the waterline.

Her touch became gentler when her hands reached his groin with their load of fresh salt. She was administering less of a rubbing or a massaging than a caress.

She stroked the length of his hard penis, first with one hand, then the other. It seemed to Longarm that the salt was sensitizing his skin there, just as his hands had felt a hundred times more sensitive when he'd been rubbing Vivian's body. He imagined he could feel the whorls of her fingertips as she ran them along the length of his erection, and his testicles felt like they were swelling to the point of bursting when she cupped her hands to lift them and cradle them in one hand, while rolling the thin flesh of his scrotum between the fingers of the other.

Longarm was throbbingly erect. He felt urgent surges sweeping up from his groin through his belly, and Vivian's hands on him caused his nerves to twitch each time she rubbed him.

"Rinse, now!" she commanded, her voice sharp.

Longarm let himself down into the tub, rolled around quickly, and stood up. Vivian dropped to her knees as he rose. Her hands cupped and lifted his testicles, and her mouth took in his erection. The warm moisture of her caressing lips brought a quick tightening to the muscles of his groin and buttocks. He wanted to be inside Vivian deeper than her mouth could take him, but did not want to lose the delicious rasping of her mobile tongue over his sensitized flesh. He felt gorged, and wanted to give himself to her in a long, spurting spasm, but was not yet ready.

Vivian did not prolong her caresses. She released him and stood up, the water streaming from her hips and thighs. Longarm reached for her, but she ducked under his outstretched arms and waded to the rim of the tub. She sat on the rim and lay back, opening her thighs in an unmistakable invitation. Now Longarm understood the long preliminary of the bath. He knelt by the edge of the tub and buried his face between her thighs. He sought her inner lips with his tongue, and ran it up their soft edges until he felt Vivian's legs grasp his head.

Distantly, he heard her say, "Oh, you've found it. That's the place. There, right there."

For a few moments, Longarm twitched his tongue from side to side in one flicking touch after another.

Vivian's thighs locked tighter around his head. He could feel the quivering of her body in response to the gentle pressure of his tongue-tip. He tasted salt, and neither knew nor cared whether it was from Vivian or from the water that still dripped from both of them. When he grew breathless, Longarm pulled his head back and brought his shoulders up. Vivian accepted his signal and opened her thighs. He stood up, his fresh erection high and ready, and went into her with a single, swift thrust that brought a sobbing cry from deep within her throat.

For a long moment, Longarm did not move. He held himself hard against the softness of her yielding body with a firm, steady pressure, and felt her inner muscles tightening around him like the closing of a warm, soft hand. Vivian stirred impatiently, and Longarm began stroking. Her soft body stirred him to thrust roughly, as hard and as deep as possible, stroke following stroke, without pausing to enjoy the sensation of her engulfing him. There would be time for that later, he knew. This first one was hers.

She took him into her silently, only the increased pulsing of her breath telling him that he was pleasing her. Again and again, Longarm pounded home, never hesitating, never stopping, until her body began quivering and then shaking, and her hips started heaving in wild convulsions until, at last, with a sudden, short scream that echoed off the walls of the small room, she stiffened and went limp.

Longarm eased his tempo then. He kept going deeply into her, letting her hot wetness engulf him, until she stirred and sighed. Then he leaned forward, relaxing slowly, until his full weight was resting on her, the soft billows of her big breasts warm against his chest.

She brought up a hand to stroke his cheek, and said dreamily, "I could just go on lying here forever, feeling you inside me. But why'd you stop? I wanted to wait, but I couldn't. I just had to let go. That pounding way you've got really set me off."

"I've got all the time in the world, Vivian. Next time, maybe, or the time after that, I'll go when you do."

She whistled softly under breath. "Jesus! You're not just built like a stud horse, you're long-winded, too."

"It takes me a while. But I like to see a pretty woman taking her pleasure."

"Would you like to start again now? Or shall we go get in bed, where we'll be more comfortable?"

"Maybe we better go in the other room. This water's getting cold around my legs."

"You're sure you can stay hard? Or get it up again without any trouble?"

"Don't worry about me. I won't lose it."

"I should hope not!" she grinned. She moved to sit up, and Longarm pulled away from her. She looked at him and sighed, "Oh, how lovely! Come on! Just seeing it standing out there makes me want to get it back inside me."

She leaned forward and ran her tongue along his engorged shaft before scrambling to her feet and taking a towel from one of the silver rods fixed to the wall.

"Here. Let me dry your legs."

She rubbed the towel down his legs, bending from the waist. Longarm fingered her gently, bringing a small shriek of surprised protest, followed by a throaty chuckle. She tossed the towel aside and took his hand. Together, they went into the bedroom. Vivian threw the folded coverlet and sheet over the footboard.

"They'd just be in our way," she said, smiling. "The only cover I want over me tonight is you!"

Longarm left Vivian Montgomery's house late in the afternoon. Despite the fact that he'd had only brief naps between their prolonged sexual bouts, he felt fine. A barber pole drew his eyes as he walked down Harrison, and after a shave, he felt even better. He stopped on the corner of State and Harrison, trying to decide whether to see if Mart Duggan had by chance come to his office early, or whether to drop into one of the saloons on State for a drink. Since his conscience was whispering that he'd taken time off when he was supposed to be scouting Leadville, he decided to try Duggan.

Knowing his friend's habits, he wasn't disappointed when the uniformed deputy marshal who was coming out of the jail just as he arrived shook his head in response to Longarm's question. He asked the man, "You got any idea where Mart'd likely be about now? I was supposed to see him last night, but I missed him."

"You might try the U.S. Hotel; that's where he lives. He was here all night last night, just like he generally is. He'd be getting up right about now, I'd guess," the man replied.

"Thanks. Which way do I head from here to find the hotel?"

"Right down the street, two squares. You can't miss it."

Longarm walked down the street. The U.S. Hotel was a one-story brick building, far from new. Its registration desk was unoccupied, but had a push-bell displayed prominently on it. Longarm tapped the bell. A door down the hall opened and a man's voice called, "If you want a room, you're out of luck. We're full up."

"I'm looking for Mart Duggan," Longarm called back.

"Try room eleven. But I won't guarantee he's there."

Mart Duggan opened the door of room eleven before Longarm could knock a second time. The Leadville city marshal was fully dressed, except for his coat. He wore his pistol in a soft leather holster, sewed to the armpit of the vest. Like Longarm, Duggan carried his gun butt-forward.

"You sure took your time, you old spalpeen. That must've been some woman you were jollying with last night," he said.

"Sorry I missed you, Mart. But I figured I'd earned a little time off, after yesterday."

"Well, don't come in and sit down. I'll get my coat on and we'll go have breakfast."

Longarm didn't remark that it'd be breakfast for him, too. He didn't feel any need to take Duggan into his confidence where his private life was concerned. Duggan came into the hall, patting his coat down around the bulge of his revolver.

"We'll go over to State Street," he told Longarm. "There's a dozen places there where we can get fed."

The hallway was too narrow for them to walk abreast. Duggan took the lead and, as they moved to the door, said over his shoulder, "You never did tell me what's brought you here, Longarm. You were in too big a hurry to get away last night. Who're you after this time?"

"That's something I don't rightly know, Mart. What I really rode here for is to take a look-see around, and to talk to you. It's your town; I figured you might be able to give me a steer or two."

"What the hell do you mean, you don't know? Billy Vail's not a man who'd send you someplace just to look at it. If that's what he's done, he's sure changed a lot since I saw him last."

"He did, though, honest fact. Surprised me, too."

"It must be something damned important," Duggan said. "Well, we can talk about it while we eat."

They were on the street now, walking slowly. The sun was a pale disc in the smoke-veiled sky, sliding steadily down toward the jagged peaks of the Sawatch Range that rose above the smelters along the railroad tracks west of the town. Duggan turned suddenly and led Longarm into a narrow alley. Refuse covered the ground under their feet, and the smell of rotting garbage overpowered the sulfuric tang that always permeated the Leadville atmosphere.

"It's no boulevard," Duggan said, half-apologizing. "It just saves us a lot walking." Longarm saw a man curled up in one of the doorways that opened into the alley. Duggan bent over him just long enough to make sure the man was sleeping, and not a corpse that would have to be removed by the city.

"My boys haul away two or three like him every week," he told Longarm. "They get tanked up on that raw bull-piss at the joints in Tiger Alley, and it's too much for them to handle."

"I guess Leadville's pretty much the same," Longarm observed.

"Maybe a *little* tamer, from what I saw when I was walking around last night."

"Tamer, shit!" Duggan snorted. "It's dead! I laid off two men last month. Might have to let two more go this month."

"It was lively enough for my taste on the way up here," Longarm said.

"Oh, I'd better tell you. I had a little chin-fest with that fellow you brought in, Blackie Spencer. Persuaded him to tell me the name of the one that got away."

Longarm glanced at Duggan's hamlike hands, clenching and opening, and imagined what the persuasion must have been like. He asked the marshal, "Anybody you know?"

"Sure. Pete Smith, generally called Telluride Pete. And the dead ones are that Riley I mentioned, and Newt Carson. Bad ones, both of them."

"Any idea where this Telluride Pete might turn up?"

"He's as apt to turn up here as anyplace else. I passed the word for my men to keep their eyes peeled for him. If I haul him in, I'll send you a wire and you can come after him."

"You give me what you got on him before I leave, and I'll have a federal want put out on him, too."

Duggan nodded. They left the alley and led the way to a white-painted frame building across State Street. It had the one word, CAFE, scrawled in thick red letters across its front.

"It don't look like much," Duggan said, "But the food won't kill you."

They went inside. The place was deserted except for a waiter who stood looking at the unoccupied tables. Duggan pulled out a chair from a table by the window, where he could look out at the street. Longarm sat down opposite him.

"Your regular breakfast, Marshal?" the waiter asked Duggan.

"Same as always, Jim." He cocked a questioning eye across the table at Longarm.

"Steak and eggs would do me fine," Longarm said.

After the waiter had left, Duggan said to Longarm,

"All right, lad. Come on out with it. There's nobody around to listen to what you say; that's one reason I picked this place. What're you really here for?"

"It's a mite hard to explain."

"Try me. My curiosity's been itching all night, and I don't like things happening in Leadville that I don't know about. Like you said back at the hotel, it's my town. If I'm going to keep a lid on it, I've got to know what's going on."

Longarm said, "Seems like I'm set to play nursemaid for a week or so. Here in Leadville, mostly, I guess. Silver Dollar Tabor's got a big high muckety-muck paying him a visit."

"Shit, Tabor don't even live here anymore, Longarm. He's got too important for a little place like this. The past few years, he's spent most of his time in Denver."

"Well, he's going to be here for a week or more, with this big important somebody in tow, and I'm supposed to see that nothing happens to him or his guest."

"If it's somebody old Haw's bringing here, then he's bound to be coming from Washington. Am I right?"

"In a way, I guess I'd have to say you are."

Duggan slitted his eyes as he stared across the table at Longarm. "The only man who comes to mind who'd get Billy Vail stirred up enough to send you along as a bodyguard would be President Arthur."

"You're close, but the president's somewheres over in Europe. Hell, no use beating around the bush, Mart. How does U.S. Grant sound to you?"

A dark cloud seemed to cast its shadow on Duggan's face.

"Like hell. I got no use for that son of a bitch."

"What'd Grant ever do to you?"

"He damn near got me killed at Cold Harbor, when I was a lard-ass recruit who didn't know much more than which end of a rifle the bullets came out of. And there was damn near twenty thousand good men who weren't as lucky as I was. Don't talk to me about Butcher Grant."

"That was twenty years ago, Mart. And men *do* get killed in a war."

"Sure, it was a long time ago. But I ain't forgot, and neither have a lot of others. I can see why Billy's worried."

"It ain't just Billy Vail. He's under orders from Washington to see that Grant gets protected. They've heard something back there about a scheme to put Grant away while he's out here visiting with Tabor."

"They can put Silver Dollar away, too, for all I care. I never could stand the high-domed bastard, even if he was the one that hired me for this job when he was mayor here. That didn't keep him and me from locking horns. I recall one time when he was trying to talk me out of putting some drunk friend of his in jail, I told him to back off or I'd knock him down."

Before Longarm could say anything further, the waiter arrived with their food. He set a platter containing three thick mutton chops and two fried eggs in front of Duggan, and a similar platter with steak instead of mutton in front of Longarm. Duggan tore into a chop hungrily. Longarm sat staring at the platter in front of him, and found that he'd suddenly lost his appetite.

Duggan didn't seem to notice. He was giving his chops and eggs his full attention. Longarm took a few bites of steak, more to give Duggan time to cool off than because he felt like eating. He'd been counting pretty heavily on the Leadville city marshal giving him a hand if one were needed during Grant's visit. At the same time, what Duggan had said made Longarm more inclined than he'd been earlier to accept Billy Vail's argument that, whether or not a plot to assassinate Grant was brewing, there were enough old hatreds left over from the War to make his job of guarding the ex-president more than just a formality.

"What's the matter with your steak?" Duggan asked when he looked up after he'd eaten two of his chops. "If there's something wrong with it, I'll tell them to cook you another one."

"No, don't bother. It's fine. I just ain't hungry."

"I guess I made you mad, what I said about Grant? Well, it's how I feel. And not just me."

"But you still wouldn't go out of your way to kill him, would you?"

Duggan chewed over the question while he was chewing up a bite of meat. After he'd swallowed, he said, "No, I wouldn't step across the street to put a bullet in the bastard. But I wouldn't go out of my way to help him, either."

"Would you feel friendly enough with me to let me know if you heard anything about somebody who *might* step across the street to put a bullet in Grant?"

Unhesitatingly, Duggan replied, "Why, shit, yes! Damn it, we're in the same line of work, Longarm. You didn't need to ask me such a fool question."

"All right. I'll settle for that," Longarm told him. He felt a little better, and cut himself another bite of meat.

After they'd eaten for a few more minutes in silence, Duggan frowned and asked, "You really believe somebody's going to make a try for Grant while he's in Leadville?"

"Hell, I don't know what to believe, Mart. Billy thinks so. The big bosses in Washington do, too. I told you, that's where the order came from." Then Longarm added, "Of course, they're nervous as a fresh-set hen, back there, after what happened to Garfield. And Lincoln before him, too."

Duggan said thoughtfully, "It sure wouldn't look too good for me if something was to happen to Grant while he was here, would it?"

"I guess you'd come in for a good share of the blame."

"Well, damn it, we'll mosey around when we get through here. Ask a question or two, see if there's anybody new come to town that I ain't been told about. I guess it won't hurt me to do that much."

"I'd appreciate it, Mart. It'd maybe help me some. Right this minute, I feel like the only blind man in a stud poker game."

They were finishing their coffee when one of

Duggan's deputies found them. He stuck his head in the door and looked around, then came to the table.

He said to Duggan, "Thought that was you I seen through the window, but I wasn't sure. I been looking for you."

"What's happened?" Duggan asked.

"That fellow you told us to keep an eye out for—Telluride Pete? He's over at Frankie Paige's parlor house."

"You sure?"

"Clancey is, and Clancey knows him from before. This Pete gave Frankie a brand-new twenty-dollar bill to pay for drinks, and Frankie thought it might be one of them twenties we put out the word on."

Duggan interrupted the man to explain to Longarm, "That mine messenger Blackie and his bunch robbed—I told you about it last night. His boodle-bag was full of brand-new twenties. I've had every place in Leadville on the lookout for them." He turned back to the deputy. "Go on."

"Well, Frankie sent the porter out to find Clancey. He's on the Main Street beat, you know. She wanted Clancey to look at the twenty. She'd already put Pete and the girl he picked in one of her peephole rooms. Clancey looked at him, and he swears it's Telluride Pete, all right."

"You talked to Clancey?"

"I swung by there when I started looking for you. Clancey swears that it's him," the deputy repeated.

"Clancey's still watching Frankie's place, then?" Duggan asked.

"Sure. He sent word by the porter over to the jail, and Flood told me to see if I could find you. I've been looking for you along State and Harrison for the last twenty minutes."

Duggan looked at Longarm. "Well, what're we waiting for?"

Longarm replied, "I sure ain't holding back. Let's go take him." He called the waiter. "Bring me the bill, in a hurry!"

Duggan said, "Forget the bill, Longarm. Hell, I never

61

pay a meal tab, you ought to know that. Come on, we're wasting time."

Longarm and the deputy followed Duggan out of the restaurant and up State Street. A few doors from the cafe he led them up an alley even more foul-smelling and garbage-strewn than the one he and Longarm had taken as a shortcut on the way to breakfast.

"Ain't you got a garbage collector in this damn place?" Longarm gasped. The odor that had assaulted his nose the instant they'd turned into the narrow alley reminded him of the waste heap at a slaughterhouse.

Duggan replied, "No use in trying to keep this one clean. This is Stillborn Alley, where the doctors all drop off the aborted babies and the whores throw away their miscarriages. Oh, I know," he went on after seeing Longarm's look of disgust. "It's a crime against nature, but we can't watch every woman every minute. I say, give them a chance to get rid of their mistakes."

They came out of the alley into the normal air. Longarm had thought its tinge of sulfur objectionable before, but now he welcomed it. He cleared his mind of all distractions, for Duggan was going up the steps of a high, narrow house. Like the houses on each side, its windows were all tightly shuttered. Before Duggan could knock, the door opened, and the three men went inside.

"Miss Frankie's waiting for you in the parlor, Marshal Duggan," said the black maid who'd opened the door.

Duggan needed no directions. He strode through the entryway and swung to the left, into a large, dimly lighted room. Its carpet was a dull purple, its shuttered windows were covered with lavender velvet drapes, and crimson-striped flocked paper covered its walls. There were sofas everywhere, and two or three tables, but only one chair, an immense high-backed affair that reminded Longarm of a throne.

A middle-aged woman wearing a lavender satin dress sat in the chair. Diamond rings crusted her fingers, and as she stood up, an ornate brooch, as big as a man's hand, threw out the sparkling arrows of light that only real diamonds emit.

"Mart," she said in a hoarse voice, "there's not going to be any trouble, is there? If there is, I'm going to send my girls next door to stay with Carrie."

"There won't be trouble if we can keep from it, Frankie," Duggan assured her. "Your girls ought to be safe."

"Good," she said. "I wouldn't want my house to get a bad name."

"Where is he?" Duggan asked the madam.

"Reba'll show you. I put him in one of my peephole rooms. After he flashed that roll of twenties, I was afraid he was a pusher, trying to get rid of some queer. That's why I sent for Clancey."

"Where is Clancey?" Duggan asked. "I thought he'd be outside."

"He's watching through the peephole," Frankie said. She snapped her fingers at the maid. "Reba, show Mart and his men how the panel works. Then you get the hell back downstairs and stay in the kitchen with the girls."

Reba nodded and turned to go, and Duggan said to his deputy marshal, "Clint, you better watch the outside, just in case. If you're standing out in front, there's not likely to be anybody ringing the bell while we're taking that fellow."

"Hey!" Frankie protested. "Me and my girls got to make a living! Do you have to scare the johns off?"

"We do for a few minutes, Frankie. And this is a dead time of day, anyhow. The smelter shifts don't change for another hour, and you know damned well your girls won't be turning a lot of tricks until then."

"Sure. You're right. Just get that bastard out of here before the night's trade starts coming in."

Duggan and Longarm followed the maid up the thickly carpeted stairs and along a hallway that was equally deeply padded. There were doors at ten-foot intervals on both sides of the hall, with wooden panels set in moldings between them. Reba led them almost to the end of the hall, and stopped in front of one of the panels.

"Now you gent'men remember to be quiet in there. You make any noise, they can hear you through the peephole," she warned them. She pressed on the wall beside the panel, and the wooden inset swung inward. Placing one finger across her lips, Reba motioned for them to go through the opening.

Duggan stepped in first. Longarm followed him and found himself in a long, narrow chamber or passageway, barely wide enough to accommodate his shoulderspan. Reba closed the panel, and darkness enveloped them; he sidled through the darkness, trying to see Duggan. His eyes adjusted to the dimness, and he could see ribbons of light streaming through holes drilled at eye level through the sides of the little enclosure. A man stood at the far end. He'd turned his eyes away from the peephole in front of him when the hall panel opened.

That, Longarm thought, *will be Clancey*.

Clancey and Duggan were talking in whispers too low to reach Longarm's ears. He put an eye to the nearest peephole, blinked when the light from the room struck it, then in a moment he could see a bed and a small area around it. A man and a girl were on the bed. Both of them were naked. Longarm looked at the man; he'd only seen Telluride Pete as a dim form riding away in the darkness, but he supposed that was who the fellow was.

There wasn't anything particularly striking about Pete's appearance; he wore a badly trimmed beard, a shade lighter than his greasy brown hair, and at some time he'd had his nose knocked sideways by a fist or a boot toe. He raised his arm, gesturing at the girl, and Longarm got a glimpse of a circular tattoo on the inside of his right forearm. He couldn't tell much about the girl, but he thought she must be young, judging by her slim figure and thin arms and legs. She was shaking her head vehemently. Her hair glinted with the off-color auburn that was the result of an overdose of henna.

Evidently Pete and the girl were arguing, but, hard as

he strained, Longarm couldn't hear what they were saying. Their words came through the peep hole as an unintelligible mumble of sound. The girl jumped off the bed, waving her arms and still shaking her head. Pete sat up and said something, pointing to some object out of the range of the peep hole. When the girl moved, Longarm saw Pete full-length for the first time, and noticed that the man was completely flaccid.

Apparently the argument was over, for the girl was no longer shaking her head. She went around the foot of the bed and disappeared briefly, then came back into sight carrying a pair of wrinkled trousers. She tossed them on the bed, across Telluride Pete's legs. He fumbled in one of the pockets and pulled out a roll of bills. Even through the peephole, Longarm could see that the bills had the uncreased sheen of unused currency. Pete thumbed a bill off the roll and handed it to the girl. She disappeared again. Pete dropped the trousers to the floor beside the bed and lay back on the pillows.

This time, when the girl came back and knelt on the side of the bed, she was facing the peephole. She wasn't as young as Longarm had thought, or the heavy makeup she wore made her look older. She bent over Pete's groin and began flicking her tongue along his limp penis. In spite of himself, Longarm felt an erection beginning, which he could see was more than was happening to Telluride Pete. The girl's continuing efforts had no effect. Pete said something Longarm couldn't quite hear, and the girl took him deeply into her mouth. This had the desired effect. Pete grasped her ankle and pulled her leg until she moved her hips to straddle his head between her thighs. Her movements didn't interrupt her pumping.

Fascinated by the peepshow he was watching, Longarm forgot about Duggan and Clancey, as they had apparently forgotten him. Then Clancey sneezed. It wasn't a mild, stop-it-with-your-finger sneeze, but a booming explosion. Telluride Pete tried to wriggle out from beneath the girl, found himself tangled with her legs and arms, but finally pushed her off the bed. He leaped to the floor, and ran out of sight for a moment.

When he reappeared, he carried a gunbelt and was tugging at a holstered revolver.

"Let's go! Quick!" Duggan called.

They began moving, but Pete had his pistol out by the time they got into motion. He fired two shots in the direction from which he'd heard the sneeze. The slugs ripped through the thin paneling. Clancey groaned, and Longarm heard the dull thud of the patrolman's body falling to the floor.

Duggan kept yelling for Longarm to hurry, but Longarm was having trouble locating any kind of latch on the panel. He finally felt a handle of some sort, and yanked the panel open. Duggan was crowded up against him, and Longarm's pull sent his elbow digging into Duggan's belly. Duggan grunted and doubled over.

Longarm stepped over the high sill made by the wall molding. He drew as he emerged into the hallway. The door of the room they'd been watching burst open, and Telluride Pete leaped out. He was still naked, and had his gunbelt in one hand and his revolver in the other.

Longarm got off the first shot, but just as he triggered his Colt, Duggan stumbled over the high step as he came out of the peephole hideaway, and lurched into Longarm. The slug from Longarm's .44 tore a gash in the corridor wall above Pete's head. Pete's shot came only seconds later, but Duggan had pushed Longarm out of the way of the outlaw's bullet.

Pete turned and ran for the stairs while Longarm and Duggan were trying to disentangle themselves from one another. At the head of the stairway, Pete turned for another shot, but Longarm had freed himself by then, and got off a shot before the fleeing bandit had his gun leveled. This time, the lead went home. The heavy, relatively slow-moving slug from the Colt drove Pete backward onto the stairs. Longarm heard his body thumping softly as it rolled from one carpeted step to the next.

At the bottom of the stairway, a woman screamed.

Chapter 4

Longarm ran down the stairs two steps at a time. Duggan was right behind him. In the hallway at the foot of the staircase, Frankie Paige stood looking down at the naked corpse of Telluride Pete. Blood was oozing from a single bullet hole above Pete's left nipple. Longarm noticed with surprise that the dead man still had an erection.

He said to Frankie, "Now just calm down and take it easy. It's finished and done, and there ain't any way to go back and do things over."

"Damn it, don't you think I know that?" Frankie snapped. "I'm thinking about the mess that's going to have to be cleaned up."

Duggan came down the stairs and stopped behind Longarm. He said, "Well, that's the end of Blackie's bunch of murdering blackguards." He put a beefy hand on Longarm's shoulder. "Sorry about bumping into you and spoiling your first shot, upstairs."

Frankie Paige was staring up the stairway. Longarm and Duggan turned to see what she was looking at. The girl who'd been in the room with Telluride Pete was standing on the steps in back of Duggan. She was still naked, too.

"Damn it, Opal, get your bare ass back upstairs and don't come down here until you're decent!" Frankie commanded. "You know my rules about parading around with no clothes on!"

"Sure, Frankie. I just thought—" the girl began.

"Never mind what you thought! Scat, now!" Frankie told her. She looked angrily at Duggan. "Mart, you'd better get those men of yours in here and haul this stiff away. I've got enough cleaning up to do before the evening trade starts, without having to worry about a dead man!"

"Sure, Frankie, right away. But I'm going to have to get some help from the station. Clancey's laying upstairs, shot."

"Well, damn you, Mart Duggan!" Frankie scolded. "That's what I get for being a good citizen and trying to help you out!"

Longarm grinned inwardly. He disassociated himself from the wrangle by removing his Colt from its holster and calmly going about the job of reloading it while Frankie and Duggan argued.

Duggan told the madam, "Now just cool off, Frankie. I've done favors for you, remember, and you'll be wanting me to do some more, as long as you're running a parlor house in Leadville."

"Well—" Frankie found Duggan's statement unarguable. "All right. But clean things up fast, will you, Mart?"

"Sure. I'll see that the bodies are out of here in a hurry. I'll even get a man in to fix up the bullet holes in the walls upstairs."

This set the madam off again. "Bullet holes! And blood all over the carpet! And here it is five o'clock, not a john in the parlor yet, and just one damn towel used all day!"

Duggan was obviously anxious to get away. He nudged Longarm toward the door. Over his shoulder, he said to Frankie, "Now quit worrying. I told you, I'll take care of everything!"

Frankie got in the last word. "See you tell your men to carry the stiffs out the back way!" she called as Duggan and Longarm went out the door.

"Frankie can be a bit of a bulcheen when she gets

upset," Duggan said, expelling a huge, relieved sigh as they walked around the shuttered house. "We'll just find Mullins back here, and turn the job of setting things straight up to him. Then you and me, we can be off about our business."

"What business is that?" Longarm frowned.

"Why, putting out lines, to be sure, Longarm. There's a few places in town that I can take you to, places run by men I trust. They'll tip me off if anybody suspicious shows up, and I'll pass the word along to you."

Longarm considered this for a moment, then said, "All right. You'd know who can be trusted, Duggan, but I'm tying one string to anything you say to these friends of yours: don't mention Grant's name when you talk to them. Just let them know you've heard there might be somebody on the way to Leadville that you'd want to know about, so you can keep an eye on him. I wouldn't want to give folks ideas."

"No more would I. You know I'll be careful." He saw his deputy standing close to the back door of the house. There's Mullins now. I'll set him to work, and we'll be off."

Duggan spoke briefly to Mullins, his big, heavy hands cutting the air with gestures that emphasized his words. Mullins kept nodding his understanding, and when their conversation ended, Duggan came over to Longarm, who'd been standing aside, watching.

"It's all taken care of," he said. "Poor Clancey's got no kith or kin hereabouts, so I'm spared breaking the sad news to a widow. Come along now; we'll see what we can find out."

They cut through the alley back to State Street. Duggan jerked a thumb toward the big, ramshackle frame structure bearing a sign that read, THE GREAT SALOON, on the opposite side of the street.

"Pop Wyman's as good a man as any of them to talk to first. We'll not have time to stop in many places before things start to get lively, so we'd best move as fast as we can."

Longarm looked around the cavernous interior of the building as he followed Duggan in through the batwings. It was less a saloon than a dance hall, from its appearance, though there was a bar that stretched from wall to wall across its back end. On one side, a group of girls in short skirts and scanty, sleeveless jumpers were gathered around a Wurlitzer Melodeon, whose red rubber pipes were bringing a jangle of pneumatic music from a roll while one of them pumped its pedals. Two pairs of the girls were dancing on the rough floor of scarred pine planks. Two bartenders polished glasses behind the bar, watching the girls without interest. The two lawmen crossed the dance floor to a closed door at the corner of the bar. Duggan entered without knocking.

A heavyset man stood in front of a high safe. He whirled at the sound of the door being opened, one hand going to the safe, where a heavy pistol lay on one of its shelves. When he saw who'd opened the door, he sighed with relief and turned to greet them.

"Duggan," he said. His voice was a deep, grating bass. "You'll get yourself shot sure as hell, busting in without a knock the way you do."

"Not likely, Pop. I'll make you acquainted with Marshal Long. He's with the federals, out of Denver."

"Marshal." Wyman nodded. "Let's step out to the bar and have a tot, if you've a mind to."

"Maybe later," Longarm said. "Thanks all the same."

"We're in a bit of a hurry," Duggan told Wyman. "Longarm, here, is trying to sniff out a bad one from the East. Killer. He got a tip the man's headed for Leadville. Have there been any dudes whirling your girls around lately?"

"None that I've noticed," Wyman replied. He asked Longarm, "What's he look like, this bad one you're after?"

"That's one of my problems," Longarm said, covering quickly. "We've got three or four descriptions of him. The only thing they agree on is that he likes fancy duds and fast women."

"Then maybe you'd do better to try the parlor houses," Wyman suggested. "My little angels aren't what you'd call fast. They're here for customers to dance with. What they do after they get through on the floor is their affair, and not any business of mine."

"We're pointing no fingers at your girls, Pop," Duggan said. "We're just spreading the word around to be on the lookout for dudes who don't have much to say, and aren't quick to talk about where they've come from and why they're in town. Now, you'll be doing me a personal favor if you'll tell your angels to look out for anybody that measures up to that, and for passing the word on to me, if they do."

Wyman nodded. "Be glad to oblige you, Mart. And you too, Marshal Long. Any time you feel like dropping in to take a look for this dude yourself, tell the boys in back of the bar your drinks are on the house."

"Pop means that, too," Duggan told Longarm. "He's always for the man who wears the badge. Well, Pop, we'll be moving along. We've got to cover the street before you boys get too busy to give us a bit of your time."

"Never too busy for that, Mart," Wyman replied. "You and your friend come back any time."

In one saloon, dance hall, or casino after another, the same conversation they'd had with Wyman was repeated with minor variations during the next several hours. Longarm learned that when Duggan accepted an invitation for a drink, it was at a place like the Catalpa, where John Kane's stock of liquor was a cut above average. When he refused, it was in one of the dance halls or casinos, where liquor was secondary to the establishment's chief attractions, girls or gambling.

As their rounds continued, Longarm began filing away in his mind the establishments that seemed the likeliest spots in which an assassin of the type he was looking for might while away his time, waiting for an opportunity to strike. He paid scant attention to the dance halls, such as Wyman's, the Odeon, Dillon's, the Silver Thread, and the Tudor. Somehow, he didn't picture the kind of man he'd be looking for as one who'd be drawn by the prospect of whirling a girl over a rough dance floor for a turn or two at fifty cents a whirl. Nor, he thought, would Grant.

From what Longarm had heard about Grant's personal habits, the ex-president enjoyed few things as much as good whiskey and sitting in a high-stakes poker game. This narrowed Longarm's list of possibilities substantially, if his conclusion was correct. He didn't think any effort on Grant's life would be made at the Tabor mansion. That left the times Grant would be appearing in public, visiting the places that offered the kind of recreation he enjoyed.

On his list of possibilities, Longarm wound up with the bars of the leading hotels: the Clarendon, Tabor's Grand Hotel, the Tontine, and the Windsor. There were few saloons catering to Leadville's upper crust: Kane's Catalpa, the Bon Ton, Monahan's. He narrowed the gambling choices down to the Board of Trade Saloon, where a high-stakes poker game ran virtually around the clock; the luxurious upstairs parlor of the Texas House; and the California Concert Hall, where music was confined to the clacking of chips, the susurrus of cards being shuffled, the rattle of dice in the chuck-a-luck cage, and the rat-tat-tat of the Wheel of Fortune against its stop.

But if I got any say in things, Longarm told himself as he followed Mart Duggan from one to another of Leadville's leisure attractions, *Grant's going to stay as far away from all these places as I can get him to. As long as he's in Tabor's house, I ought not to have too damn much to worry about. But if I let him roam free where anybody who takes a notion can get at him, God knows what might happen.*

A little after nine o'clock, when the amusement places were getting crowded and their proprietors were busy with their own problems, Longarm said, "I reckon we've laid enough lines for tonight, Mart. And I know you got other things to do besides help me. Why don't we call it quits for now?"

"There's still the whorehouses," Duggan pointed out. "We got that spalpeen Pete today because he went to Frankie Paige's place. And hers ain't the best parlor house in Leadville. I'd put Frankie's about fourth, after Molly May Price's and Sal Purple's, and Carrie Sunnel's. Then there's Minnie Purdy's place, too. All of them are right there on Main Street, and it's still too early for them to be very busy."

Longarm shook his head. "No, I've had enough for today. I'll tell you what. When you've got some time, you lay the lines into the whorehouses. It don't have to be done tonight."

"Well, I'll be glad to do that." Duggan grinned knowingly. "It sounds to me like you're sort of anxious to get back to whoever the lady was you spent so much time with last night. Guess you've got the lead back in your pencil again."

"Well, I did say I'd drop in on her," Longarm admitted. "But I'll have to be getting the morning train back to Denver. I think I've done what I came here for. I know the layout of the town, and I know that if I get in a bind, I can get you to lend me a hand."

"You'll be wanting to take your prisoner back with you, then," Duggan said. "The morning accommodation train on the DSP&P pulls out at about seven, and the chances are I'll be around the office until six. If I leave before you come to pick up Blackie, I'll leave word with Flood to look for you."

"Thanks, Mart. You've been a real big help. I'll likely be back in a week or so; it just depends on when Tabor pulls in from Washington with Grant in tow. The telegraph's working every day, though. If you hear anything I ought to know, send me a wire."

"I'll do that. But I thought you'd be here another day. Hell, we didn't get a chance to see the elephant and hear the owl together."

"We'll do it for sure, when I come back. Or when you're in Denver. Anyhow, I'll try to get here before you're gone in the morning. One of those lines you laid out today might be getting a nibble before then."

Apparently, Vivian Montgomery hadn't bothered to dress after Longarm had left her, still sleeping soundly, in the late afternoon. When she opened the door for him, she was wearing a flowing negligee as thin and transparent as gauze. It was designed to emphasize, not conceal, the rosettes and erect nipples of her large breasts, and even through the doubled folds of the garment wrapped around her, Longarm could see the deep saucer of her navel and the light tan of her pubic hair. He tossed his cheroot behind him, into the yard, before he went in. She moved into his arms even before the door was closed.

"Ain't you afraid you'll scandalize your neighbors?" he asked, when she'd released him from her embrace after a deep and prolonged kiss.

"I don't really give a damn about my neighbors on either side, Longarm. They're not at home much. They spend most of their time in Denver, like almost everybody who's made a pot of money out of Leadville silver. It took you a long time to get back. I thought you'd forgotten me."

"Now, I'd never forget a pretty lady like you."

"I sent the cook home two hours ago. But I've waited for you and kept our dinner hot. I've kept myself hot too, just thinking about last night." She pulled the knot from the sash that held her negligee. Her smooth white skin gleamed like the silk of the thin garment in the soft light. "But which would you rather have first, me or dinner?"

"There ain't but one way a man in his right mind would answer that question, Vivian." He moved to grasp her, but she stepped back.

"We'll go upstairs, then," she said. "And while you're getting your clothes off, I'll turn on the water in the bathtub."

Longarm stretched out with a grateful sigh in the seat of the DSP&P accommodation coach as the little narrow-gauge engine puffed to a start. He was planning on getting some sleep during the ten-hour trip to Denver. Though the Colorado capitol was less than a hundred miles from Leadville on a straight line, the railroad looped north and south and zigged and zagged so much to avoid the foothills of the Mosquito Range that they'd cover twice that many miles, and the long line of gondola cars bearing smelted concentrate held the train's speed down.

He looked across at Blackie Spencer, whose arm and shoulder were encased in overlapping layers of bandages that kept the arm useless. His right wrist was held by handcuffs to the arm of the seat. There'd been only a handful of Denver-bound passengers waiting when Longarm and his prisoner had arrived at the depot, and he'd been able, by showing his badge, to persuade the conductor to put all of them in the first passenger coach. He wasn't looking for Spencer to make trouble, with one arm useless and the other one chained, but if the outlaw did pull any tricks, Longarm didn't want to be slowed down by a bunch of passengers in the car.

Spencer was staring glumly out the window at a landscape that was treeless and desolate, as was all the country around Leadville. The smelters' insatiable appetite for fuel had eaten up every tree within sixty miles before the railroads had come in with their loads of coal and coke.

Longarm lighted a cheroot and let his eyes slit almost shut. Two nights with Vivian had been wearing. He stayed awake while the train chugged through the Blue River valley to its first stop at Climax, then, for the rest of the trip, he slept most of the time, waking up every hour or two—just long enough to glance at Spencer and make sure he was still anchored to the seat.

By the time the train stopped at the Denver depot, Longarm was feeling wide awake again. He looked out at the platform sliding by, and was surprised to see Billy Vail loom suddenly out of nowhere and start walking beside the slow-moving train. Before the engine had braked to a full stop, Vail swung aboard the coach and came in by the back vestibule door.

"What's wrong?" Longarm asked his chief.

"Wrong? There's nothing wrong. Why?"

"I guess I'm just sort of surprised you met the train, Billy, that's all."

"If you want to know, I met the train because I knew

damned well, when I got your wire saying you were on the way, that you'd deliver your prisoner to jail, have supper, and then go home. And I don't intend to wait until tomorrow to find out what you dug up in Leadville."

"Washington's been sending you some more messages, have they?"

"Two or three a day."

"Well, about Leadville—"

Vail stopped Longarm with an upraised hand. "Not now. Wait until we get rid of this fellow." He indicated Spencer, who was listening to their conversation with the first sign of interest Longarm had seen on his face during the entire trip.

Vail went on, "I've got a hack waiting outside the depot. We'll ride over to the jail and book Spencer in. You can do the paperwork on the case tomorrow."

"Thanks a lot," Longarm put in.

Vail ignored the interruption. "Then, after we get rid of him, we'll have supper while we talk. I don't suppose you've eaten, have you?"

"Now, Billy, you know the DSP&P don't run any dining cars. What I had since breakfast was a stale cheese sandwich the butcher-boy came hawking when the train stopped at Breckenridge. That was a while before noon, and that damn sandwich didn't even have mustard or butter on the bread."

What Longarm didn't add was that Vivian Montgomery's cook had fixed them one of the finest breakfasts he'd ever eaten: grilled veal chops and eggs, and tiny button mushrooms sauteed in sweet butter and served on crisp toast.

When they got back in the carriage after the brief formality of committing Blackie Spencer to the Denver City Jail to be held for trial on a federal charge of attempting to rob the U.S. Mail coach, Vail said, "All right. What did you find out while you were in Leadville? Anything that'll help you?"

"No. If there's anybody plotting to do Grant in while he's staying there, they're sure keeping mighty quiet. I spent some time with Mart Duggan, though. We put out lines to all the places where a hired killer might spend some time while he waited for his chance. Mart'll wire me if he hears anything."

Vail nodded. "Duggan's a pretty good man. He keeps a tight rein on his town and sees that his men toe the mark. What bothers me is that there's a good chance no hired killer's going to be used. The Justice department's convinced by now that it's politics more than anything else that's got somebody gunning for Grant."

Longarm decided it was time for him to come out with the speech he'd been framing during his wakeful moments on the train ride from Leadville.

"Look here, Billy," he said. "This kind of case just ain't up my alley. Now, you know I don't pull back from much. When you put me on a case, I stick with it, whether I like it or not. But this here's something different. Politics calls for a lot of skullduggery, and I ain't much good at that. Don't you think you could see your way clear to taking me off this, and putting somebody else on it?"

For a moment, Vail said nothing as the hack rumbled along Colfax Avenue on the way to Magruder's Restaurant. Finally, after Longarm had just about decided his chief was going to ignore his request, he said, "No, I'm not taking you off the assignment. If a hired killer's going to take a crack at Grant, you'd be the man to take him out. If it's an amateur, well, I know you'll do the best you can. But I've made up my mind, and that's final. You're going to stick with Grant while he's in our jurisdiction—whether you like the job or not."

Longarm stationed himself at the spot the stationmaster had pointed out earlier, where Silver Dollar Tabor's private railroad car would be when the Limited pulled up to a stop in the Denver station. The train was due in ten minutes or less, and after a hurried lunch, Longarm and Billy Vail had been on hand for the better part of two hours. They'd come early, at Billy's insistence, to watch the crowd as it assembled and to examine Tabor's second private car, this one a narrow-gauge, which would carry the party to Leadville. The second coach was standing on the narrow-gauge track that paralleled the mainline standard-gauge. It was enamelled a bright blue, and its metal fittings were plated in silver.

Billy Vail swung off the car and came across the dozen feet of brick walkway between the two tracks, then jumped up on the station platform to join Longarm. "I went through the car with a fine-tooth comb," he announced. "Nobody's hidden in it, everything looks fine. I've got the vestibule door keys in my pocket, and I'll go over and unlock it when they get ready to go aboard."

Longarm nodded. He suspected that Billy had volunteered to look over the car more because he was curious to see the kind of luxurious accommodations the richest man in Colorado provided for himself and his friends than because he had been afraid an assassin might have hidden himself there.

Longarm contributed to his chief's peace of mind by adding, "I ain't seen any suspicious characters in the crowd yet."

Billy looked at the people. There were fewer than a hundred—mostly women bringing their children to get a look at a man they'd read about in their history books. "Not a very big crowd, is it?"

"It ain't such a much," Longarm agreed. "I'd say most of the men are old enough to have fought with Grant in the War. Or against him."

"They don't have to have been on the other side to carry a grudge against him," Billy said thoughtfully.

Longarm recalled Mart Duggan's outburst of anger when he'd first mentioned Grant's name to the Leadville city marshal. "You're right about that," he agreed. He fished out a cheroot and a match, then, before he lighted up, shoved both of them back in his pockets. This wasn't any time to have his hands busy, with the train due so soon.

As though responding to his thought, the Limited's whistle echoed through the half-tunnel made by the snowshed that extended over the tracks. In a few moments, the engine came in sight, a thread of smoke trailing back from its conelike funnel and clouds of steam spurting from its massive cylinders as the engineer throttled down more and more, preparing to stop.

"You handle things on this side," Vail said. "I'll cover the space between the cars. Then I'll be there to open the doors when they're ready." He took a long step off the platform and hurried across the tracks in front of the slowing engine.

A half-dozen blue-helmeted Denver policemen appeared, opening a passageway through the crowd. Behind them came Governor Pitkin and a handful of legislators. It was no secret that Pitkin and Tabor had been bitter political enemies only a short time ago, but the governor had bought peace by appointing Tabor to a month-long unexpired term in the U.S. Senate after thwarting Silver Dollar's expensive efforts to win a full term. And everybody in the crowd knew, from the news stories in the *Denver Post* and the *Rocky Mountain News,* that Grant, not Tabor, was the reason why Pitkin was there at the depot.

While the policemen were pressing the crowd back to make space for the governor and his party at the platform's edge, the engine passed. It left a smell of hot oil and coal smoke in its wake, and a few cinders bounced off the ceiling of the snowshed; the people on which they fell began slapping and brushing to rid themselves of the hot, sooty particles. The Limited's passenger coaches wheeled slowly past Longarm, giving him a blurred glimpse of faces pressed to windowpanes. Then the train crept to a creaking halt, with the Tabor private car—painted bright blue like its narrow-gauge counterpart on the next track—stopped almost exactly where the stationmaster had promised it would.

There was a bit of pushing and a great deal of scurrying on the platform as the crowd redistributed itself. A few passengers, stepping down from the forward coaches, came back to join the Denver residents.

Longarm hadn't counted on this happening. He frowned in sudden worry, and started forward. Then he stopped as it came to him that if an assassin had been on the train, there would have been ample opportunity for him to do his job under more favorable conditions than on a crowded and well-policed platform in the Denver station.

He leaned against the lamp standard again, and turned his attention back to the crowd. He didn't really expect anything to happen in Denver. Leadville, where Grant could be expected to move around, on the streets or in the surrounding countryside, would offer better opportunities. He relaxed again.

A man in a long frock coat ambled with a shuffling, hesitating gait onto the private car's observation platform. He wore a high silk hat, and sported a handlebar mustache that protruded at least two inches on either side of his thin face. Longarm was sure, from descriptions and prettied-up likenesses he'd seen on political campaign posters, that he was looking for the first time at Horace A. W. Tabor.

If Tabor saw Governor Pitkin on the station platform —and it would have been impossible to have missed the governor and his party—he gave no sign of it. He raised his hands, the familiar gesture of a speaker requesting silence. The small crowd quieted down.

"My friends, of the great city of Denver—" Tabor began.

Governor Pitkin stepped up onto the observation platform beside Tabor. The silver magnate had no choice but to notice the governor now. He extended a hand. Pitkin took it for the briefest possible handshake. Tabor turned back to face the spectators as though he intended to resume his interrupted speech. Pitkin tapped him on the shoulder.

Longarm alone was near enough to the private car to hear what the two men said to one another. They spoke under their breaths, but their hushed voices didn't diminish the vigor of their words.

"I came to introduce General Grant," Pitkin said. "As long as you're about to start, go ahead. Introduce me, and I'll present the general."

"I will like hell!" Tabor snorted. "Grant's my guest. I'll do the introducing."

"Damn it, Tabor, it's part of my job to welcome visiting dignitaries! Now, introduce me and then stand aside to give the general front place."

"You didn't bring Grant here; I did. If you want to say something after the general's spoken, I won't object. But *I'm* going to present him," Tabor retorted.

Longarm began to notice that the crowd was getting restive, and Pitkin's politician's instincts gave him the message. He solved the problem, and not to Tabor's liking.

Turning to face the crowd, Pitkin said, "My friends and fellow Coloradans! All of you know Senator Tabor, one of our leading citizens, who's just returned to us today after completing his term in the United States Senate." He paused for applause, and a few mild handclaps came from the spectators.

Then Pitkin went on, "We're happy that Senator Tabor has brought with him, to renew his acquaintance with the beauties of our state, the savior of the Union and our former president, the Honorable Ulysses S. Grant!

This time, the applause was louder. Grant must have been waiting just inside the vestibule door, for when he heard his name followed by the crowd's applause, he stepped out to the observation platform. He shook Pitkin's outstretched hand, and the governor waved to the crowd. The faltering applause became a bit more enthusiastic than the first spattering had been.

Grant waved a hand, and the clapping subsided. He said in his light, monotonous voice, "I'm very glad to be back in Colorado, even for a short visit. Senator Tabor has invited me to inspect some of your sources of wealth in the mountains, and I won't be staying in Denver at the moment. But on my way back East, I do want to stop here for several days, and I'm sure I'll meet you then. Thank you for coming to greet me."

With that, Grant gave another wave and disappeared into the car. Tabor and Pitkin glared at each other for a moment before remembering they were under observation from those spectators who hadn't already turned to go, and managed to smile and nod. Pitkin stepped off the observation platform and rejoined his aides. As a group, they turned and marched toward the exit.

Longarm had been watching the crowd, rather than Grant, once the ex-president had appeared. When he turned back, it was just in time to see Grant's coattails vanishing through the back door of the railroad coach. For a moment, he stood there trying to decide whether he should go into the standard-gauge car and introduce himself, or whether it would be better if he went to the narrow-gauge car and waited for the Tabor party there. His boss made up his mind for him. Vail's head appeared around the back of the observation platform of the standard-gauge car.

"You'd better get moving, Long. While that speechifying was going on, Tabor's servants moved the baggage over to the other car. If you don't hustle, you'll be left behind." the chief marshal said.

Longarm jumped off the platform and started toward the narrow-gauge car. A yard donkey was just backing up to couple onto it, and Tabor was helping a woman— the new Mrs. Tabor, Longarm guessed—up the steps.

He told Vail, "I'm on my way," then he crossed the space between the two cars in three long strides and swung up its steps just as it began to move. He opened the vestibule door, but found his way blocked by a pallid-faced, husky man in a black suit.

"Better let me go through, friend," Longarm said. "I've got business with Mr. Tabor and the general."

"Sir, this is a private railroad car," the man said. "If you don't remove yourself at once, I shall be forced to put you off."

"Now hold on," Longarm replied. "I got business here, I told you."

"Senator Tabor can't be disturbed for a business discussion now. See him when he returns to Denver, at his office in the Tabor block."

"You mind telling me just who in hell you are?"

"My name is Forbes. Mr. Tabor employs me as his—" the man paused and frowned, as though searching for the precise word— "as his factotum."

"Well, whatever that means, Forbes, my name's

82

Long. I'm a deputy U.S. marshal, and my business here is to see that General Grant stays safe as long as he's in the state."

Forbes's manner changed at once. "Yes, of course. Senator Tabor mentioned that you'd be with us in Leadville. Ah—when you meet the senator, Marshal, you might keep in mind that he prefers to be called 'senator' now, instead of plain 'mister' Tabor? And Mr. Grant prefers to be addressed as 'general.' "

"Thanks for the tip. I'll remember it. You figure it's all right if I go in there now, to let them know I'm on the job?"

"Yes, indeed, Marshal. I think that's an excellent idea." Forbes opened the door into the private car's main salon, and let Longarm enter ahead of him. There were three people in the narrow room, sitting in easy chairs arranged in a semicircle around a low table that held bottles and glasses. Longarm knew who the men were, Grant and Tabor, and assumed that the plump blonde woman with a cluster of frizzy hair arranged low over her forehead was the new Mrs. Tabor.

Forbes cleared his throat and addressed Tabor. "Senator, this is Deputy U.S. Marshal Long. He's been assigned as the general's escort while he's in Colorado."

"Assigned?" Grant asked. Longarm was struck again by the ex-president's high-pitched voice. "Who assigned you to your job, Marshal?"

"My chief, General. In the Denver office. Billy Vail."

"His idea was it? To provide me with an aide? Or is it 'bodyguard?' " Grant went on.

Longarm thought fast before answering. He didn't want to get Billy into trouble, and he wanted to stay out of trouble himself.

He said, "He didn't tell me whose idea it was, General, and I didn't ask him. Whenever my chief gives me an assignment, I just go on about it. I don't ask questions."

Grant nodded. It was the kind of reply a military man would understand and approve. He looked at Tabor, and said, "Your idea, Horace?"

Tabor shook his head. "Not for a minute. You told me you just wanted to rest. I didn't ask for an aide for you."

"Well, I suppose it's all right," Grant said. From the tone of his voice, Longarm could tell he was still a bit puzzled. "All right, Marshal. Carry on."

There was a moment of silence. Tabor seemed lost in thought. Longarm, getting his first close look at the Silver King, as he'd heard Tabor called, was struck by the magnate's strangely shaped head. Tabor's brow was tall and bulbous, with two large and clearly defined frontal lobes that rose above his sparse, flat-combed hair. Behind the rising forehead, the top of Tabor's skull was flat, and the back of it receded to a taper, almost to a point.

Seen at eye-level and without the top hat he'd worn during his brief observation-platform appearance at the station, Tabor's mustache didn't seem quite as wide; it protruded something less than the two inches beyond his cheeks that Longarm had first estimated. His nose was long and straight, his mouth hidden by the mustache, but his clean-shaven chin was firm above an incipient wattle.

Tabor finally aroused himself from his abstraction. He said, "Well, Marshal, we're glad to have you with us. It had slipped my mind for the moment, but Attorney General MacVeagh did mention, before I left Washington, that he planned to have one of you men from his department go along to Leadville with us, if I approved. I suppose I did approve, since you're here."

"I'll try to keep out of your way—yours and the general's—as much as I can," Longarm told Tabor. Then he turned to Grant. "Of course, General, you know I got orders to tag along with you, no matter where you go. I sure hope you don't mind."

Grant smiled. "I'm used to it." He looked and sounded tired, Longarm thought, and acted as though he had something on his mind. Grant didn't look like the pictures Longarm had seen of him. His face was lined, and under a receding hairline, his brow showed deep furrows. His beard, beginning to go white, was cut shorter than in most of the pictures of him.

"It'll be like old times," Grant added. "We'll get along all right, Marshal Long, I'm sure we will."

"Thank you, General." Longarm looked at Forbes. "Now, if you'll just show me where I'm supposed to ride, I won't bother the senator and the general anymore."

For the first time, Mrs. Tabor spoke. Her voice was clear and soft, like a muted bell. "Put the Marshal in the small stateroom, Forbes. It's a short trip; he should be comfortable there."

"Of course, Mrs. Tabor." Forbes bobbed his head and said to Longarm, "If you'll just come with me, Marshal . . ."

Longarm followed the man through the salon and along a narrow, door-lined corridor. One of the doors near the end of the car was ajar, and Longarm got a glimpse of a small galley stove and an expanse of white wooden counter with cabinets above it. Forbes, looking back, said, "We'll just have a picnic supper on this trip. But you won't go hungry, Jean-Pierre will see to that. And I—" he hesitated— "I hope you won't mind eating with the staff this evening. Unless the senator gives me instructions—"

Longarm interrupted, "Listen, Forbes, I don't mind who I eat with, as long as I'm fed. I guess I see what you're up against. I ain't exactly a servant hired by Mr. Tabor, and I ain't part of his bunch, either. I don't look for him to invite me to sit down at the table with him and his wife and the general. You just stop worrying about where I belong. I'm used to taking care of myself."

Forbes's tone of voice showed his relief. "I'm glad you're a practical man, Marshal. I'll admit, I've been puzzled about exactly where you were going to fit in."

"Just wherever there's room," Longarm assured him.

They were almost at the end of the car now. Forbes opened one of the corridor doors and stood aside to let Longarm enter the small compartment, a bit larger than a Pullman car's drawing room, that the door led into. With its berth folded against the wall, there was room for two chairs and a shelflike desk.

Longarm looked around the compartment. Forbes asked, "Is there something wrong?"

"No. I'm just wondering about my baggage, though. My chief said he'd see that it got put on the car."

"There's a baggage car ahead of this one, with the trunks and suitcases the senator and Mrs. Tabor brought from Washington; perhaps your luggage is in there. And there's a small compartment on this car where it might be. Tell me what you have, and I'll see if I can find it. The senator isn't likely to need me for a while."

"It ain't much. A man in my job gets used to traveling light. Just a sort of carpetbag and my Winchester."

"I'm sure they're here somewhere. Now, is there anything else you'd like? A drink, perhaps?"

"That's something I sure won't turn down. If you got some Maryland rye someplace—"

"Of course. The senator keeps an ample supply of liquors on hand, wherever he might happen to be. Just make yourself comfortable, Marshal. I'll be right back."

Longarm settled into the more comfortable-looking of the two chairs. He glanced out the window. The car was rolling through Denver's warehouse section now, enroute to the Denver & Rio Grande Western station, where it would be coupled to a narrow-gauge engine that would haul it and the baggage car on to Leadville.

Forbes came back in carrying a tray; on it were an almost full bottle of Maryland rye, bearing a very respectable label, several glasses, a siphon of soda, a carafe of water, and a silver ice bucket.

"I think this will be everything you need," he said. "Unless you'd like a lemon and some maraschino cherries. I neglected to put those on the tray, but there are plenty in the galley."

"I don't aim to be mixing up any pink lemonade," Longarm assured him. "All I drink is the whiskey. Why don't you set down and have a swallow with me?"

Forbes hesitated for a moment before saying, "I—I don't suppose there's any reason why I shouldn't. But I'll mix our drinks first. Do you prefer water or soda, Marshal?"

"Neither one. Just pour me a tot of plain old barefoot whiskey."

Forbes poured the drinks, mixing his whiskey with a squirt of soda. Longarm settled back into his chair and motioned for the Tabor factotum to take the other. Again Forbes hesitated, but finally lowered himself into the chair.

Longarm sipped the smoothly biting rye. He asked Forbes, "Is this the kind of whiskey the senator drinks himself?"

"Oh, my, no. Senator Tabor usually drinks very little except champagne during the day. In the evening, he prefers bourbon before dinner and brandy afterward."

Longarm shook his head. "I guess that's all right for rich folks like him. Me, I'm afraid if I mixed up all them different kinds of liquor, it'd make my stomach turn over."

Forbes smiled. "It makes the senator's turn over sometimes. Though I'll appreciate it if you don't mention that I said so."

"I vow I won't breathe a word to nobody," Longarm promised. "You been the senator's—whatchamacallit —a pretty good spell, have you?"

"Only for the past three years, since he began spending most of his time in Denver. Why do you ask, Marshal?"

"No special reason." Longarm had no intention of admitting why he was showing any curiosity at all about Tabor's habits and surroundings. "You know, I'd look on it as a favor if you'll hold back on so much of that 'marshal' stuff. I ain't one of Tabor's big, rich friends that you got to be bowing to and calling by whatever fancy handle they put ahead of their names."

"It wouldn't be quite courteous if I simply called you Long, though," Forbes pointed out.

"Then call me Longarm. That's what my friends do, mostly."

"I'll be pleased to, if you don't mind."

"You'll find I answer to it a lot quicker than I do to 'marshal.'" Longarm took another sip of the rye. "Good whiskey. But I guess the senator can afford the best there is."

"He insists on it. Not just whiskey, either. Everything."

"How about you, Forbes? You got a front handle, or some kind of name your friends call you by?"

"My given name's Geoffrey, but it's been such a long time since anyone's used it that I'd prefer you just to go on calling me Forbes."

"Whatever you want."

Longarm sipped again, relishing the good whiskey. He lighted a cheroot and puffed on it for a moment before asking, "Tell me something. A minute ago, you said the senator's got a staff on board the car, here. Who-all does that take in?"

"Just myself, Mrs. Tabor's maid, Suzanne, and the chef, Jean-Pierre. Of course, the regular household staff will be on duty when we get to Leadville. They stay at the senator's home there the year around. And he has a staff at his house in Denver as well."

Longarm whistled to hide his consternation. There'd be a lot more people to check out than he'd thought. "Like I said a minute ago, I guess he can afford it. How many at his place in Leadville, now?"

"Let's see. There's the cook—though Jean-Pierre will be preparing the main meals, of course—and a kitchen maid. There's the housekeeper, Mrs. Morgan, and two or three maids. Then the outside staff: coachman, stableman, a groom."

"You know all of them, I guess? Have most of them been working for the senator a pretty good while?"

"Well, yes and no, Longarm." Forbes used the nickname a bit uncertainly. "The house staff hasn't changed, except for one of the upstairs maids. But the outside staff changes, especially the stablemen and grooms."

"Are there any new ones on the job since you were there last?"

"Mrs. Morgan's last report to me, when I wired her to be sure the house was ready for the senator's arrival, mentioned that she'd hired a new groom. Why do you—" Forbes broke off as the train began slowing down. He looked out the window, as did Longarm, who recognized the D&RG yards. Forbes said, "Oh, my! I'd better go and attend to my work; Senator Tabor doesn't like for the engineer to go too fast on the curves. And I'll check up on your missing luggage, too, Longarm."

"No hurry. If it ain't with us now, it's too late to go back for it. I'll just buy me a new shirt in Leadville. I'll see you at supper, I guess," he called to Forbes's disappearing back.

Longarm decided to go out and watch the switching, too. A railroad yard was a pretty convenient place for somebody who didn't have any business on a train to hop on the blinds.

He walked out to the front vestibule and clambered up on top of the private car, where he could watch both sides of it, and the baggage coach as well. Nobody tried to hop the cars, but he waited until the D&RG engine had picked up the cars and was on the main line out of Denver, gathering speed, before he crawled down the grab-bars and returned to his compartment. He poured a fresh drink and lighted up a cheroot, then settled down into a chair to do a little more thinking.

Chapter 5

Longarm made several discoveries during the trip to Leadville. The first was that staff and minor visitors ate only after dinner had been served to the Tabors and their guests. By the time Forbes came to invite Longarm to sit down and enjoy supper with the staff of the private car, he was so famished he could have eaten bare beef bones raw.

On seeing the table, set up in the large compartment shared by Forbes and the French chef, next to the galley, he learned that what Forbes had described as a "simple picnic supper" was more than a plateful of drying sandwiches, cold chicken drumsticks, and hard-boiled eggs, when the "simple picnic supper" had been prepared by a French chef and was served in a millionaire's private railroad car.

Here were sandwiches, but they were open-faced and spread with truffled *pâté de fois gras*. The chicken was thinly sliced white breast meat, accompanied by hot, flaky rolls and a rich, creamy spread. The eggs were halved and stuffed with their yolks, in which fresh caviar had been blended. As a final touch, there was a cream of asparagus soup that was almost as satisfying as a full meal. Privately, Longarm would have preferred steak and potatoes, but he was so hungry that he tackled the food with gusto and found himself enjoying it.

He discovered, too, that when the chef dines with the staff, the food served does not consist of millionaire's leftovers. Every dish on the table had been freshly prepared, and even the delicate white wine that accompanied the meal was poured from a newly opened bottle. His final discovery, though, was delayed until after dinner.

Forbes had arranged the seating. Longarm sat at his right, and Suzanne, Mrs. Tabor's maid, sat at his left, with the chef, Jean-Pierre, across from the factotum. Longarm thanked Forbes silently for the seating arrangements. He'd much rather be looking at Suzanne, a tiny brunette with the high coloring that so often complements the attractiveness of dark-haired women, and flashing brown eyes under thick eyebrows. The severe black dress she wore failed to hide her full breasts that jutted proudly above a thin waist and flared hips.

On Longarm's right side, the French chef made no secret of his evil mood. He muttered under his thin, pointed mustache while Forbes was seating them at the table, and the compliments of the diners on his food elicited only grunts and nods, although the chef's bad temper did not seem to affect his appetite. Longarm paid him little attention. He was kept busy returning the sultry glances sent him across the table by Suzanne.

Finally, Forbes broke the silence that the glowering chef had imposed on the table. He asked, "What's wrong, Jean-Pierre? It isn't something Suzanne or I have done, is it?"

"*Non, non!* It is the general! He insults the first meal I have prepare for him!" the Frenchman scowled.

"But, on the trip—" Forbes began, then stopped, thought for a moment, and went on, "But that's right. The senator and Mrs. Tabor and the general ate in the dining car while we were attached to the Limited."

"And just as well!" Jean-Pierre exploded. "Or I would have quit before we came to this uncivilized place!"

"What did General Grant do to rile you?" Longarm asked.

"My good food! My *pâté de fois gras,* with the shreds of delicate white truffles! My chicken breast with béchamel sauce! Even my eggs *farcis!* All of them, he pushes away like garbage!" Jean-Pierre demonstrated by shoving his own plate halfway across the table.

"Maybe the general just don't like rich-seasoned food," Longarm suggested mildly.

"Bah! My dishes are not rich! They are perfect in seasoning and texture!"

Forbes showed his surprise in his voice. "I hadn't heard about all this, Jean-Pierre. The senator told me to serve them and leave, that they wanted to talk privately. I put the platters on the table, and left."

Jean-Pierre was not through. He ignored Forbes and went on, "Then what is take place? So, I will tell you! Mrs. Tabor herself comes to my kitchen. 'Oh, Jean-Pierre,' she is say, 'the general wants plain meat for his dinner.' Plain meat, *mes amis!* Only beef! No herbs, no spices, nothing but salt! And cooked *noircire,* black, like a coal dead in the ashes!"

Longarm still tried to soothe the chef's feelings. "I'd say the general's got too used to army food. They cook everything till it's plumb mushy."

"Then he should get used to food prepared in a civilized manner!" Jean-Pierre exclaimed. "*Non!* When we get to this place called Leadville, I will resign! I will not cook in such a way! Beef, beef, beef! No mutton, no pork, no *venaison*! Beef! Bah, bah, *bah*!"

Suzanne asked Longarm, "How about you, Marshal Long? You were taking General Grant's side, as near as I could tell."

"Well, now, you didn't see me picking at what Jean-Pierre fixed up for us, did you?"

"No. But looking at you, I'd bet you like a lot of good meat. Most big, strong men do."

"Oh, I won't deny I like a good steak," Longarm said. "And I bet Jean-Pierre could cook up a dandy one, if he put his mind to it."

None of them were prepared for Jean-Pierre's

explosion. The chef flung up his arms, then jumped to his feet, kicking his chair over backward. He looked with wild eyes at the window, then started for the door, as he shouted, "Steak! Steak! It is all you *sacré Américains* know!"

While the others were still staring at him with surprise, the Frenchman rushed out of the compartment.

"I'd better go try to calm him down," Forbes said, rising hastily. "He might do something foolish, like throwing himself off the train, in the mood he's in." Forbes followed Jean-Pierre out into the corridor.

Suzanne smiled across the table at Longarm. "If you're concerned about Jean-Pierre, you don't show it, Marshal."

"There's nothing wrong with him except he's got a full head of steam up," Longarm told the girl. "Soon as he blows it off, he'll settle down."

"I'm sure you're right. French chefs are always getting into a pet of some sort, but they get over it fast."

"You talk like you've known a lot of them," Longarm commented.

"I've seen a few, at places I've worked before Mrs. Tabor hired me. Rich people seem to think they've got to have one, just to stay in style."

"So I've noticed. Senator Tabor's got another Frenchie cooking at that hotel he owns in Leadville. But I never had much to do with them, myself."

"And I've never had anything to do with a real Western marshal. You're the first one I've seen."

"Lived in the East all your life, I guess?"

"Marshal, I've never been farther west than Pittsburgh. But I've heard a lot about you marshals, how you have gunfights with badmen and things like that," Suzanne said.

"You know, you can't believe everything you read nowadays. Half of it's made up by Eastern dudes who never got past Pittsburgh either."

"Well, I intend to find out for myself. I can't believe some of the things I've heard and read."

Forbes came in, mopping his forehead. "Jean-Pierre's all right. I talked to him for a few minutes, and managed to calm him down. He won't do anything foolish. We'd better finish our supper. We're going to have a busy time when we arrive in Leadville."

After the trio had finished eating, Forbes and Suzanne went about their jobs and Longarm started back to his compartment. The train was wheeling up the grade to Trout Creek Pass now, and with the memory of his earlier trip still fresh in his mind, he decided to step into the vestibule and look around. The moon's phase had changed, and the night was dark. The little engine pulling the special train had only two cars behind it instead of a full load and even on the steep upslope, it was clipping along at a healthy pace. He leaned out of the vestibule and looked in front of the engine, where the headlight's glare revealed the trees along the right-of-way flashing past.

He thought, *There just ain't much of a way anybody's going to hop on board, this trip. Not at the speed we're making.*

Satisfied, he returned to his compartment and poured himself an after-dinner drink. The first sip cleared his throat of the creamy taste left from the sauce Jean-Pierre had concocted to go with the chicken, and a cleared throat with half a glass of good Maryland rye waiting to be savored called for an after-dinner cheroot. He lighted up and puffed the blue smoke with satisfaction, thought about pulling off his boots and propping up his feet on one of the chairs, but decided he'd better leave them on. He sat down and leaned back, propping his feet up on the extra chair, boots or no boots. He was just beginning to relax when the click of the knob on the compartment door brought him to his feet, whirling cat-quick as he rose, to face whoever might be coming in.

Suzanne opened the door just wide enough to slip into the compartment. Her eyes widened when she saw Longarm whipping around to face her. "My goodness!" she gasped. "You'll scare the goodie out of a girl if you're not careful! I didn't know a man as big as you are could move so fast!"

Longarm told her severely, "Don't talk about careful

to me. You took a fool's chance, girl. A man with a job like mine has got a habit of shooting when he hears somebody trying to sneak up on him. You're lucky I saw you in time. Why didn't you just knock before you came in?"

"I didn't dare risk it," Suzanne replied. "I'm not supposed to be here at all. I ought to be in my room, in case Mrs. Tabor decides she wants me to do something."

"Then you're taking another chance," Longarm told her. "What if she does?"

"She won't. I peeked at her and the senator. They're still talking to General Grant. And a girl in my job learns to use what few minutes she's got to herself if she wants to get any pleasure out of life."

"And you want your pleasure now?"

"If you didn't know that the minute you saw me, you Western men aren't what I've heard they are." Suzanne moved up to Longarm and pressed her body against him. "I've been wondering about you ever since I saw you get on at Denver. If we hadn't been sitting so far apart at supper, I'd have found out a lot more about you by now." Her hand crept up his thigh to his crotch, and began exploring. After a moment, she shook her head. "I guess it's not true, what I've heard."

"Depends on what you've heard." Longarm was beginning to get interested in this forward girl who came looking for what she wanted.

"One thing I've been told is that a man out here in the West is always ready to take on a woman." While she spoke, she was inserting her fingers into Longarm's fly, seeking its buttons.

He said, "We generally are, if the woman's willing and ready."

Suzanne's fingers had done their work now. Her entire hand was in Longarm's trousers. She sought and found what she'd been after. The gentle pressure he felt from her warm hand was bringing him erect.

"Maybe I was wrong," she said, liberating his swelling shaft. She looked down and her eyes grew wide.

"I guess I was. And what I've heard about Western men being big—well, I'm beginning to believe that now."

"If you're really looking for me to pleasure you, I better drop down that bed that's folded up against the wall over there," he said. He brought a hand up to the buttons of her dress, high on her back.

"No. I haven't got time to undress. Not now." She took his hand and pressed it to her breast. "You'll just have to feel me through my clothes, this time."

Longarm said, "If you ain't got time to undress, you ain't got time enough to take all the pleasuring a woman needs."

"I've learned to take what I can get, Marshal," she answered. "You don't know what it's like, being on call all day and all night, having to steal a minute here and there from a woman who thinks she owns every second of your time."

"I know what it means to be on duty, all right."

Longarm thought of the times in the past when his own pleasure had been far more hurried than he'd liked. He said philosophically, "I guess we better just do the best we can." He rubbed her breasts, feeling her nipples harden under his fingers.

Suzanne quivered and wrapped her hand around him. Longarm was erect now, and she gasped, "My God, it *is* true! Hurry up, sit down!"

Longarm backed up to the chair. Suzanne did not let go of him as he sat down and stretched his legs out in front of the chair. She raised her skirt with her free hand. Beneath her dress, Suzanne wore nothing but a slip and long hose that came halfway up her thighs. Longarm got a fleeting glimpse of the coal-black fur at the juncture of her plump white thighs before she turned her back to him.

Her buttocks were as white as her thighs, as firm and as well-rounded. Suzanne straddled his legs and lowered her body an inch or two. She took her hand away and leaned forward. He could feel her thigh muscles grow taut as they took her weight. A small murmur like the satisfied purring of a giant cat began in her throat as she lowered herself slowly. The murmuring grew louder as he felt himself sliding into her wet, warm depths. Suzanne prolonged his penetration as much as she could. It seemed several minutes before Longarm felt the full weight of her body come to rest on his hips.

Looking at him over her shoulder, Suzanne said, "Now I believe what I've heard. I hope you feel as good as I do right now."

"You'll feel better when I get all the way in," he told her.

"Oh, no! I'm full right now! I don't think there's room for any more of you!"

"There's always room. No use in letting anything go to waste."

Longarm grasped Suzanne's hips and pulled her down on him. She squealed as she felt the penetration of his last inches, and gasped, "I didn't think I could do it, but I am! And, oh, how wonderful it is! Oh, damn it! Why do we have to hurry right now!"

As though suddenly aware that time was passing faster than she'd realized, Suzanne began to rock her hips back and forth. Longarm held them firmly and helped her to move faster until he felt her breathing begin to turn to panting. He stopped her then, and held her motionless. Suzanne moaned and swayed and tried to move, but he held her motionless until her breathing was once again slow and even.

When she felt Longarm release the pressure on her hips, Suzanne began to gyrate them, revolving her torso in quickening circles. Longarm knew she was getting ready to climax, and he was far from reaching that point yet. He stopped her movements for a second time, grasping the soft flesh of her hips between his strong fingers and bringing a whimper of painful pleasure from deep in her throat.

"Don't do that!" she begged. Then, "Don't stop doing it, either!"

"I don't aim to stop, not until I catch up with you."

"You'll have to catch up fast, then," she warned him.

Longarm knew what he needed to do. He stood up, holding Suzanne impaled on his shaft, and turned her around so they faced the chair. He touched Suzanne's shoulders and she understood. She bent over, resting her hands on the chair's seat. Relieved of her weight on his hips, he could now stroke and pace himself.

His first thrusts were slow and deliberate, deep and smooth. Suzanne moaned, not with pain now, but with ecstasy brought by Longarm's prolonged, almost leisurely penetrations. Her lubricity was beginning to work on him. He speeded his stroking, hurrying now to respond to Suzanne's urging to catch up. She helped him by turning her hips from side to side. His thrusts were no longer going into her freely; now the hot flesh of her wet inner lips scraped softly along his shaft as he pounded in.

Longarm felt himself building. He knew Suzanne was holding herself back; her inner muscles were tightened against his plunging. He began stroking faster, getting caught up in the excitement that radiated from her with each short quiver of her writhing body. When Suzanne began to jerk convulsively, Longarm was almost ready to let go. He held back until her spasms were coming in waves, and she was whimpering with each recurring convulsion. He felt her peak and pass the peak, and felt her muscles relax. He pushed himself harder with a few final, fierce thrusts, and stopped abruptly, his hands on her hips, pulling her to him as he spurted and shook and let himself go. Then he held her close until her quivering stopped and her gusting breaths subsided.

For a moment or two after Longarm released her and stepped back, Suzanne did not move, but stood bent over, clutching the chair. Longarm could see that her knees were trembling. She stood up and gave her shoulders a vigorous twist to shake her dress down, then turned to him.

"If all the men in the West are like you, I'm going to like it out here," she said with a smile. Then she shook her head. "But I know that's too much for a girl to hope for. I know one thing: I'm sure going to hate to say goodbye to you in Leadville. I'd give a lot to be in bed with you some night, when we could take our time."

"No reason why you can't. I'm going to stay at the Tabors' house as long as General Grant's in Leadville."

"Why, you devil! If you'd told me that before, I'd have waited—" She shook her head. "No, I wouldn't have waited. I was getting goosebumps just thinking about you all during supper. There wasn't a thing that would've kept me from getting in here as quick as I could manage to."

Longarm grinned. "I had a thought or two about that, myself. It's the finest way I know for us to get acquainted."

"Damn it, I wish we had time for another one, right now," she said, brushing back a wisp of hair that had fallen over her forehead. "Listen, Marshal, I've got to go. I don't know how long I've been here, but it's longer than I should be. Maybe I can get away later tonight, after things settle down at the Tabor house . . . if you'd like for me to, that is."

"I can't think of anything I'd like better."

"Good. Now, I've got to run." Suzanne pressed a quick kiss on Longarm's lips, and slipped out the door.

Longarm shook his head. *I'll never figure Eastern women,* he thought, recalling some of those he'd encountered who were traveling through the West. *Most of them act like every day is the last day they'll be alive.* He poured a fresh drink, settled down in the easy chair, and propped his feet up again.

Might as well rest while I got a chance. If Suzanne gets away later on, it could be real long night. But she saved me a lot of time, coming in here like she did. Now I've got a pair of eyes and ears where they could be right handy, if there's trouble. Yes, sir, that little girl might turn out to be a real ace-in-the-hole.

He leaned back and closed his eyes. Things were beginning to work out.

With a gust of steam pouring from its cylinders and a long shriek of its tenor-toned whistle, the special train pulled in and stopped at the Leadville depot. Longarm had gone out to the private car's observation platform the moment he'd been able to distinguish, in the general blur of light, the fires of the individual smelters ringing the town. He was surprised at the size of the crowd waiting beside the tracks; half of Leadville seemed to have turned out to welcome Tabor. Or more likely, Longarm thought, Tabor's guest.

Behind him, the door's latch clicked. It was his signal to step down to the station platform, but he'd put to good use the few minutes he'd had to scan the crowd. He'd seen nothing alarming, which didn't surprise him. Any effort to get to Grant would be more likely to be made after the general had established some sort of routine that would give an assassin a clue to his probable whereabouts at favorable moments. He swung off the platform just as Tabor came out with Baby Doe on his arm. The Silver King smiled and waved, and held up his arms; it was the same gesture Longarm had seen him use at the Denver depot.

"My friends and neighbors," Tabor began, as the bustle diminished, "We're glad to be back with you. As you know, I've been fortunate enough to find a lovely wife, and I present her to you now."

He waited for applause; when it came, it was less than deafening. Not a bit perturbed, Tabor waited until Baby Doe had made a nodding bow, then said, "And now, my honored guest, who is the man I know you've been waiting to see. The former President of the United States, and General of the Armies, my good friend, Ulysses S. Grant!"

This time the applause was genuine. Longarm shot his eyes here and there among the spectators, trying to locate those who were standing glumly silent, or glowering angrily, instead of applauding. His range of vision, as he stood now at the same level as the crowd, was limited to the front rows, but all those at whom he looked appeared to be in the ranks of Grant's well-wishers.

An inevitable amount of shifting was going on in the throng, as those in the back pressed forward and those in the front shifted to one side or the other, trying to get a better look at the famous visitor. Through the gap that opened momentarily, Longarm spotted Mart Duggan. Wearing his usual derby hat and blue suit, the Leadville city marshal was leaning against the depot wall. Duggan saw Longarm and waved.

Longarm began pushing through the crowd toward Duggan just as the engineer let off a series of whistle blasts. An instant later, Longarm almost jumped out of his boots when the engine's whistles were drowned by a louder, higher-pitched cacophony of shrieking. It sounded to Longarm like a million goats had selected the same moment to protest some overpowering indignity.

Almost to a man, the spectators turned, trying to locate the source of the new noise. From around the corner of the depot came a trio of bagpipers, their pipes shrilling some tune that sounded vaguely familiar to Longarm, but which he couldn't put a name to. Then he forgot the wild music. Following the pipers, there came rank after rank of men marching four abreast, wearing uniforms that would have put a rainbow to shame.

Longarm blinked at the dazzle of color. The marchers wore short black jackets faced with cording of scarlet and bright blue—the same blue, Longarm realized belatedly, with which the Tabor private railroad cars were painted. The marchers wore kilts of scarlet plaid, the bright red background chequered with lines of green, black and white, and capes of the same tartan pattern draped rakishly over one shoulder.

Creamy goatskin sporrans bounced at mid-thigh with each step they took, the silver-clasped black tassels that adorned the sporrans sparkling bluely. The marchers' knees were bare, and the exposed skin looked a dull, faded pink between the bright patterned kilts and the calf-high stockings of the same color and design. The crowning touch was provided by their caps: black velvet berets worn drooping to one side, while, on the other side, silver buckles supported long white plumes that nodded as the men marched.

Longarm stopped short and stared in blank amazement as the pipers shouldered through the crowd. Very little pushing on their part was necessary, for at close range, the earsplitting wail of the bagpipes was so loud that it was painful to hear. The spectators parted, leaving a lane through which the pipers led the ranked marchers to the observation platform.

Longarm got a look at Grant's face. The general was staring as wide-eyed as any of the other onlookers, his habitual cigar drooping from his half-opened mouth.

With a final skirling of pipes, the uniformed men halted. The pipes whirred into silence. Tabor stepped to the edge of the observation platform and took a long, white-encased package that the leader of the uniformed group handed up to him. Then the Silver King turned to face Grant.

"General," he said, "as a remembrance of your visit to Leadville, the greatest silver-producing city in the civilized world, it's my pleasure to present to you, on behalf of Mrs. Tabor and myself, and for the citizens of our city, this solid silver sword."

He ripped the wrappings from the package and held up the sword in its gleaming silver scabbard. Then he went on, "Not only does this sword symbolize your victorious leadership of our nation's armies in war, but your strong hand at the helm of the ship of state during your terms as president."

A burst of applause began from the crowd; those who had little use for Grant as a military commander responsible for the South's defeat felt obliged to acknowledge his leadership of the nation he'd done so much to reunite.

Tabor waved for silence and continued, "But this sword symbolizes even more. It indicates that, for the duration of your stay in Leadville, you are once more a commander of a military force: Tabor's Highland Guards, who will provide an escort of honor to my home this evening, after you have said a few words to our good citizens."

Grant took the sword, extended to him by Tabor. He held it above his head for the crowd to see. He began to speak, his light voice almost lost until the crowd subsided, straining to hear.

". . . for this sword," Grant was saying when his words became audible. "It is a memento which will always remind me of your city when I look at it. And Senator Tabor," he went on, addressing Tabor directly, "I don't expect to have any occasion to give your Highland Guards any commands while I'm here, but it's an honor to be given the leadership of such a fine-looking group of men. Thank you, all of you."

"Short and sweet, wasn't he?" a voice said in Longarm's ear. He turned to see Mart Duggan, who'd come up behind him while the Highland Guards were marching into position.

"Mart, tell me one thing. Where in hell did Silver Dollar get that ragtag bunch?" Longarm asked. He kept one eye on the observation platform, where the spectators were crowding up to shake Grant's hand.

"Oh, they go back quite a few years. Back to when there wasn't any law to speak of here. Tabor wasn't the only one who had a little private army to guard his mines and smelters. Why, there was the Carbonate Rifles and the Wolf Tone Guards and a half-dozen more. Got to be a sort of race between the mine and smelter operators, to see which one could get up the fanciest outfit."

"Well, I'd say Silver Dollar won, hands down," Longarm said.

"Oh, this bunch ain't what it used to be, when I was in command of 'em," Duggan said. "Hell, I had 'em looking like *real* soldiers."

"I didn't know you'd ever worked for Tabor."

"I did, as long as I could stand it. It beat freezing my ass off in a mine, or sweating in a smelter. Then, after I got picked for city marshal, I stayed with the Guards for a while before I gave it up."

"I'll be damned." Longarm looked around to see if there was anyone listening. He dropped his voice and asked, "Your lines get any nibbles?"

Duggan shook his head. "Not yet. They're still out

there, though. I suppose you'll be at Tabor's house as long as Grant's in town?"

"I suppose. Unless the general moves someplace else, which ain't very likely."

"I'll send word there, if I hear anything," Duggan promised.

"Thanks, Mart. I'll look in on you, whenever I can get away long enough. We'll have that night on the town yet."

"Sure."

A patter of hooves sounded from behind the station, and grew louder, attracting the attention of both Duggan and Longarm. A barouche came in sight, drawn by as fine a pair of horses as Longarm had ever seen.

Duggan anticipated Longarm's question. "It's Tabor's rig. I guess him and the new missus and Grant are going to ride."

"Damn it, I'm going to have to run to keep up!" Longarm exclaimed. "No place I can get a horse real quick, is there?"

"Not a one. Closest livery stable's three blocks away. You don't have to worry, though, I'd bet. If I know Tabor, he'll have his Guards march alongside the carriage all the way to his house. You won't need a horse to keep up."

"I got to get my gear off the train, though," Longarm said. "Looked like it was lost for a while, but Forbes, that factu-whatever of Tabor's, dug it up for me out of the luggage closet."

"I'll look for you to drop in, then," Duggan said.

"First chance I get," Longarm called over his shoulder as he hurried toward the train.

Forbes appeared in the vestibule just as Longarm started up the steps of the private car. "I was wondering where you were, Marshal Long," the factotum said. "There'll be a carriage here in a few minutes to take the staff to the mansion, if you'd care to ride with us."

"I'd appreciate it. Not that it's much of a walk, but I'm supposed to keep pretty close to the general."

"So the senator's informed me. I've changed the bedroom arrangements I had in mind, then, and put you in the room opposite General Grant's. Will that be satisfactory?"

"Suits me fine," Longarm told Forbes. "I'll just step into the car and pick up my gear, and then I'm ready to go."

"You needn't worry about your luggage, Marshal. There's a wagon waiting to haul all the bags and trunks to the mansion. Your bag will be on it, and your rifle."

"I think, if it's all the same to you, I'll carry the Winchester myself. I don't feel real easy when anybody else gets their hands on it without me watching to see what they do to it."

"Suit yourself," Forbes replied, "if you feel that strongly about its being safe."

"Oh, I ain't worried about the gun being safe, Forbes," Longarm explained. "It's my hide that concerns me. If I need to use that Winchester and it don't work right, if somebody's monkeyed with the sights or the action, I might get some holes put in me."

"I hadn't looked at it that way," Forbes said. "I don't blame you a bit for wanting it with you."

When Longarm returned carrying the Winchester, Suzanne and Jean-Pierre had joined Forbes, and a closed carriage was just pulling up beside the train. The men stood aside to let Suzanne get in first, and she managed to flounce around in the center of one of the seats while Jean-Pierre was boarding. The chef had to take his place on the facing seat. This left the space beside Suzanne for Longarm, and placed Forbes with Jean-Pierre.

They were several minutes behind the carriage in which the Tabors and Grant were riding, escorted by the Highland Guards, but the escort marched slowly, and when the little procession turned into Harrison Street, the second carriage had caught up with the first. In the dark passenger compartment, Suzanne had captured Longarm's hand and tucked it under her skirt. His fingers roamed along her thighs, and she twitched occasionally as he caressed their warm softness.

In a strained voice, she asked Forbes, "Have you

chosen rooms for each of us yet, in the house we're going to?"

"Certainly. Your bedroom will be at the head of the stairs on the third floor. It's directly above the Tabors' bedroom, and there's a bell-pull which Mrs. Tabor will use when she wants you. Jean-Pierre, you will be across the hall from Suzanne."

"You told me I was going to be opposite the general's room," Longarm said to Forbes, understanding now the reason for Suzanne's question. "I take it that's on the second floor?"

"Yes. Just down the hall from the Tabors', at the rear of the mansion. And my own room will be on the—" Forbes's words were interrupted by a fusillade of shots from the street ahead of the carriage.

Longarm sprang from his seat, thrusting his rifle toward Forbes, who sat across from him. He was drawing his Colt as he wrenched open the carriage door, and he hit the street running. He could see the barouche and its occupants quite clearly in the always-bright Leadville night. Grant and Tabor were sitting in the back seat, waving their hats. Baby Doe Tabor sat facing them. All three of them seemed unharmed. More shots sounded. Longarm looked around, trying to locate their source. He saw Mart Duggan walking behind the last line of the Highland Guards, and hurried up to him.

"Mart, what in hell's going on?" he demanded.

Duggan looked around, with surprise on his face. Then he burst into a wide grin that set his sandy mustache to twitching and bristling. "Oh, hell, that's just some of the boys, hoo-rahing for Grant. They was shooting in the air, not *at* anybody."

Longarm breathed a relieved sigh. He'd overlooked the custom of spectators applauding with sixguns. "Jesus! Had me going for a minute there."

"Yeah, you looked right determined when you come at me waving that Colt. I thought for a minute you was after me."

Longarm smiled sheepishly. "Makes a man feel like a damn fool, don't it? Just the same, I'll walk along with you till this parade gets to the Tabor house, and I see Grant safe inside."

"You plan to tuck his nibs in bed, and pull the covers up around his whiskers?" Duggan asked, poking Longarm in the ribs with his big thumb.

"It ain't funny, Mart. If I ever let Billy Vail shove me into another job of nursemaiding like this one, I hope somebody kicks my ass from the South Platte to the Mississippi River!"

Longarm devoted most of the next morning to exploring the Tabor mansion. He was just as glad the Tabors and Grant had decided to stay indoors part of the day and rest from the long train trip West. He'd just begun to doze the night before, when Suzanne had come in to fulfill her wish of getting into bed with him when they could take their time, and they'd taken so much time, between the time she'd slipped into his bedroom and sunup, that he'd gotten almost no sleep.

Throughout the morning, Longarm wandered through the big house with seeming aimlessness. Like all the other miniature palaces the silver magnates had built along Carbonate Avenue, the Tabor house was huge and ornate. Longarm covered it from the basement, with its kitchen, storage rooms, and wine cellar, to the bare, echoing attic under its slate roof.

He began to get an idea of the wealth H. A. W. Tabor must control, to be able to build such a house in Leadville and another, even bigger, in Denver. The rooms on the main floor of the Leadville house were enormous, scaled to twelve-foot ceilings. On the second floor they were a bit smaller; the ceilings on this level were only ten feet high. It wasn't until Longarm got to the staff quarters on the third floor that he began to find rooms that were similar in size to the one in which he lived. Here, the ceilings were cramped down to a mere eight feet, and the rooms were of a more usual size.

Everywhere Longarm looked, there was silver. He didn't know how much of it was solid and how much was plate, but the doorknobs, the exposed gas pipes that supported the lighting fixtures, and even the latches on the stained glass windows of the first and second floors, were made of the shining white metal. So were the bathtub and lavatory faucets in the bathrooms on all but the top floor; the staff-level bathroom had faucets of brass.

Massive furniture cluttered all the rooms on the two main floors. On the first floor, mahogany and tapestry predominated in all the rooms except Tabor's study, which was lined with unopened books. There, the upholstery was leather. On the second floor, canopied beds towered to the ceilings, and marble-topped chests of drawers and vanity dressers stood against the walls.

Oddly, there were few pictures in any of the rooms, though a large oil painting of Tabor occupied a prominent position in the main salon. Next to it, an obtrusively bare spot hinted that a matching portrait of the first Mrs. Tabor, divorced only a few weeks before the Senator's marriage to Baby Doe, had recently been removed.

Satisfied that he'd be able to find his way around in the big house, even in the darkness, Longarm sought Tabor and Grant. He found them in the conservatory, a pleasant, glassed-in room, bare now of plants, that looked out over the town and caught any rays of sunshine that managed to filter through the ever-present haze of smelter-smoke that shrouded the sky. A tray with glasses and a bottle of sherry sat on a table between the wicker chairs in which the two men sat.

Longarm stopped in the doorway and cleared his throat by way of announcing himself. Tabor looked around.

"Oh, Marshal Long. I heard from Forbes that you were looking over my house. Did you find something you wanted to tell me about?"

"No, Senator," Longarm replied. He took the chair that Tabor indicated with a wave, and returned Grant's nod of greeting before sitting down. "I just need to talk with you and the general for a minute, if you've got the time to spare."

"Certainly. What's on your mind?" Tabor asked.

"Like I told you on the train yesterday, I want to keep out from underfoot as much as I can and still do my job," Longarm began. "But I've still got my orders to carry out. I'm going to have to be wherever the general is, as long as he's in Leadville."

"I told you yesterday that it's all right with me," Grant said.

"Yes, sir, General. But if it's not too much bother, I'd like to know where you gentlemen plan to go and when, so I can be ready and not have to run to catch up with you, like last night."

"I didn't mention that welcome at the station yesterday, because I was saving it as a surprise for the general," Tabor explained.

"Oh, I understand about that, senator. But I don't mind telling you, I got upset when the men in the crowd there on Harrison Street begun shooting their guns, saluting the general."

"It upset me for a minute too," Grant chuckled. "I'd forgotten your Western custom, and I haven't heard a lot of firearms being discharged since '65."

"It didn't hurt anything, of course," Longarm said quickly. "Only, it just shows how a man can be taken by surprise. And it might not be just funning, the next time."

"Nonsense!" Grant snorted. "Now listen to me, Marshal Long. I know what sort of bee the attorney general's got in his bonnet. He's always been overcautious. It's not at all likely that I'm in the least bit of danger here."

"Well, General Grant, I can't say yes or no to that," Longarm said soberly. "But it still don't change my orders. Now, I don't imagine you'd cotton to a man who didn't follow whatever orders you gave him, would you?"

Grant thought about this for a moment. He nodded and turned to Tabor. "The marshal's right, Horace. We're not being fair to him, even though he didn't put it quite that bluntly. We owe it to him, as a man under orders, to keep him informed of our movements and plans."

"I suppose so," Tabor agreed. "Very well, Marshal Long. This afternoon, after we've had luncheon, the general and I are going to stroll around for about an hour on Harrison and Chestnut Streets. We'll just be shaking hands and letting him say hello to the ordinary folks here in Leadville. If there's time, we might go over to State Street for a few minutes, so the sporting element won't feel they're being left out."

"You don't plan to do anything special?" Longarm asked. "You're just going for a simple little walk?"

"Oh, I imagine we'll be forced to go into two or three of the better saloons. Some of our more prominent men are sure to insist on treating the general to a drink, and I don't see how we can refuse such a reasonable request. Then we'll come back here for dinner."

Longarm nodded. "That's fine, Senator. What about supper tonight? And after supper?"

"Just the family for dinner," Tabor replied. "After dinner, I've invited a few of the mining and smelting leaders in for a small reception. And I'll personally vouch for each one of them." Tabor's voice had taken on a slight edge. He went on, "Tomorrow I'm taking the general for a drive. We'll go look at a few mines and smelters. We won't get out of the buggy at any of them, unless it's the Little Pittsburgh or the Matchless. I suppose you know I own both of them, and I feel I can trust my employees. If you think you should go with us, I'll take a chaise instead of a buggy, so we'll have room."

"I'd appreciate it if you'd do that, Senator. If it'll help any, I'll handle the reins," Longarm offered.

"No," Grant broke in. "That's reserved for me. You might not know it, Marshal, but my only real pleasure is harness driving. And poker, of course. But I haven't had a set of reins in my hands for quite a while, and I know Horace has some fine horses. I've already put in my bid."

"So you have," Tabor agreed. He leaned his head back and thought for a moment. "There'll be nothing besides the drive, then, day after tomorrow. But the following day, Mrs. Tabor is holding an afternoon soirée for the ladies of Leadville, to get acquainted with them herself and to present them to the general. In the evening, General Grant's insisted on being host at a dinner for the leading families in Leadville. It will be at the Tabor Grand Hotel, and since it's also one of my properties, I think you'll agree that there's little possibility of any danger there."

Tabor paused and looked questioningly at Longarm. After a momentary hesitation, Longarm nodded agreement, although he had a few private reservations. This wasn't the time to mention them, though, he'd decided quickly.

"On the following day," Tabor went on, "I've invited some of my most influential political associates for a dinner, with the general as guest of honor. I'm providing a special train to bring a number of them from Denver, and I've selected the guest list very carefully. That should be enough to say on the subject of the dinner. And on the day after that, Mrs. Tabor and the general and I will go back to Denver."

"Senator, I sure thank you for your help," Longarm said. "I got all that tucked away in my mind now, so I'll know where I ought to be, and when. So, now that it's settled, I won't take up any more of your time." He made a clumsy little half-bow to the two men. "General, Senator. I'll bid you good day until it's time for us to go into town."

As he walked out of the conservatory, Longarm thought, *Well, old son, you sure got handed a nice job this time. Just how the billy blue hell am I supposed to keep a man safe who don't believe he's in danger, and how am I supposed to get the richest man in Colorado Territory to listen to me, when he ain't used to paying attention to anybody, or doing anything except what he damn well feels like?*

Chapter 6

Longarm didn't enjoy his luncheon. He was thinking about the afternoon ahead, wondering if Tabor's Highland Guards with their shrieking bagpipes were going to serve as escorts. The Guards would assure the gathering of a crowd, and after the barrage of shots on Harrison Street the night before, he'd been very much aware of just how easy it would be for almost anyone, close pistol-wielder or distant sniper, to make Grant a target.

He paid no attention to his table companions: Suzanne, Jean-Pierre, Forbes, and the mansion's resident housekeeper, Mrs. Morgan. They ate in the small staff dining room in the mansion's basement, sitting down as soon as Jean-Pierre had dished up the last of the food that the waiters would carry upstairs to the main floor dining room where Grant, Tabor and Mrs. Tabor were eating. As soon as he'd finished, Longarm took his hat and went looking for Tabor and Grant.

He found them sitting in Tabor's study, their coats draped over chair backs, finishing their after-dinner coffee and cigars. He hesitated for a moment in the open door, but the two didn't seem to be having much conversation, so he went in.

Tabor looked up. "Well, Marshal, you're right on

time. We're almost ready to go. Find a chair. It'll be a few minutes yet."

Longarm sat down and waited silently while the two men drained their coffee cups and snuffed out their cigar butts in a silver spittoon that stood at the corner of Tabor's massive desk.

"Well," Tabor said, slipping his arms into his coat-sleeves, "I suppose we'd better get started."

They walked the short distance to the end of Carbonate Avenue and turned south on Harrison Street. Tabor pointed proudly to his Grand Opera House, which towered above the Clarendon Hotel next to it. He said, "It's too bad the season hasn't opened yet, General. I wanted to arrange a gala night for you, but my manager couldn't get any really good performers here on such short notice."

"I won't miss it a bit, Horace," Grant replied dryly. "Opera's not exactly a favorite of mine. I'd rather sit in a good stud poker game or buck the tiger at a faro table anytime."

They walked on down Harrison Street. There were few people in sight, far fewer than there would have been moving around on the streets at midnight in another town of Leadville's size. Leadville was a somnolent place until evening arrived, except for brief flurries of activity in the dawn hours and late afternoon, when the shifts changed at the mines and smelters. The town didn't usually come to life until around six o'clock, then activity continued until nearly midnight. On State Street. it seldom slacked off until daybreak.

Grant's appearance changed that situation quickly. By the mysterious grapevine that exists in most small communities, the news spread quickly that the former president and wartime commander-in-chief was walking around town, and more and more people appeared to swell the throng that soon trailed in the trio's wake.

Their first stop was at Buchanan's Dry Goods Emporium, because, as Longarm heard Tabor say in an undertone to Grant as they went in the store, "He's a good Republican, one of our strongest supporters."

For the first few moments following their entrance, the few women poring over the bolts of yard goods on the tables and counters tried to look the other way. Then, after Grant had shaken hands with Jonas Buchanan and swapped a few comments about the weather, one of the shoppers approached the General somewhat timidly.

"You really are President Grant, aren't you?" she asked.

"No, ma'am," Grant replied, doffing his hat. "Now I'm just plain Mr. Grant, a citizen just like everybody else."

"Well, you'll always be General Grant to my husband, and President Grant to me," she told him. "And I just couldn't keep from coming over to shake your hand."

Grant had just lighted a fresh cigar; he'd taken it out of his mouth when the woman came up. Now he shifted it quickly from his right hand to his left and extended his right.

"My pleasure, ma'am."

Flurried by the handshake, the woman gave Grant a quick nod and hurried away. She'd broken the barrier, though. The rest of the women in the store flocked around Grant and Tabor. The Silver King stayed close to the general, but Longarm stepped aside a few feet and watched as hand after hand was shaken.

With very little variation, the same sequence of events took place in the next store and the next. As the three men slowly worked their way south on Harrison toward Chestnut Street, the number of shoppers in each store, as well as the number of strollers waiting on the sidewalk in advance of the three, grew larger and larger.

By the time they got to the corner of State Street, Grant had kissed five grandchildren of Union Army veterans, and had exchanged a few words with a score of veterans of the conflict who'd heard somehow that their former commander-in-chief was appearing in public. Most of the veterans had never seen Grant before, except perhaps at G.A.R. conventions, but one of them recalled having been under his direct command during the grim days when Grant was working his way up from an obscure colonel of a group of raw Illinois volunteers, fighting guerrillas in the border states.

"Well, you'll just have to come have a drink with me," Grant told this man. "It's not often that I see one of my real veterans, these days." He turned to Tabor. "Horace, which one of those saloons across the street do you recommend?"

Tabor glanced across Harrison to the corner of State Street, and said, "Er—either the Texas House or the Cabinet Saloon. They're both quality houses."

"Good," Grant said. He took the veteran by the arm and started across the slag-paved roadway. The crowd followed, and the men went inside with Grant and his group, leaving the women standing angrily on the sidewalk. Tabor, Longarm thought, was ill at ease while drinks were passed around. He seemed anxious to get them on their way again. Longarm understood why, when they were finally back on the street and moving south on Harrison again. They'd gone only a short distance, and entered only two stores, when Tabor stopped and pointed to a square brick building across the street.

"Well, what do you think about it?" he asked Grant. "There was too much excitement the other night for me to point it out to you."

Longarm had recognized the building from a distance, but it hadn't registered on him then. He knew what Tabor was referring to, but his eyes followed the magnate's extended finger, just as did Grant's. The two-story building, plain and classically severe in its design, had on its roof a replica of a silver dollar at least ten feet in diameter. The big disc glistened in the haze-filtered sunlight.

"My bank," Tabor explained, proudly but superfluously.

Grant lowered his eyes from the shining disc and smiled at Tabor. "I've heard your friends call you 'Silver Dollar,' " he said, "but I never did know until now how you came by the name. That's quite an idea, Horace, quite an idea."

"If you'd like to rest a minute, we can go inside." Tabor dropped his voice to a loud whisper and suggested, "Or we can go up the street, to the Tabor Grand Hotel."

"I can wait until we get to the hotel, if that's what you're asking me," Grant said. "But if you're in a hurry to go, I'll be glad to visit your bank for a few minutes."

"No, no," Tabor replied. "I'm all right. We'll just go along the way we're heading, then."

They set out again. The crowd had diminished somewhat after the stop at the saloon. Longarm trailed Grant and Tabor far enough behind so that he'd look like one of the group following them. He was feeling better than he had when the tour had first begun. So far, there'd been nothing but friendliness shown toward Leadville's distinguished visitor.

At the hotel, Tabor led the way inside. "If you'd like a room to yourself, I'll get a key at the desk," he offered. "I'm going to step into my office here for just a minute."

"I don't need a room." Grant said somewaht testily. "I'm not too good to use the public convenience. Just show me where it is. You take care of your business, and the marshal and I will wait for you in the bar."

For a moment, Longarm thought Tabor was going to insist that Grant take the private room, whether the general wanted it or not, but the Silver King finally nodded and indicated the opposite side of the ornately decorated lobby.

"It's right next to the door into the bar. Tell Powder House Billy you're my guests when you go in."

Longarm followed Grant into the public toilet. Like the bathrooms at the Tabor mansion, it was solid marble throughout, though the fittings of the urinals and washbasins were of brass instead of silver. Grant stepped into a urinal stall, and Longarm went into the one beside it. The slabs of marble that formed the partitions came to Longarm's shoulders.

116

Grant looked across the partition and said, "I don't know how you feel about the kind of public show I'm putting on, Marshal Long. To tell you the truth, I don't much enjoy it. It gives me the feeling that I'm running for office again, but I know I've finished with all that sort of thing."

"Well, now, General, if you don't enjoy it, I don't see what a man in your position does it for, then." Longarm said.

"Oh, I've got my reasons. Accommodating Horace is one of them. He put a lot of money into the Republican Party, these last two general elections. And there are other reasons," he added cryptically. "But shaking hands and kissing babies never did appeal to me."

Longarm came out of the stall and took a step backward toward the door. He was just turning when the door to the lobby swung open and a man rushed in. Longarm was in the midst of his second backward step, buttoning his fly. The man bumped into his left side, grinding Longarm's Colt into his hip.

"Oh! Excuse me!" the stranger gasped. He scurried into one of the toilet compartments and closed the door before Longarm got a look at him.

Grant backed out of the urinal stall and moved to the washbasins. Longarm joined him and they rinsed their hands.

The Tabor Grand Hotel sure don't hold back on towels, Longarm thought as he picked up a thick, fluffy hand towel from a rack holding perhaps two dozen. *But I guess the senator can afford to go first-class in just about everything he takes a notion to do.*

"I'll pass on the drinks this time, Marshal," Grant said as they returned to the lobby. "But if you feel like having one, I'll be glad to go in with you."

"No need, General. I'd just as soon pass too, this time."

As had been the case from the beginning of their walk, a crowd soon gathered around Grant. Longarm stepped back, as usual, and watched while Grant shook a dozen hands; the only sign of his professed distaste was the shifting of his cigar from one side of his mouth to the other. Tabor appeared from somewhere and stood beside Longarm for a moment, before joining Grant. After a few more conversational exchanges with the men in the crowd, the two began edging toward the lobby door. Longarm followed them to the street, and on across it to Chestnut Street.

Their stroll along Leadville's secondary business thoroughfare was a virtual repetition of their earlier progress along Harrison. Though Chestnut rivaled Harrison in importance, its stores and hotels—except for Walsh's Grand Hotel, which had had the name before Tabor's Grand Hotel—were smaller and less patronized.

Their tour along Chestnut was completed in far less time than it had taken to cover Harrison, and as they came back to their starting point and turned up Harrison and across State Street, Grant suddenly said, "Horace, didn't I hear you say this is the street with all the theaters and gambling houses on it?"

"Well, not all of them. Just the biggest ones."

"My feet are getting a little bit tired of walking," Grant said. "Why don't we step into one of these places and sit down? I might even risk a dollar or two in a game, if you can guarantee me it'll be an honest one. I haven't been in a gambling house since Mrs. Grant and I made our world tour, and stopped at Monte Carlo and some of the other famous places over there."

"Don't look to find anything like them in Leadville, General," Longarm said. He was walking with his companions now that the crowd had thinned to a dozen or so. "I heard some of them places make a man doll up in an evening suit before they'll even let him get inside."

"That's true enough," Grant said. He turned to Tabor and asked, with an impassive face, "Horace, I don't suppose they'll turn us away here because we're not wearing boiled shirts, will they?"

"Of course not!" Tabor replied indignantly. "Why, if they did—" He stopped, a belated smile twitching his lips, then went on, "We'll stop in at the California, if you want to turn a card or two."

Tabor led the way up State Street to a huge frame building that covered a good fourth of one of Leadville's small-sized city blocks. Inside, the establishment didn't look quite as large. It had been divided in half by a wall down the center, and the long rectangular room formed this way was cut into compartments by head-high partitions jutting from the walls. There were voices coming over the partitions, accompanied by the clicking of a roulette wheel and the rattle of chips.

A young man—Longarm judged him to be in his late twenties—sat behind a long desk just inside the door. He was coatless, but wore a vest, and his shirtsleeves were covered by black muslin protectors held by rubber bands just below his elbows.

"Mr. Tabor!" he exclaimed. "What brings you—" He caught sight of Grant and stopped short, staring. "That looks like—my God! It is!" He leaped up, hurried from behind the desk, and stopped in front of Grant.

"General, I'd heard you were in town, but I never thought I'd see you here in my place."

"Why not?" Grant asked. He ran his eyes over the streaked paint that covered the partitions. "It looks all right to me. I've *lived* in places worse than this one."

"This is Jeff Whinney, General," Tabor said. "He owns the California."

Grant extended his hand. "Glad to meet you, Mr. Whinney."

"Not half as glad as I am to meet you," Whinney said, pumping Grant's hand.

Tabor said, "The general wanted to sit down at a table and try his luck, Jeff. I thought about that fine faro dealer you've got here—"

"Why sure, Mr. Tabor. I don't think the faro table's getting a big play right now. If you gents will follow me . . ."

Whinney led them down the aisle that had been left between the partitions. Each held tables devoted to some different type of game: stud poker, draw poker,

119

chuck-a-luck, roulette, paddlewheel, keno. He stopped in front of the last partition.

"You'll be bucking the tiger against the best faro dealer in Colorado, gents: Miss Kitty Crawhurst."

"A woman?" Grant exclaimed. "Why, I've never—" He stopped and smiled. "Well, I suppose it had to come, someday." With a shrug of one shoulder, he followed Whinney into the enclosure. Tabor and Longarm were close behind him.

A half-dozen players, most of them miners or smelter workers, judging by their clothing, were spaced around the faro layout on the big, green, felt-covered table, but they might as well not have been there. On Longarm and the general, who'd never seen her before, Kitty Crawhurst had the impact of an explosion.

Her hair, piled high on her head and held in loose loops with silver-inlaid tortoiseshell combs, was a deep, brilliant red, from which her forehead curved downward, creamy, unmarred by lines, to dark brows and flashing green eyes. Her nose, on close examination, was a bit too wide for beauty, and her lightly rouged cheeks were a bit too plump, but these small flaws went unnoticed in the overall effect. Her generous lips were parted in a smile that showed good white teeth. Her chin was square, her jaw wide. Her dress was cut low, and a thin silver chain held a single large pearl in the cleavage between breasts squeezed tightly together by her sheer white satin dress and the corset underneath it.

"General Grant," Whinney said, "Miss Kitty Crawhurst, my top faro dealer."

Grant said, without smiling, "I think you must be hired by Mr. Whinney to keep players' minds off the game, Miss Crawhurst. But I'm old enough to be immune to beautiful women."

He took a long leather snap-purse from his coat pocket and shook some coins into his hand. Picking out five double eagles, he lined them up on the green felt, saying, "But I'll see if I can't concentrate on the cards."

"Thank you, General," Kitty said. She began stacking chips in front of him. "The limit's twenty-five dollars on any combination. The winner's still in the case, and I'll hold up my next turn until you've looked at the case-keeper." She asked Tabor, "Will you and the other gentlemen be bucking the tiger, Mr. Tabor?"

Tabor was whispering something to Whinney. He looked up and shook his head.

Longarm answered for himself, "No, thanks, miss. This is the general's fling."

Whinney disappeared and returned quickly, carrying a chair. He placed the chair behind Grant, who sat down without taking his eyes off the buttons of the case-keeper, which indicated the cards already drawn. When he'd finished studying the case-keeper, Grant turned back to face Kitty.

"Do you deal a brace game here, Miss Crawhurst?" he asked.

"No, General. But I will, to oblige you, on the next deal."

"Thank you, but I prefer singles." He dropped a chip on the layout, splitting his bet between the nine and the five. Two of the other players hurriedly dropped chips beside Grant's.

By now, word had spread around the gambling house that Grant was at the faro table. Players from the other compartments began to trickle in, and several of them bought chips for the game. A flurry of betting followed, and the layout was strewn with chips. Kitty waved her hand above the silver box, the "case" that held the deck, with its last winning card exposed. It was the faro dealer's traditional signal that no more bets could be placed on that turn.

Delicately, using only the tip of her forefinger, she pushed the card at the top of the case through the slit in the side of the box. The losing card thus revealed was a four. Kitty pushed it through the slit to show the winning card. It was a nine.

"Your card sense is working for you, General," she commented, dropping chips on top of the winning bets of Grant and the players who'd followed him in betting the five/nine combination.

A ripple of chatter passed around the table. Grant

picked up his winnings and dropped two of the chips on the seven, isolated at the end of the layout. The players who'd followed the general's bet in the last turn hurried to do the same. So did one of the newcomers to the game, who stood at the end of the table.

"Might as well follow you here, General," the man said. "I followed you to a win at Shiloh in '62."

Kitty waved her hand to close the betting, and put her forefinger on the nine that showed in the top of the case. Those around the table were watching her hand. So was Longarm, who stood beside Tabor and Whinney at the far end of the table, which was now lined with players.

The new player's mention of the Battle of Shiloh jangled in Longarm's mind, conjuring up for him a sense-memory of the odor of apple blossoms. As a raw, teenaged volunteer from the hardscrabble farm country of West Virginia, he'd killed his first man—a boy, really, no older than his own fifteen years—under the blossoming apple trees of 1862, in the hills surrounding Shiloh Chapel. Occasionally, in reverie or dreams, he still saw the quizzical, dead face staring up at him from its pillow of fragrant white petals.

Under the influence of this memory, the cacophony of the gaming room faded away, and the tall lawman's gaze narrowed, focusing on the new player. There was something familiar about the man . . .

Then two things struck Longarm at once. The man wasn't looking at the case, but had his eyes fixed on Grant. And Shiloh was the Confederate name for what the Union troops had called the Battle of Pittsburg Landing.

Grant was watching Kitty's hand as she shoved the nine out of the case to expose the losing card. So was every other player around the table, with the exception of the newcomer; that man's hand was stealing into his coat pocket. Longarm could see the man's fingers move to grasp something inside the pocket.

Then recognition flashed through Longarm's brain. The faro player had been in the crowd on Harrison Street, and was also the man who'd jostled into Longarm while he and Grant were in the men's room at the Tabor Grand Hotel, the man who'd ducked with such haste into one of the toilet compartments.

Longarm moved more by instinct than by plan. There were players all around the table, so he couldn't get a shot at the man, standing where he was. He took one step to his right, bumping into Tabor and Whinney and pushing them aside. Then, with a single giant stride, he leaped to the dealer's side of the faro layout, beside Kitty. He was drawing as he leaped. The stranger's coat pocket bulged out now, the unmistakable shape of a pistol barrel outlined by its cloth.

Longarm's shot caught the man an instant before he could turn the muzzle of his weapon toward Grant. The player began to sag. His dying reflex triggered the gun he was holding in his coat pocket. The cloth showed a patch of black as a slug from the hidden gun tore through the pocket and into the center of the faro layout.

For an instant following the two shots, the players around the table were frozen into statues. Then they all began to talk at once. Longarm raised his voice to cut through the babel.

"All of you men get back over there against the wall! I'm a U.S. marshal, and that's an official order!" he called.

Slowly, the players moved to obey. The shots had drawn men from the other compartments, and they packed into the corridor between the partitions. A few of them started to come inside the faro room, but a quick sweep of Longarm's Colt sent them backing out.

Without turning his head, Longarm said, "Whinney! Get some of your dealers and housemen, and herd everybody who wasn't at the faro table out of the way. Get them back where they were before the shooting."

Whinney was apparently no stranger to shootings. He spotted his housemen and dealers among the newcomers, barked a few quick, sharp commands, and within minutes, the faro room and the corridor in front of it were cleared of onlookers. Those who'd been at the faro table were still pinned by Longarm's revolver against the wall of the partition. Tabor was still in the corner where Longarm's bump had shoved him. Grant still sat at the faro table, his face expressionless. Kitty Crawhurst had backed up to the wall behind the table and was standing there, watching.

Longarm ran his eyes along the line of men who'd been playing at the table before the shooting. There were eleven of them; six or seven had been there before Longarm, Grant, and Tabor had arrived, and the others had come in afterward. None of the players seemed more nervous or upset than would anyone who'd witnessed an eruption of violence ending in sudden death.

"Now, then," Longarm told the players, "I guess you've all looked at dead men before. I want you to step up one at a time and take a look at that fellow on the floor, then tell me if you ever saw him before."

He gestured with the muzzle of his Colt to the man at one end of the line of players. The man stepped up to the body, bent over it, studied the dead man's face briefly, and shook his head.

"Far as I know, I never saw him before," he said.

Longarm nodded, and motioned for the next player to look. The player looked and shook his head. One by one, the players stepped up, inspected the corpse, and went back to their places.

One of them volunteered, "I noticed him when he first come in. He didn't act no different from anybody else."

Another said, "He shoved in between me and that fellow there, at the end of the table. Seemed to me like he was real set on getting a place there, instead of going where there was more elbow-room."

Longarm looked for confirmation to the player the speaker had indicated, who nodded.

"That's about what happened, Marshal; he just pushed in between us. I recall thinking he must be a piking player, he just bought in with twenty dollars."

"Miss Kitty?" Longarm said to the dealer. "You

mind looking at him and telling me if you remember him playing your table before?"

"I don't need to look at him, Marshal," she replied. "When I see a new face in a game I'm dealing, I pay special attention to it. I never saw that man before, in the California or anywhere else."

Whinney was standing guard in the opening of the faro room. Longarm asked, "Whinney? Is this fellow a stranger to you, too?"

"I don't remember his face, Marshal," the owner answered. "But we get a lot of men through here, and I might not recall him, unless he was a regular." Then Whinney went on, "I haven't had a chance to ask you yet, but do you want me to send one of my housemen over to tell Mart Duggan about this?"

Longarm nodded. "I guess you better. You got some kind of private place, a room where we can put this body to get it out of the way?"

"There's another faro room down the line," Whinney said. "It won't be in use until evening. You want my boys to move him down there?"

"I'd appreciate it. I ain't had a good look at him yet, and neither has Senator Tabor."

From the corner where he stood, Tabor said, "I don't need to look at him again, Marshal Long. I've never seen that man anywhere before, at any time."

Grant had not risen from his chair during the time spent by Longarm in questioning the witnesses to the shooting. Now he spoke for the first time. "I've never seen the man either, that I can recall, Marshal. Not unusual, though I've got a pretty good eye for faces. But there were a lot of men in the army. For all I know, this one might have been in one of the units under my command at Pittsburg Landing."

"If he was, it was because he was a spy, General," Longarm said.

Grant frowned. "I don't follow you."

"That's what tipped me off first, what he said about being there. You called it the Battle of Pittsburg Landing. That dead man, he called it what the Confederate side named the fight—Shiloh."

125

"You're right," Grant said, surprised. "It didn't occur to me when he spoke. That was quick thinking on your part, Marshal. It saved me from getting shot. I appreciate your fast action."

"Thank you, General."

Whinney's men came in, interrupting Longarm. He said, "If you'll excuse me now, I want to go along with these men Mr. Whinney's brought in. There might be something in that fellow's pockets that'll give us some idea why he came gunning for you."

"Take your time," Grant said. "Unless Miss Crawhurst's too nervous, or Mr. Whinney objects, I'm planning to stay right here and finish out my game."

Longarm followed the men carrying the sagging body. They went down the corridor, past the open compartments where poker, chuck-a-luck, and keno games were beginning to resume. Some of the players turned from the tables to look curiously at the little procession, while others paid no attention. At the last room on the corridor, the housemen turned in. Three or four chairs had been lined up in the center of the compartment, and they laid the body face-up across the chair seats.

"Thanks for your help," Longarm told Whinney. "I'd be grateful, if you've got a man who knows how to shoot, if you'll set him to keep an eye on the general while I'm in here. I don't reckon there's much chance anything else might happen to him, but I don't aim to take any chances, either."

"Sure," Whinney said. "I've got a couple of good men. I'll see to it, Marshal, don't worry. Damn it, I'd hate to have the General hurt or killed in my place." Then he added thoughtfully, as he turned to leave, "I'll bet it'd sure bring the crowds in, though."

Longarm first removed the gun from the dead man's pocket. It was an old Smith & Wesson "Russian model" revolver, with its barrel sawed off to reduce the size of the weapon. Longarm broke the gun, and the ejector plate lifted its .41 caliber cartridges up where he could pick one out. The cartridge was shiny-new, as new as the sawmarks on the shortened barrel. Longarm could tell at a glance that the gun had been modified to make a pocket weapon of it, a revolver that could be as easily concealed as a derringer, but gave its user five rounds instead of the derringer's one or two, and though its accuracy was poor, the sizable load its cartridge cases carried made it a deadly short-range weapon.

"Somebody did a lot of thinking about this," he muttered, hefting the pistol. "And put in a lot of work on it, too."

Laying the pistol aside, he searched the coat's other side pocket. It yielded a purse, heavy with gold coins. He didn't stop to count the money, but estimated that there must be something close to five hundred dollars in the purse. He returned the purse to the coat pocket and lifted the garment's lapel to get to the breast pocket. A folded paper was all that it contained.

Longarm studied the paper for a moment or two before unfolding it. The paper was bloodstained, and had a ragged tear in it where his bullet had ripped through. The blood on the paper was still moist. He unfolded the paper. It was a letter, dated just the day before. The handwriting was well-formed, though here and there a scratched-out word gave evidence that it had been written hastily. Longarm's bullet had torn away part of the superscription and a word or two in the letter itself.

Longarm's eyes widened when he saw the two remaining words of the superscription: *Dear Senator*— The third word had been removed by his bullet. He read the few lines on the unfolded page:

Devil Grant is now here. I will take the first chance I can find . . . blood of my brother and my father, shed when they died at Shiloh under the guns of his bluebellies, will be revenged by his own. And I . . . not be taken. When I have seen him die, I will turn my gun on myself. My mission will be completed. If I should fail, and fall before I remove Devil Grant, I know that you

. . . others who will follow me. If I fail, they must succeed . . .

Frowning, Longarm tried to decipher the signature, but it too had been ripped by the bullet, and he could only guess from the loops of the words above the torn-out spot that the name might have been Phillip or William. There were the loops of a double L, barely visible at the top edge of the missing part. The rest of the word was gone, as was the name of the senator to whom the letter had been addressed.

Longarm tucked the letter into his own breast pocket and went on with his search. The dead man's right-hand breast pocket yielded nothing except two crumpled cigars. A handkerchief was in one of his trousers pockets, a small penknife in another. The other pockets were empty.

Mart Duggan came in just as Longarm was finishing his search. "Hear you had a little trouble," he said.

"Nothing I couldn't handle." Longarm jerked his head at the corpse. "You know this fellow?"

Duggan studied the dead man's features. He shook his head. "I can't recollect seeing him around Leadville before, Longarm. But that don't signify. Men come and go here so much, I sure can't keep up with all of them."

"Chances are, he ain't been here more than a day or so."

Longarm didn't mention the letter, which gave a pretty good hint that the man had arrived only a short time in advance of Grant.

"I'm right sure he was tagging along with us while we went through town, earlier," he continued. "And he followed me and Grant into the toilet at Tabor's hotel. I didn't get a real good look at him, but enough to know he's the same one."

"Well, what do you want me to do?" Duggan asked.

"Hell, Mart, there ain't a whole lot you can do. If you can get a tintype artist to make some pictures of his face, and give them to your men and ask around, it might help. I don't believe this fellow was a loner. I think there's others mixed up with him."

"You mean you still believe somebody's out to get Grant," Duggan said flatly.

"I believe it a lot more than I did before."

Again, Longarm held off mentioning the letter. He knew he was being unfair to Duggan, but he wanted to see what he could get out of that document himself before revealing its existence to the Leadville marshal. He went on, "I asked that Kitty Crawhurst if she'd seen this man before, and asked Whinney, too. Neither one of them had, that they recalled. You might ask the housemen if any of them have seen him in here, but I suspicion you'll just be wasting time. The way I got it figured, he's been tagging along after the general all afternoon, waiting for his chance."

"Lucky you were around when he took it," Duggan said. He noticed the gun on the faro table, where Longarm had put it. "That what he let go with?"

"Yep. Cut-down S&W Baby Russian. Fresh shells in it, fresh sawmarks where the barrel was cut off. He fixed that gun for the try he made, Mart. The only reason for toting a gun like that is to hide it in your pocket till you can get close enough to shove it up against whoever you're after."

Duggan had lifted the revolver and was looking it over.

"I'd have to agree, Longarm. With this damn thing, you couldn't hit a bull steer from more than three or four feet away."

"Take it along, if you like," Longarm said. "You might find some smith in town who worked it over, or maybe a store that sold him those cartridges. I'd say .41 Russian caliber's not too common."

"There's damn few guns chambered for it," Duggan agreed. He tucked the revolver in his pocket. "Well, I'll get the meat wagon to come pick this one up. And I'll see what else I can find out for you."

He turned to go, then faced back to Longarm and said, "I guess I sounded off out of turn, when I said what I did about Grant the other day. Forget it, will you? And let me know if there's anything else you need."

"Sure. Thanks, Mart."

Longarm waited until Duggan had left, then took out the letter he'd found in the dead man's pocket and reread it, trying once again to make out, by deduction or by guessing, the missing portions, particularly the names. He gave up after a few minutes of staring and juggling letters in his mind, folded the letter, and returned it to his pocket. He took out his Colt and slid the spent shell from its chamber, replacing it with a fresh cartridge from his coat pocket. He inspected the new cartridge carefully before inserting it in the chamber. He stood looking down at the face of the corpse for a few moments, but he'd learned long ago that dead men don't talk, even though this one had told him more than he'd expected to learn. He shook his head, gave up, and returned to the faro room.

Grant was still sitting at the table. The pile of chips in front of him had grown moderately, and the number of players around the layout had increased tremendously. Now, men were packed four deep on all three open sides. Only the back, where Kitty Crawhurst and the case-keeper sat, was free of players.

Tabor came up to Longarm. His face showed his worry.

"Well? What did you find out, Marshal?"

"A little bit, but a lot less than I need to go anywhere from here."

"Just exactly what do you mean, Marshal Long?"

"Senator, I mean I learned enough to bother me, but not enough to give me much in the way of answers. I got to do a little bit of studying and putting things together before I can come up with anything right solid."

"I'd appreciate it if you'd be a bit more specific," Tabor said sharply. "You know I feel responsible for bringing the general in here and exposing him to danger."

"You don't have to worry about that part of it," Longarm assured Tabor. "That fellow would've made his play for the general anyplace. There's not a bit of it you're to blame for."

"Well, that relieves my mind a little. Now, what did—"

Longarm interrupted Tabor. Respectfully but firmly, he said, "Senator, I'd take it as a favor if you don't make me go into everything until we get back to your house, where we can talk private, just you and me and the general."

"Why, of course, if that's what you'd prefer."

"It ain't just what I want to do personally, Senator." Longarm nodded at the faro players. "Might be, one of those men's got bigger ears than we can see. There ain't much use in us having a private confab where so many people can catch part of what we're saying."

"Yes. Yes, of course," Tabor nodded. "You think there might be further trouble here?"

"Not likely here, Senator. Whoever set that fellow on the general, he'd be too smart to push his luck like that."

"But you think there will be—"

Again Longarm interrupted Tabor. "Let's talk about that later, too, Senator, if you don't mind."

"Very well. I think the general's about ready to leave, anyhow." Tabor shook his head. "You know, Marshal, I've heard a lot of stories about him, how cool he was under fire, how nothing seemed to ruffle him up. I didn't quite believe those tales until I watched him today, going calmly on with his game just after somebody'd tried to kill him."

"I'd imagine he got sort of used to that, during the War," Longarm suggested. "How's he been doing, bucking that lady dealer's tiger?"

"He's been winning pretty consistently, four turns out of six since the shooting. He hasn't made any big bets, but he's won twice as many turns as he's lost."

Longarm smiled. "I just wish I could do that good."

Tabor frowned. "You don't think—" He stopped short and shook his head. "No. It couldn't be. I've watched every turn that woman's made. Besides, I've always understood that Jeff Whinney runs his games straight."

Grant looked up from the table and saw Longarm. He motioned for him to come over. Longarm skirted the ranks of players packed up to the table, and walked up behind Grant's chair. Out of deference or shyness, the players on both sides had refrained from crowding Grant too closely.

Over his shoulder, Grant asked Longarm, "Did you find out anything when you searched that man?"

"Some. Not as much as I'd have liked to."

"What?"

"Begging your pardon, General, but I guess I better ask you the same favor I just asked Senator Tabor."

"Which is?"

"Don't ask me any questions right here and now. There's too many people standing around that might hear what I'm saying."

Grant frowned, a mere tightening of his eyebrows. "You sound like you've turned up something serious."

"It looks that way to me, General. Now, if you don't mind, let's us wait until we get to the senator's house, where we can be sure we're talking private."

"All right, Marshal. I'm naturally a bit curious, you understand."

Before Longarm could reply, Kitty Crawhurst raised her voice and said, "Are you going to buck on this turn, General?"

Grant glanced at the case-keeper's marker and shook his head. "No, Miss Crawhurst. I think I'll stand out. You're getting right close down to cases now, and I don't want to take advantage of the house."

Kitty shrugged. "It's your choice, General. Shall I cash you in, then?"

"If you will."

Grant shoved his pile of chips over to her. Kitty tallied them with lightning flicks of her fingers and pushed a small stack of double eagles back across the layout. Grant took off the top coin and handed it to her. "My thanks for an enjoyable hour."

"I'm glad you enjoyed it, General," she said, smiling.

"Come back when you can stay longer, and give the house a chance to get even."

"I just may do that, Miss Crawhurst."

Grant touched his hat to her and beckoned to Tabor, who moved up to join Longarm and the general. A few of the players nearest him, seeing Grant getting ready to leave, extended hands to be shaken. In the corridor, they encountered another line of outstretched hands, as the players from the rooms they passed on the way to the door rushed to bid him farewell. Grant's handshakes were short now—a grasp, a downward jerk, and a quick release. He was obviously impatient to leave.

As they went out to the street, Tabor said, "I've got one of my carriages waiting at the bank to take us home. I didn't think you'd relish walking back, after being on your feet all afternoon."

"Right thoughtful, Horace," Grant muttered distractedly.

He looked around the street and, seeing no one within earshot, said to Longarm, "All right, Marshal. This is private enough for me, whether it is for you or not. Don't force me to exercise my rank on you. I want to know what you've found out about that man who tried to kill me."

"I ain't trying to keep from telling you, General," Longarm replied. "But I sure don't reckon you're going to like what I've got to say."

"Don't be too sure," Grant snapped. "I got over being scared by much of anything about the second time I took my men against Fort Henry, and that was quite a while ago. Out with it, man!"

"I wasn't suggesting you're scared," Longarm said. "I just told you that you ain't going to like it. General, that man who threw down on you at the faro table wasn't any hot-headed never-say-die Secesh who's been nursing an old grudge all these years. He was mixed up in some sort of scheme. I'm a long ways from unraveling it yet, but I intend to. Except I got to ask you to do one thing while I'm working it out."

"What's that?" Grant asked.

"Help me to keep you alive long enough to do it," Longarm said. "I got something in my pocket that I'll need to show you, but I don't aim to take it out here on the street. Let's wait till we get to the senator's house, then we can sit down and see what's what."

Chapter 7

Tabor picked up the torn, bloodstained letter from his desk, and looked at it for the tenth or twelfth time; Longarm had lost count. Grant had read it through once, and tossed it back on the desk with a noncommittal grunt.

"I can't believe it!" Tabor said, repeating himself for the fifth or sixth time. "But I'm not sure you're right in your deductions, Marshal. The 'senator' this is addressed to could either be a member of the U.S. Senate or the state senate." He faced Grant and went on. "You know you've got enemies in Washington—perhaps more than you have in Colorado."

"I'd say it's about a toss-up," Grant said calmly. "The senators from the Western silver states and territories have never forgiven me for signing the Mint Bill back in '73. The ones in Washington have never forgiven me for being elected president in the first place."

Longarm was getting tired of pointless debate. The three of them had been going around in circles since they'd gotten back from town and shut themselves up in Tabor's study. That had been two hours ago, and all their discussion had gotten them nowhere.

And it sure ain't the general, Longarm thought. *It's the senator. He can't seem to get it through his head that whether the senator that letter's intended for is in*

Colorado or in Washington, it don't matter a damn. There's a plot, and it's going to run on till I get onto the trail that'll let me bust it up.

He said to Grant, "General, I think you got the right idea about it not making much difference *where* there's people who don't like you very much. The thing I'm getting at is, are you going to be careful where you go when you leave the senator's house, and be sure I'm along with you all the time?"

"Marshal Long, I get the idea you're planning to treat me like a baby who needs a nursemaid," Grant said. His voice was sharp, almost angry. "I don't think I need that kind of attention."

Longarm met the general's angry glare. Grant's jaws were clamped tightly on his cigar, and under his graying beard, his chin jutted out like a bulldog's.

"You know, General," the lawman said mildly, pretty certain that Grant's ingrained soldier's thinking would govern his reaction, "that's just what I told my chief when he gave me my orders. No, sir, I don't feel like you need a nursemaid any more than I do. But if I get orders to tag along after you and keep you from getting shot or something, I've got to obey them. And I'd take it kindly if you'd help me all you can."

Grant sighed. "All right, Marshal. I'll do what I can to see that your chief's orders are carried out."

Longarm turned back to Tabor. "Now, Senator, how about this shindy you're throwing tonight? Would there happen to be any state senators invited?"

"Two or three, mostly from the other party. There'll be a half-dozen at the dinner later this week, of course. I think I mentioned that I'm having a special train run from Denver to bring some of the dinner guests. Forbes has the guest list for both affairs; get it from him."

"You know most of them personal, I reckon?" Longarm asked.

"All of them, Marshal. I'm not as well acquainted with those from the other party, of course, but I still can't agree with you that this letter's addressed to a state senator."

He picked up the letter and looked at it again, as

though, during the few minutes it had lain on the desk, the missing parts might somehow have been restored.

Longarm said patiently, "Now, Senator, that just stands to reason, the way I see it. The fellow who wrote that didn't expect to get himself killed. My guess is he was writing to somebody who'd get that letter in a day or two—likely somebody in Denver. He finished the letter, then he didn't have a stamp or envelope, which I'd judge means he was a stranger to Leadville. He put the letter in his pocket, aiming to mail it later on."

Tabor nodded reluctantly. "Yes, I suppose your deductions do make sense."

"Anyhow, that letter's about all we've got to go on," Longarm pointed out, "unless Mart Duggan comes up with something. I'll talk to him later tonight, after your party, and find out."

"You're going to attend the reception?" Tabor asked.

"Oh, I don't expect to be there like I was invited. I'll just hunker down, look as small as I can, and try to keep out from underfoot. But I sure am going to be on hand."

"I don't suppose there's anything more we can do now, is there?" Tabor asked. "It's getting late, and I've told Mrs. Morgan to serve dinner an hour early, so we'll have some time to get ready before the reception starts."

Grant stood up. "Keep me informed of what you find out, Marshal." Somewhat grimly, he added, "If you find out anything."

Longarm was even less attentive to his table companions at dinner than he'd been during lunch. Suzanne acted out of sorts from the beginning of the meal, because Jean-Pierre had chosen to take the chair between her and Longarm; she got even angrier as the meal progressed, and Longarm ignored her efforts at conversation. It improved her temper not at all that he was equally inattentive to the others at the table: Forbes, Mrs. Morgan, and the chef.

As soon as he'd finished, Longarm went upstairs to his bedroom. He poured an after-dinner drink from the fresh bottle of Maryland rye that had appeared on his dresser while he was gone. He supposed he had Forbes to thank for that; Tabor's factotum seemed to think of just about everything. He took off his coat and tossed it on the bed, then remembered he'd want it to be unwrinkled when he went back downstairs, and hung it over a chair. He draped his vest over the coat, unbuckled his gunbelt, and laid it on the dresser. Sliding his Colt out of its holster, he rummaged in his carpetbag until he found a small can of gun-oil and a flannel rag, then he unloaded the weapon to clean it.

While he was working, he glanced up at his face in the mirror. No question about it, he could do with a shave. He was trying to decide whether he had time to visit a barbershop before the reception, when Suzanne slipped in the door.

"Why are you mad at me?" were the first words she said. "I didn't do anything to you, that I can remember."

"I never said you did, Suzanne. And I sure ain't mad at you."

"You didn't say two words to me at lunch, or at supper, either. You acted like I wasn't even there," she pouted.

"Maybe that's because I got too much on my mind right now." Longarm gave the Colt a final rubbing with his cleaning rag and restored the gun to its holster.

Suzanne came up behind him and began to caress him. Longarm pulled away.

"Honey, you're a sweet girl, but I just ain't got time to love you up right now. I got to get to town and have me a shave before that shindy starts up tonight."

She ran a hand over his cheek. "Why do you have to go to town?"

"Because I don't like to scrape my own face. I don't even carry a razor with me, because if I did, I'd always be having to use it."

"I can shave you as well as any barber can," she told him.

"Do tell? Even if I ain't got a razor?"

"Senator Tabor has a set of razors, one for every day of the week, in his dressing room downstairs."

Longarm was tempted. "You'd borrow one of them, without telling him?"

"Why not? They're still at the dinner table downstairs. Baby Doe had a bath this afternoon; she won't be calling me until it's time for her to dress. And you *do* need a shave. She stroked his cheek and made a small face. "I've shaved men before. I won't scrape you or nick you."

"Well—all right. But you better hurry up."

Suzanne went after the razor. In a very few minutes, she was back, carrying not only the razor and a silver shaving mug with a brush in it, but a fluffy towel and a pitcher of hot water as well. Longarm had taken off his shirt in preparation. He sat down in a straight-backed chair. Suzanne sloshed a few drops of water into the shaving mug and began working up the lather. She brushed it on Longarm's face, then put the mug aside and began massaging his bristly skin with her fingertips, lubricating them with the lather.

"I like the feel of a man's face when it's all soapy and wet and warm and slick," she whispered as her fingers roamed over his skin. "It makes me break out in goosebumps."

"Feels good to me, too," Longarm told her. "You got a lot nicer touch than any of the men barbers who've worked on me."

"Well, of course I have!" she said indignantly. "Now, close your eyes and lean back a little farther."

Longarm obeyed. He missed her touching him for a moment, then felt the delicate, caressing touch of a single fingertip on his lathered cheek. He began to relax. His eyes were still closed. The soft pressure wandered over his jaws and chin, continuing, with brief pauses between touches, until Longarm began to wonder when she was going to start shaving him. He could feel the warmth of Suzanne's body on his face, and the heady aroma of her perfume grew increasingly stronger.

Under the sensual massage, Longarm began to harden. That wasn't in his plans. He sat up in the chair and opened his eyes. He got a brief, flashing glimpse of

Suzanne bending over him, each of her hands cuddling one of her breasts, and suddenly realized that for the past several minutes she'd been massaging his face with her erect nipples. In the few seconds before his movement broke the spell, he saw Suzanne's head thrown back, her eyes closed, her lips parted ecstatically.

Her eyes snapped open. She said angrily, "You weren't supposed to move or look!"

"You were supposed to shave me, Suzanne, not get me all worked up."

"That was the only way I could think of to get you worked up," she confessed. "Come on, Longarm. We've got time, if we hurry."

She unbuttoned his trousers to free him, and, as she'd done in their first encounter on the train, straddled him and let her body down to take him inside her.

"Now!" she said urgently. "Go ahead! Fast and hard! Hurry!"

Longarm grasped her by the waist and helped her to raise and lower her hips. She worked wildly, rotating her body in his hands, while he brought himself up beneath her with quick, hard jabs. It was a tempestuous coupling, sudden and fierce as a summer storm, both of them hurrying, until Suzanne began shaking. Longarm stood up, bringing her with him, her legs locking around his hips, and her hips hanging free to let him move them back and forth with his strong hands. Suzanne went limp with a moaning sigh, and Longarm sank into her with a final flurry of thrusts, until he was ready to let go with her.

He held her to him for a few moments after their frenzy died away, until she stirred and said, "You can let me down, if you want to. And I promise that I'll just shave you now. Not anything else."

Longarm nodded. He sat down again. Suzanne smiled at him in the mirror as she went to get the shaving mug and add more hot water to it. This time she did shave him, with swift, gentle strokes as expert as any barber's he'd ever felt. After she'd finished one cheek, she asked, "You do feel better, don't you? I know I do."

"You can shave me any day you feel like it,

Suzanne," he said, smiling. "Or any night you feel like it. Whether I need shaving or not."

"Later tonight?" she asked, beginning on his other cheek.

Longarm said, "I ain't sure when I'll be back. I've got to go to town after this shindy's over with, to see the city marshal."

Suzanne had wet the towel and was washing the last flecks of lather off Longarm's face. She asked him, "Is it true, what Mrs. Monroe told Forbes? Did you really shoot a man today?"

"I had to. Don't let it bother you; it's happened before."

"You don't want to talk about it, do you?"

Longarm could tell that Suzanne *did* want to talk about it, but he said curtly, "Not especially. It's over and done. No use worrying it now."

"All right, I won't." She stepped back and indicated his face in the mirror. "Now. Did I do a good enough job to satisfy you?"

Longarm looked, felt his cheeks, and nodded. "You sure did. Shaving and the extra, too. Now, you better get the senator's mug and razor back where they belong, before he misses them and starts raising hell."

"I guess I'd better, at that. Don't stay in town long tonight. I'll be here waiting, whenever you get back."

Longarm poured a fresh tot of Maryland rye to sip on while he dressed. He pulled a clean gray flannel shirt out of his carpetbag and slid into it, knotting his black string necktie before tucking in his shirttail. He took his time adjusting his gunbelt and holster; after what had happened that afternoon, he was convinced that his job wasn't the waste of time it had seemed to be when Billy Vail had first given him his new assignment. The letter in the dead man's pocket today was proof of that.

Satisfied at last with the set of his holster, Longarm put on his vest and reached for his coat. The tips of the cheroots sticking up from the inside pocket drew his fingers; more out of habit than because he felt the desire to smoke, he lifted one of the slim cigars out and bent to the lamp chimney. He puffed until the tip of the cheroot glowed red. Only after he'd lighted it did he become consciously aware of what he'd done.

Old son, he told himself, *you ain't got the hold-back of a gander that's been stuffing himself on green corn. There wasn't a reason in the world why you had to light this damn thing. Not a one. If you knew what was good for you, you'd put it out this minute.*

The half-inch of still-unswallowed rye in the glass on the dresser caught his eye. *Well now,* he thought, *that's as good a reason as a man needs to enjoy a cigar. Besides, look at the general. Cigars don't seem to've hurt him any.*

He tipped the rye bottle over the glass to bring its level up a bit, and with the cigar in his mouth trailing a thread of smoke, he stepped over to the window and stood gazing out, swirling the rye in its glass.

It was a typical Leadville night; the darkness was held away from the town by the smelter fires. To the east, on Carbonate Hill and Fryer Hill and up the slopes of Strayhorse Gulch, the furnaces glared brightest, but wherever Longarm looked, the sky was far from dark. The yellow puddles of light from the open fronts of the furnaces merged and overlaid one another, and mingled with the blue of the night sky to give the entire area a light greenish cast, not daylight-bright, but not night-dark, either.

Occasionally, a freshly charged furnace sent a fireworks burst of white sparks from the top of its stack to flare against the pale night. On the far slopes, the pinpoints of light marking the mineheads matched the closer pinpoints from the windows of Leadville's houses. Even through the closed window, Longarm could get a faint whiff of the fumes that always hung in the air.

Like all the mansions on Carbonate Avenue, the Tabor house was without landscaping. Water was more important to the mines than to the trees and shrubs and grass their owners might grow around their imposing dwellings. In any case, the few who tried to create a green setting for their homes soon discovered that the earth had long ago been made sterile by the fallout of chemicals from the smelter fumes. It was not an inviting landscape, and a short look at it was enough. Longarm was just turning away from the window, his drink finished, when he saw the shadow moving between the Tabor mansion and the house that stood next to it.

At first he thought it was a trick his eyes were playing on him, some stray reflection caused by the glowing end of his cigar. He took the cheroot from his mouth and held it to one side of the window, keeping his eyes fixed on the place where he thought he'd seen something move. After a moment or so, it moved again. Longarm tensed as he saw what it was: a man emerging from the shadow of the house next to Tabor's. He walked slowly—*sneakily*, was the thought that registered in Longarm's mind. In one hand, the dimly visible man carried a long, thin object that Longarm was certain was a rifle.

Longarm's first instinctive move was to reach for his Winchester, which stood leaning against the wall in the corner nearest the head of his bed. There was enough light to give him a clear shot, and from the height at which his window stood, picking off the intruder would be a simple matter—a single round. His hand hadn't yet touched the rifle barrel when better judgment halted his reaching arm. The prowler would be worth a lot more, alive and talking, than he would be as a corpse. The man on the ground hadn't moved since emerging from the shadows. He seemed to be surveying the mansion's grounds, reconnoitering. Grabbing his hat from the bedpost, Longarm started for the stairs.

He took the steps three at a time until the clatter of his own heels reminded him that he didn't want to rouse the Tabors and Grant. There was no point in getting them all stirred up, maybe running out and getting in his way. He slowed his downward rush, completed it in silence, and turned down the hallway. By going through the kitchen and out the back door, he'd come out in the deepest shadows. As he passed the door of the staff dining room, he saw Forbes and Mrs. Morgan sitting at the table, with coffee cups in front of them. Forbes called an invitation to join them, but Longarm waved and hurried on outside.

Moving slowly and carefully now, to avoid scraping his feet on the rock-studded soil and revealing his presence, Longarm walked in the thin shadow of the mansion to its corner. During the time it had taken him to get downstairs and outdoors, the prowler had gotten still closer to the mansion. Peering around a corner of the house, Longarm saw him, still moving toward the Tabor place with a strange, stumbling, halting gait.

There was something very odd about the way the man moved, Longarm realized. He acted as though he had sore feet, and was being forced to use his rifle as though it were a cane. The course the intruder was taking would bring him to the back corner of the house, where Longarm stood. Hunkering down, he waited for the man to get closer.

When the intruder was within a dozen feet of his hiding place, Longarm slid out his Colt. The approaching man might be fast enough to bring his own weapon to bear as fast as Longarm could draw, though he still used the rifle like a cane, putting it to the ground in front of him with each step he took in his queer, hesitating walk. Longarm waited until the stranger had gotten to within an arm's length of the corner, then he moved. He leaped from his shadow and was at the prowler's side in a single, long stride.

He shoved his Colt into the man's ribs and grabbed for the rifle barrel with his free hand, saying, "Stop right where you are! And get your hands in the air!"

Before he'd finished speaking, Longarm's hand was closing around the rifle barrel. The instant he touched it, he knew something was wrong.

What Longarm felt was not the cold, hard steel of a rifle barrel, but the wooden shaft of a sturdy cane. The intruder didn't resist when he felt the prodding of the Colt, but raised his arms obediently.

"What you sticking me up for, mister?" he asked in a thick voice. "I ain't got nothing you'd want."

Although he was beginning to suspect that the man might be telling the truth, Longarm took no chances. "Come along," he commanded. "Let's get you in the kitchen, where there's enough light so I can see who in hell you are."

"Sure, I'll go with you," the stranger replied. "I was heading there anyways."

"Well, move faster, then! I get nervous when I got my gun on a man in the dark!"

"Don't go killing me now," the prowler pleaded. "I ain't hurt nobody, and I ain't about to."

By now, Longarm's uncertainty had vanished. He'd started his course, though, and he stayed with it. He kept his prisoner moving until they reached the back door. Without his cane, the man moved slowly, in hesitant, lurching steps. Inside, Longarm saw at once that he'd captured no desperate, would-be killer. His captive's clothes hung in tattered rags, his face was grimy and unshaven, and his eyes were rheumy and bloodshot.

"What'd I do, mister?" he asked. "I didn't set out to cause nobody no trouble."

"I reckon I believe you," Longarm admitted. "Just what in hell's your name, and what're you doing here?"

Forbes and Mrs. Morgan appeared through the door of the staff dining room. The housekeeper said, "My goodness, Marshal! What are you holding a gun on that poor old man for?"

"You know him?" Longarm asked.

"Why, of course I do. Everybody in Leadville knows Limpy Joe," she smiled. "He got crippled a long time ago, in a mine accident. I guess he didn't have anyplace else to go, because he just stayed on here in Leadville. Everybody sort of looks out for him."

"I come to the party," Limpy Joe told her. "I'd a been here sooner, but it was a while before I heard about it. I bet you got something good, ain't you?"

"Joe always shows up at the back door, wherever there's a party," Mrs. Morgan told Longarm. "He loves cookies and cake and everything sweet. And he knows there are usually leftovers that we'll give him."

Feeling like a fool, Longarm said, "I seen him from the upstairs window. From up there, it looked like he was trying to sneak up on the house with a rifle."

Forbes said, "I can't blame you for feeling anxious,

Marshal. And there's no harm done. Mrs. Morgan will take care of Joe."

"Of course I will!" the housekeeper said. "Come on, Joe. I'm sure there are some broken cookies put away for you. I'll fix you a nice sack of them."

She started for the kitchen. Limpy Joe followed her. Just before he reached the door, Joe looked back over his shoulder and stuck out his tongue at Longarm. The last glimpse Longarm had of him was of a dirt-streaked face with its mouth spread in a wide grin that showed the broken stumps of three or four yellowed teeth.

You just better buckle down and get a hold of yourself, old son, Longarm thought.

He was standing in his bedroom, looking out the window through which he'd been tempted to fire at Limpy Joe a short time earlier.

Why, hell, you're acting spooked worse'n General Grant, and it's him they're gunning for. Good thing I thought twice before I shot once, or I'd have killed that poor old cripple. Made enough of a fool out of myself, too, bullhiding him in with a gun in his gut. But maybe it's a good thing I didn't take a chance. If I hadn't stormed down there, it could've been a shooter like that fellow at the faro table. He said in that letter that if he didn't get the general, there'd be another man along to take his place. So maybe I didn't make such a big fool out of myself.

Sounds of music, filtered through many doors, reached Longarm's ears. It brought him sharply back to the present. He put on his coat and vest, and started downstairs. As he got closer to the main floor of the mansion, the music grew steadily louder. There was nobody in the big salon, or in the formal dining room that opened on it. Still tracing the source of the music, Longarm crossed the dining room to the conservatory, and found a string quartet sawing away. He stood and watched the group for a moment, decided again that he had a tin ear, and was turning to go just as a woman spoke from behind him.

"Enjoying the music, Marshal?"

Longarm checked himself and turned back. Baby Doe Tabor was smiling at him. Her hair had been freshly fluffed, and shone golden above her straight, dark brows. Her large eyes looked troubled, though, in spite of her smile. Her cheeks were flushed pink, whether from nature or from Suzanne's skill at applying rouge, Longarm couldn't decide. The senator's wife had dressed for the reception in a full-skirted silk gown of palest blue. The only jewelry she wore was a mammoth diamond, which hung from a thin chain at her throat and rested on the soft, rounded shelf of her full breasts.

Longarm said, "It sounds right nice, Mrs Tabor. And you're sure a pretty picture tonight."

"Why, thank you, Marshal." She hesitated before confessing, "To tell you the truth, I'm as nervous as a kitten in a strange room. This is the first real party I've given here, and I'm just afraid nobody's going to show up."

"Why wouldn't they? You and the senator being Leadville's leading citizens, so to speak."

"You don't have to pretend you haven't heard the ugly things people are saying about me, Marshal Long. And I'm sure Horace's former wife has a lot of friends here."

"Now, don't pay a bit of mind to what folks say, Mrs. Tabor. There's always some that's going to meanmouth and backbite. Just keep on smiling like you are, and they'll soon shut up."

"I hope you're right." She glanced nervously around at the empty dining room. "I was just taking a last look, to be sure everything's all right. When I saw you, I wanted to tell you how grateful we are, Horace and I, for your quick action this afternoon. Horace says there's no doubt in his mind that you saved General Grant's life."

"Well, you know I'm supposed to be here to keep the general safe. All I did was what I'm paid to do."

Baby Doe asked anxiously, "You don't think there'll be any more terrible things like that—" She broke off, reading the answer to her unfinished question in Longarm's eyes. "You do, though. Am I right, Marshal?"

"I ain't one to borrow trouble, Mrs. Tabor," Longarm hedged. "I just take things as they come."

"That's what I've always done myself," she said.

"You're right, though. I wouldn't make any bets that we've seen the last of it. No, ma'am."

Baby Doe sighed. "I know you'll be doing your job well. I'll keep on trying to take things as they come, then."

A rustling behind them caught their attention. Two liveried menservants were carrying in a washtub-sized silver punchbowl on a massive tray of the same metal. They put the bowl on the large round table that sat in the middle of the dining room. Mrs. Morgan came in carrying another tray on which were plates of cookies and thinly sliced pound cake. A kitchen maid followed her with a load of silver cups, which she arranged around the punchbowl. Baby Doe and Longarm watched until the housekeeper finished arranging the table to her liking and left.

"I've never tasted Mrs. Morgan's punch," Baby Doe said. "Let's try it and see if you approve."

"I'm afraid I wouldn't be much help to you in tasting punch, Mrs. Tabor. Neat whiskey's more my style."

Baby Doe led him to the table, but before they could dip into the punchbowl, Tabor and Grant came in. Grant had his inevitable cigar clamped in his mouth.

They nodded to Longarm, and Tabor said to Baby Doe, "Ah, my dear, ready to welcome our guests, are we? I hope you're not nervous."

"Well, I am Horace," she confessed. "But I'm not going to show it."

"Good. It's going to be—" Tabor began, but voices from the main salon interrupted him. He said, "I think they're beginning to arrive. We'd better go." He offered her his arm, and Grant moved to walk beside the couple as they went into the salon.

Longarm waited for a few moments before following them. The arrival of the first guests seemed to have been a signal for others to begin trickling in. Longarm found himself an inconspicuous place at the end of the entrance hall—a small settee shaded by the stairway, where he could sit without attracting attention and watch the guests as they entered. He wasn't exactly sure who or what he was looking for, but he intended to look, just the same.

Most of the guests wore evening clothes. The women sparkled with jewelry, the men were as sedate as penguins in black and white. Longarm saw a few familiar faces. Three or four of the men he recognized as having been among the store proprietors he'd seen briefly earlier in the day, but he could put names to none of them. One of the Tabor housemaids was on duty to take the cloaks and wraps worn by the women and put them in a room off the foyer; it was a warm evening, and few of the men wore topcoats.

In spite of the variety in the faces and figures of the guests, waiting and watching soon came to be monotonous, and Longarm's attention relaxed. He was debating giving up the post he'd chosen and making a tour of the salon and dining room—perhaps even taking enough time to go up to his own room for a wake-up drink and a cigar—when Vivian Montgomery arrived.

Longarm hadn't thought of the possibility that she'd be there. He looked curiously at her escort, a man of perhaps forty, tall and singularly thin, almost bald, but with a full mustache and a carefully trimmed chin beard.

Vivian didn't see Longarm at first. She was turning around after handing her velvet evening cloak to the maid, when she glanced down the hallway and saw him sitting there. Her face showed her surprise, but after an initial widening of her eyes and lifting of her eyebrows, she relaxed into impassivity. She said something to the man at her side, and he followed her the few steps down the hall to the settee Longarm occupied. Longarm rose as they approached.

"What a pleasant surprise, Marshal," Vivian said. "I didn't have any idea you'd be here this evening. In fact, I didn't even know you were back in Leadville."

"I just got in yesterday evening, and I've been a mite busy, or I'd have called on you, ma'am," Longarm replied. He didn't know the relationship, if there was one, between Vivian and the man with her, and wanted to spare her the embarrassment of seeming too familiar.

Vivian's almost imperceptible flicker of an eyelid told him she understood. She turned to her escort. "Senator, let me present U.S. Marshal Long. He's the man who saved our smelter payrolls from train robbers a few days ago. Marshal, the Honorable Wilkes Purvis, of the Colorado State Senate."

Purvis held out his hand. "I've heard of you before, Marshal. I understand you also saved General Grant from an assassin's bullet today. You seem to have the knack of being in the right place at the right time."

"Just happened I was close enough to do something," Longarm replied. "It wasn't such a much."

"You didn't mention Marshal Long's name when you told me about the attempt on General Grant's life at dinner, Wilkes," Vivian said. "I got the idea it was just someone in the crowd who shot the gunman."

"Did you, Vivian? I suppose the marshal's name just slipped my mind," Purvis replied. "Now, hadn't we better go in and greet our hosts, my dear?"

She nodded. "I suppose we should." To Longarm she said, "If you're going to stay through the evening, perhaps we'll have a few moments to chat, later."

"Sure, Mrs. Montgomery," Longarm said. "I imagine I'll be here for a while."

Vivian opened her mouth to say something more, but Purvis had put his hand over hers, where she'd rested it on his arm after he suggested that they go. She had no choice but to accompany him toward the salon door. Longarm watched them until they disappeared.

Wonder how she likes washing Purvis's skinny back, Longarm thought. *The way he looks, it'd be about the same as rubbing your knuckles across a washboard. I'd say there's something between them, all right. Or has been. He acted real put out when she came down the hall to say hello. And he didn't waste much time hustling her away, either. Unless it wasn't her he was concerned about.*

He chewed on that idea for a moment, then shook his head. *Not likely, though. It'd be stringing too long of a*

150

bow for him to be the senator that fellow was writing about. Things don't tumble into line all that neat. Just the same, I'll keep him in mind while I'm nosying around.

Longarm stayed in the hall for a short time longer, but the number of arriving guests had dwindled to an occasional latecomer, and he began thinking about prowling through the house for a change. Inactivity, except when on a stakeout, had always struck him as being time wasted.

Wandering through the salon and dining room was pretty much a waste of time too, he decided after he'd made the circuit twice. The guests had split into several groups. The largest was centered around Grant, who stood in the middle of the salon. Vivian Montgomery and Purvis were in this crowd. In the dining room, Tabor and Baby Doe formed the nucleus of another knot of guests. This one seemed to be chiefly composed of women. Longarm thought they must be anxious to find out what the new Mrs. Tabor was like.

There were three other separate small conclaves in the dining room. From the scraps of conversation Longarm heard as he skirted them, the women were dividing their chatter between the newest fashions and Horace Tabor's new wife. One group of men were discussing conditions along Harrison and Chestnut Streets; another group—mine and smelter operators—were worrying about the activities of the Knights of Labor. After being defeated in the strike it had organized in Leadville a few years earlier, the militant miners' union had surfaced again in the copper diggings in Montana, chiefly around Butte.

Longarm heard nothing that would be useful to him, or was even of much interest, during the two circuits he made of the rooms. He looked at the punchbowl, which was kept replenished by one of the menservants, but decided that sugared wine with a little brandy to give it a whisper of authority wasn't what he wanted. He'd started toward the stairs, to go up and get a sip of Maryland rye from the bottle in his room, when Vivian beckoned to him to join her. She was standing alone, near the door of the salon. Longarm looked around for Senator Purvis, and saw that he was still among the group surrounding Grant. He nodded to Vivian and joined her.

"I think I'm angry because you haven't come to see me since you got back," she said, her voice pitched just above a whisper. "But not angry enough not to want you to stop in, when you have the time. Quite a bit of time, preferably."

"You know I ain't forgotten you, Vivian. I was aiming to come see you tonight while this blowout was going on, but something came up, and I figured I better stick close by Grant. Then, later on, after him and the Tabors have gone to bed, I got pressing buesiness to take care of in town. Maybe tomorrow night, though."

Vivian smiled, "That would be very nice. I'll look for you." She glanced past Longarm and added, "Wilkes is finally getting away from the crowd around the general. I'll have to join him. I haven't paid my respects to the new Mrs. Tabor yet."

She left Longarm, and he took a step or two toward the stairs, then changed his mind. He'd better stay on the main floor, and not get too far away. He reversed his course and went to the staff dining room, where Forbes or Mrs. Morgan could probably rustle him up a drink.

"Of course," Forbes said, when Longarm asked if there was a bottle of rye anywhere handy. "I'll get you one." He vanished, and before Longarm had a cigar lighted, he was back with an almost full bottle. It bore the same label as the one on Longarm's dresser.

Forbes explained, "The senator likes full bottles in the cabinet in his study. I refill those that are only partly full until the labels don't look new, then I open a fresh bottle."

"It must be nice to be rich," Longarm said with a grin, pouring himself a drink. He pushed the bottle across the table to Forbes, who shook his head.

"Not now, thanks. I'll wait until bedtime, and have a brandy."

"When's bedtime for you, Forbes? Whenever the senator goes to bed himself?"

"Just about. But I like it better than being in an office. At least I only have the senator to satisfy, instead of a whole set of bosses."

"I guess." Longarm sipped the whiskey. "This blowout that's going on out there, when's it going to be over with?"

"Quite soon, I'd imagine. The senator wasn't feeling too good after dinner, and the general remarked that he was very tired and hoped he'd be able to get to bed early. Why?"

"I got to go into town for a spell, as soon as everybody leaves."

"Something in connection with the attack on General Grant today?"

"In a way. Mart Duggan's trying to find out who the fellow was who tried to put the general away, and I want to find out if he's got anything yet."

"If you're going to be very late getting back, I'd better give you a door key. The staff will want to go to bed as soon as the cleanup's finished." Forbes closed the door and took a key from a board on which dozens of keys were hanging.

Longarm frowned. He hadn't gotten around to making sure the mansion would be securely locked while he had to be gone. He asked Forbes, "Who's got keys to the outside doors of this place?"

"Why, the senator and Mrs. Tabor, of course, and Mrs. Morgan and myself. The stableman keeps one, in case he has to let in somebody who gets here at an inconvenient hours."

"You keep the doors locked when everybody's in bed, I guess?"

"Certainly. And Mrs. Morgan checks all the windows on the lower floor before she goes to bed."

"Good. I'd hate to think just anybody could walk in whenever they felt like it." Longarm pocketed the key and stood up. "That being the case, I don't see much need for me to put off going to town. Those folks out there ain't going to hurt the general."

As bad as Leadville's sulfur-tinged air was, Longarm breathed a lot more freely when he got outside. He took his time walking to Pine Street. Duggan was in his office at the jail, sitting at his desk going through wanted fliers.

"I'm damned if I can find out anything about that fellow you shot today, Longarm," he said, as soon as they'd exchanged hellos. "I did what you asked me to, and had the tintype artist come in and take some pictures of him. Nobody my men have showed them to so far has ever seen him around town."

"You think it'd be a pretty good guess that he came here for just one reason?" Longarm asked.

"I'd say so. I've been looking at all the flyers I got lately to see if any of them fit him. So far, they don't."

"Nobody at the train station recalls seeing him come in?"

"No. He could've come on horseback, but the livery stables both say they haven't got any horses waiting to be picked up." Duggan shook his head and said with a grim smile, "Far as I can see, he might've come here in a balloon, for all anybody knows."

"Or in a wagon or buggy with somebody else who took the rig and left. Or somebody who lives here and keeps a stable," Longarm added with a thoughtful frown.

"That'd take in a good part of the town. Now, you're not going to expect my men to go asking all over the place about him, are you?"

"No. I ain't unreasonable, Mart, and I know you're curious too. But I got good reasons for thinking that fellow was working in cahoots with somebody else, and that somebody else just might live in Leadville."

"Or out of town, but close by," Duggan suggested. "Maybe in a claim shack, or maybe in what's left of Oro City."

"Well, one thing's for damned sure," Longarm said, shaking his head. "If nobody recalls seeing that shooter before, he's likely to've had some place to hole up, likely with somebody who knows his way around town and steered him to where Grant was. And that's the party we're looking for, Mart."

"You said you had reasons for being sure there was somebody else in cahoots with this fellow. You feel like telling me a little bit more? Why you're so certain, for instance?"

Longarm couldn't see any reason for withholding any longer the contents of the letter he'd taken from the dead man's pocket. He quoted the missive as best he could remember, then said, "Now, there's only two things I can see about that letter. Either it didn't get mailed, or it wasn't intended to be mailed."

"If it wasn't meant to be mailed, why'd he write it?"

"To hand to somebody who'd hand it on to this senator it was addressed to."

Duggan thought this over for a moment, then said slowly, "If it wasn't going to be mailed, then whoever would do the handing-over has got to be somebody living here in town."

"That's how I see it," Longarm agreed. "You don't have any senators or ex-senators living here do you, Mart?"

"Not unless you count our friend Haw Tabor."

"I don't. I thought about him a lot, but it just ain't his style, Mart. I can't fit him into anything like this thing's shaping up to be."

"Well, we're still noplace, then. We're still right where we started."

"Looks that way."

For a moment, the two men sat in silence, then Longarm asked, "Mart, what do you know about this Wilkes Purvis? He's in the state senate, so I guess you've heard his name. He wouldn't live here in Leadville, would he?"

"No. He don't live too far away, though. He's got two or three mines and a part-interest in a little smelter up at Climax."

"You got any idea where he was before he settled down in Climax?"

Duggan frowned. "It was someplace over in South Park that he got started, I'm pretty sure. Fairplay,

155

Alma, Tarryall . . . Damn it, I can't remember things like that about a man who's never started any trouble here in Leadville."

"He never did live here, then? Or in Oro City?"

"Oh I guess he might have. Oro City, now—that'd be before my time here. They'd already moved everything here from Oro City before I hit town," Duggan said.

But he's in Leadville, I guess?"

"Now and again. But you'd have to ask somebody besides me, if you want anything beyond that. Why? You figure he might be the senator we're looking for?"

"He might be, he might not be; it's a tossup. Take your choice."

"You take it, Longarm, it's your case. I told you I'd help all I could, but when it comes to mixing in politics—well, I've held onto this job as long as I have because I don't mess with politics at all."

"Can't blame you." Longarm paused before adding, "There's one way you can help me a lot, if you will, Mart."

"Go ahead. I'll tell you whether I can or not, after I hear what you want."

"Grant's going to be here two or three days longer. I can't stay with him every minute of every day. Have you got a man you can put to keep an eye on the Tabor place when I get caught up in something I can't get away from?"

"No, damn it, Longarm, I haven't. I'm shorthanded all the time, and I still haven't found a man to fill Clancey's place."

"It won't be much—a little while tomorrow night, and maybe somebody to back me up the next night, at that party the general's having at the Tabor Grand Hotel."

"Hell, let Tabor hire a guard or two. He's got plenty of money. Plenty of men, too. He's got guards at all his mines and smelters. At the bank, too. Why come to me?"

Longarm caught Duggan's eyes and held them with his own. "Because I don't want to go to Tabor."

"Jesus!" Duggan exploded. "You just got through

saying you didn't think Tabor had anything to do with this business of somebody trying to kill Grant!"

"I don't. But I don't want him to know there's anybody besides me keeping an eye on things."

Duggan sat silently for a moment, then he sighed and nodded. "All right, Longarm. I'll squeeze out a man to help you tomorrow night—and the next, at the hotel. What's he supposed to do?"

"Nothing, unless there's trouble. Tomorrow night, now, if he'll just stake himself out on the porch of the house next door to Tabor's—"

"That'd be the Daly place," Duggan interrupted.

"I reckon. Just stay out of sight, except to walk around every hour or so, make sure there's no prowlers." Longarm grinned wryly. "I damn near killed one of your good citizens tonight. Mistook him for a prowler, when all he was doing was coming to beg some cookies at Tabor's back door."

Duggan said, "Sounds to me like Limpy Joe. He'd eat a cow turd if it had sugar on it."

"That was his name, all right. But making a mistake that way got me started thinking. If he could just walk up to Tabor's place, so can anybody else. As long as I'm in the house, it won't matter, but if I've got to be away for a while, like I am tonight—and maybe tomorrow night too—or if there's a big crowd like there'll likely be at the hotel, I could use an extra set of hands and eyes."

"Which you're looking to me to supply. I can't do it, Longarm. I'll tell you again what I said a minute ago: let Tabor hire his own guards."

Longarm didn't answer Duggan for a moment. He'd learned long ago that federal lawmen risk more than they stand to gain by pushing a local officer, even when their authority overrides his. He shrugged at last and said, "All right, Mart, it's your town; you know what you can and can't do. But if something should happen to Grant here in Leadville, I'd sure hate to be the one answering the questions you're going to be asked. You know how jittery they are in Washington, after what happened to Garfield."

"Wait a minute now!" Duggan said. "I don't go back on my word. I told you you could count on me to help when I can, and it looks like this is one of those times. I'll see that you have a man."

"That's a real big help, Mart." Now Longarm felt it was time to sugar the dose Duggan had swallowed. "You know, we've been putting off making the rounds together. Every time we run into each other, here or in Denver, we say we'll do it next time. Why don't we do it now?"

"You mean the elephant and the owl?"

"Up to a point. Damn it, I need to get my mind off Tabor and Grant and all the rest of it. Are you on?"

"You're buying, I guess?"

"I asked you, didn't I?"

"And I waited long enough for you to do it. Sure, I'm on. I'll just step back and tell Flood to shift for himself tonight. Then we'll be on our way!"

Chapter 8

Wearily, Longarm mounted the three steps leading up to the back door of the Tabor mansion. He'd tried to cut the night on the town short, but Mart Duggan wouldn't hear of it. They'd covered Leadville, from the Clarendon Hotel for a late supper to the most squalid alky joint on Tiger Alley. Along the way, they'd danced with the ticket girls at Pop Wyman's Great Saloon and the Bon Ton; listened to the maudlin songs of the performers at the Grand Central; sat in for a few hands of stud poker at the Board of Trade Saloon and in the plush upstairs gambling room of the Texas House; bucked the tiger at the Little Church Casino; and paid their respects to Kitty Crawhurst at Jeff Wyman's gambling house.

After they'd lubricated their throats at the Catalpa, Monahan's, and the Windsor and Tontine bars, Longarm lost track of the names of the places they'd visited. He'd found that when he was with Duggan, his money was no good. He'd tried to pay for the drinks every time they'd stopped, but all of the barkeeps had pushed it back to him. The gambling houses, though, took both his and Duggan's money without hesitation. So did the fifty-cents-a-ticket girls at the dance palaces, and the scantily clad women described as "waitresses" in the theater.

Longarm fumbled in his pocket for the back door key, but before he found it, the door swung open. He looked up to see Mrs. Morgan staring at him with open surprise.

"My goodness, Marshal Long, but you gave me a real start!" she exclaimed. "You're certainly out early, this morning. Did you get roused up with Mr. Forbes and me, when the senator was taken ill an hour or two ago?"

"No, ma'am, I'm just getting back. I've been downtown with Mart Duggan all night. I hope Senator Tabor's not bad sick."

"He's not. It happens every time he eats them."

"Eats what?"

"Dill pickles."

Mrs. Morgan led the way into the staff dining room, where a coffeepot with a plume of steam still rising from its spout stood on the table. "If you've been out all night, you'd probably relish a cup of fresh coffee." She righted one of the cups that stood upside-down on the table, placed it in its saucer, and filled it. She went on, "It happens every time he eats them. Now, the *first* Mrs. Tabor would never let him eat them, but this one—" she shook her head disapprovingly—"this one doesn't know any better."

"How'd he get hold of the pickles?" Longarm asked, trying to make sense of what the housekeeper was saying.

"He sent for them, after the guests had gone. One of the housemen got them for him; he didn't know any better, either. So, about an hour or two ago, we were roused up to tend to the senator."

"Did you have to send for a doctor?"

"Oh, my goodness, no! I knew what to do, as soon as I found out what he'd eaten. He used to sneak into the hotel kitchen and eat one, when the *first* Mrs. Tabor was—well, when they were still married—and then he'd come home sick. But he's not going to be able to take the general for that trip around the diggings that they were supposed to make today."

"Has anybody told the general yet?"

"No, he's not awake yet. Unless all the fuss roused him."

Longarm drained his coffee cup. "Can I ask a favor of you, Mrs. Morgan?"

"Of course."

"Wait till after breakfast to tell the general. And tell him I'll be in my room, if he wants me for anything. Right now, I need to get me an hour or two of shut-eye. After that, I'll be fit as a fiddle and ready to go."

Longarm took off only his coat, vest, boots, and gunbelt, before falling into bed. He snapped into quick wakefulness at once when Forbes touched his shoulder, and had his hand on the butt of his Colt, hanging in the holster on the bedpost, before he saw who had roused him.

"What's the trouble?" he asked.

"There's no trouble, Marshal," the factotum said. "The general was asking for you, and I thought you'd like to have time for a bite to eat before he finishes his own lunch."

Longarm sloshed water on his face and toweled dry. He stamped into his boots, buckled on his gunbelt, and followed Forbes downstairs to the staff dining room, while putting on his vest and coat. He and Forbes ate the meal in silence. They'd only half-finished when Grant appeared in the doorway.

"Thought I'd find you here, Marshal," the general said around his cigar. "I guess you know Horace is under the weather today?"

"Yes, sir, I'd heard about it, general."

"I was glad enough to rest, myself, this morning," Grant went on. "But I'm not going to let Horace's delicate belly do me out of holding the reins of a good harness horse. How well do you know the country hereabouts?"

"Not as good as Senator Tabor does, General, but I guess I can find my way around, if you're bent on seeing the sights."

"I don't care much about the sights," Grant said with a smile. "I'm after a little fresh air and an afternoon drive. I suppose you're free to go along?"

"Why, sure, whenever you're ready."

"As soon as you're through with your meal, then." He said to Forbes, "You tell the stableman that I'll expect the best nag he's got out there to be in the shafts of the buggy. I suppose by the time he's got it harnessed up, the marshal will be ready to go."

"Longarm said, "I'm ready now, General, if you are."

"No hurry, Marshal. Finish up, and meet me at the stable."

Grant turned and left, trailing a cloud of cigar smoke.

Longarm took only enough time to go upstairs and get his Winchester before going to the stable. Grant was already there, watching the stableman fastening the last buckles of the harness.

Grant indicated the big chestnut gelding, its eyes rolling in their sockets, its legs shifting in anticipation of movement. He said. "That's as fine a piece of horseflesh as I've seen anywhere. Reminds me a lot of my old Butcher Boy. But we'll see how he compares when we get out where he can run."

"You'd better keep a tight rein on Sovereign for the first few miles, General," the stableman cautioned. "He ain't been out of his stall for the last two weeks, except for what little exercise I can give him, walking him around the neighborhood."

Grant grunted. "I can handle him. I like a spirited beast, anyhow." He turned to Longarm, and noticed the Winchester. "Going to get in some target practice, Marshal? Or looking for trouble?"

"Neither one, General. I don't go looking for trouble, but if it catches up with me, then I do my target practice."

A quick smile split Grant's face. He said, "Maybe we'll get along without either one, today. All right, Marshal, we might as well go. The horse is getting impatient, and so am I."

Longarm remembered enough from his visit to Leadville a few years earlier to be able to direct Grant through the outskirts of town and onto the road that led through the diggings, and eventually to Mosquito Pass.

The road wound erratically, and its surface was rough, still rutted with the deep grooves cut by ore carts in the days before the railroads had come to Leadville and pushed sidings out to the more distant mines.

"I won't be as good a guide for you as Senator Tabor'd be," Longarm said as the buggy bounced over the rough road. "He'd be able to tell you which mines belong to who, and all about the smelters and everything else. I don't know all that much about Leadville, but I'll do the best I can."

"Don't worry about trying to tell me too much," Grant said. "If Horace was along, I'd listen to him, but the real reason I wanted to take this ride wasn't to look at mines or smelters." He swung his head to take in the minehead shacks, which stood almost as thick as the houses of Leadville on the slope of Carbonate Hill, and on the other side, up the slanting walls of Strayhorse Gulch. "Anyhow, they all look about the same, don't they?"

"Pretty much," Longarm agreed. "I'd be hard put to tell which one was which."

Grant went on, "No, Marshal, I'm not that interested in the mines. I wanted to get out in a buggy, with a good horse ahead of me. That's the only real pleasure I get, these days. New York's so big now, and so crowded with people, that the only place to take a rig out is Central Park. There's not much variety in it, after you've covered all the roads it has three or four times. Washington's getting to be the same way. There used to be some right pretty country out along Rock Creek, but it's getting covered with houses."

"I'd bet anyplace is prettier than here, though. Anyplace where there's trees and shining water, that is."

Grant surveyed the rugged, gulley-scored slopes that rose on both sides of the road. The ground was raw and treeless. No bush, no sprig of grass showed anywhere. There were fewer mineshaft sheds here, though, and they'd passed the last of the smelters. The air was clearing up, and the smell of sulfur that persisted everywhere in Leadville was no longer noticeable.

"When I went through the Rockies before, in '72, I

remember there were trees everywhere I looked," Grant said, frowning, "but I don't see any here."

"General, you won't find a stand of trees anyplace inside of twenty miles. Those smelters we just passed eat wood like a sty of hogs that ain't been slopped for a week."

"Isn't there a lot of coal mined in Colorado?"

"A right good lot, but coal costs money. Trees are free."

Grant nodded, and lighted a fresh cigar as the buggy bounced over the long curve around Fryer Hill. Between puffs, he asked Longarm, "Are all the roads around here as full of curves and bends as this one? I've got the feel of the horse now. I want to run him a little bit."

"I disremember this particular stretch of road, General. But in these parts, the roads mostly curve around hills."

Grant peered ahead. The road rose on the flank of Fryer Hill and vanished over the crest of its broken slope. He said, "Well, if this is the best we're going to find, I'll give him a little workout here and now."

Longarm settled a bit more firmly into the buggy seat. Grant eased the reins, clucked to the gelding, and slapped the leathers on its back.

"Go, Sovereign!" Grant commanded. "Let's see how you measure up to Butcher Boy!"

For a moment, the big chestnut seemed unaware that it had been given its head. Grant slapped the reins again, and Sovereign's ears twitched. Then the horse's pent-up energy asserted itself. Its hooves drummed a bit faster on the sun-baked dirt of the rutted road, and when the first tentative increase in its gait went unchecked, the animal's hooves drummed yet faster.

Grant was leaning forward in the buggy seat, his chin outthrust, the smoke from his cigar a thin blue thread flowing over his shoulder. Longarm gripped the side of the seat and pushed his boots against the dash as the buggy began to careen on the rough road. The butt of his Winchester was beating a tattoo on the floor, and he held the gun with his free hand, bracing it on the dash beside his feet. Grant slapped the horse with the reins for the third time, and Sovereign responded. The thudding of his hooves took on a quicker tempo as he pulled the light buggy with effortless ease up the hillside.

Now Grant was holding the reins with both hands, but as far as Longarm could tell, he was putting no pressure on them. The general seemed content to let the horse run. His eyes were fixed on Sovereign's legs and flowing mane as they swept up toward the top of the rise. They were within a few hundred yards of the crest when a team came in sight over the low hump the road made. It was a loaded wood wagon, hauling fuel for the smelters. The jagged stumps of the logs that made up the load jutted far out on both sides of the wagon and spanned the narrow road almost completely.

Longarm clamped his teeth together and felt like closing his eyes as the gap between buggy and wagon closed swiftly. The sides of the road were cut with rain-washed gullies, and strewn with massive white boulders bigger than buggy itself. He shot a quick glance at Grant. The general's eyes were fixed on the approaching wagon, the teamster was on his feet now, sawing on the reins, but his team was feeling the downslope underfoot, and, as far as Longarm could judge, was moving faster every second.

For a few moments, a collision seemed unavoidable. Then Grant braced his feet on the dash and twisted his body as he sought the leverage necessary to turn the speeding Sovereign. The horse responded. The buggy bounced off the road and tilted crazily from side to side as its wheels rolled over humps and dropped into gullies. They shot past the wagon, the teamster's head turning, his mouth open, as he followed the buggy's erratic, sliding progress over the rough ground beside the road.

By the time they had crested the slope, Grant had slowed Sovereign's mad dash to a trot. Bit by bit, he kept increasing the presure on the reins until the creaking, lurching buggy was rolling at a more sedate pace. He pulled back onto the road and let the horse keep moving at a good clip over the smoother surface until the animal cooled down. They reached a spot at the end of the grade, on the other side of Fryer Hill, where the road widened. Grant pulled the horse up and turned the the buggy off the road.

He turned to Longarm. "Now, that was something like!" he exclaimed. His eyes were glowing, his mouth spread in a wide smile. "That's the best drive I've had in years! It was worth the trip, if I don't get another bit of good out of it!"

Longarm found his voice. "Well, I'm sure glad you enjoyed it, General. And, I got to say, that was as neat a job of handling as I ever did see."

Grant was lighting a fresh cigar. When it was drawing to his satisfaction, he said. "That was the kind of run that makes a man forget his troubles. You know, Marshal—" he stopped and frowned— "I hate to call a man by his rank; I've had too much of that in my life. What's your first name, anyhow? After we've shared that kind of ride, I can't just call you 'Marshal' or 'Long.' "

"Well, my first name might not make much of a hit with you, General. It's Custis."

"I see," Grant said. He looked at Longarm narrowly. "You're related to General Lee's wife's family, then?"

"If I am, my folks never did tell me about it."

"It wouldn't make any difference to me if you were." Grant told him. "I have a high regard for General Lee, though I never did meet any of his wife's kin that I can recall. But that war's over and best left where it belongs, in the history books. You might've seen service it it, but I'm not going to ask whether you did, or if you did, which side you fought on."

"Well, I was right young, back then. Old enough to get into a little bit of it, though. But I'm like you are, General. I try to disremember all of it, right on down to which flag I was under."

"Yes. That's the best way," Grant replied, nodding. "I'm certainly not asking you any questions." He relighted his cigar. "Let's see, we were talking about your name, when we got off on the War."

"Mostly, my friends call me Longarm."

"I suppose we're friends, aren't we? We're still talking amiably enough, after that scrape I got us into. It'll be Longarm as far as I'm concerned, then. And I still say that was the best drive I've had in quite a while."

"I was enjoying it, right up to the time that woodcutter's wagon started for us."

"I'll take it easier on the way back," Grant promised. He reached for the reins, then drew back his hand and shook his head. "I'm not really in a hurry to get back. It means I'll have to start thinking about my problems."

"Sorry to hear you got any, General. Seems to me a man in your position's sort of earned the right to just coast along without having to worry."

"Oh, I worry. Right now—" he looked at Longarm— "you know, it might do me good to talk to somebody. Somebody I could rely on to keep things to himself."

Longarm studied Grant's suddenly troubled face. He said, "If it's me you mean, I got a way of forgetting things folks tell me they don't want repeated."

Now it was Grant's turn to study Longarm. At last he said, "Yes. I've seen enough to know you'd be that kind of man. And I need to talk out my problems."

He slapped the reins on Sovereign's back and the chestnut moved slowly forward. Grant turned the horse back in the direction of Leadville. He said nothing for several minutes, then began, "I'm in a dilemma, Longarm. It started after Mrs. Grant and I got back from our world tour a few years ago. My son Buck had formed a partnership with two other young men, James Kirk and Ferdinand Ward, in an investment banking house, Grant & Ward. Buck was so enthused about its prospects that I invested just about everything I've got in the firm. Now—well, now it looks as though the business is headed for trouble."

"That's the way businesses do," Longarm said after the general had stopped talking and stayed silent for a short while. "They go through good times and bad ones. Chances are, it'll work out."

"I'm not so sure. I've gotten hints that young Ward's been engaging in some questionable practices. I know Buck's very worried. That's one reason I decided to take this trip, to see if I could attract some more capital into the firm. But now I'm not sure I want to, even if I could." He flung his cigar away in sudden anger. "The cold fact is, I think Ward's a crook, and both Buck and I are going to wind up not losing just our money, but our reputations."

"I wouldn't think you'd have to worry about your good name," Longarm said. "General of the Army, President of the United States—nobody's ever going to be able to take that away from you."

"Don't ever think that about any man who's picked up a certain amount of fame as he's gone through life, Longarm," Grant cautioned. "I'll tell you something I've learned. When a man's winning, nothing and nobody can touch him. When he's losing, everybody tries to take a bite out of him. Believe me, I know. I've lost, and I've won."

"You've always wound up winning, though, "Longarm reminded him.

"Don't think my losses have been forgotten, Longarm. I don't believe they ever will be. If Grant & Ward goes under, especially in any kind of scandalous way, there'll be plenty of people ready to say, 'Well, that's Grant for you. He was a damn fool when he took his men into the Wilderness, he was a damn fool when he was president, and he hasn't changed a bit.' "

Longarm said, "Maybe things ain't as bad as they look to you right now, General. You'll come out ahead this time, too. Just wait and see."

"I hope you're right," Grant said soberly. His cigar had gone out. He relighted it, took a puff, and tossed it away. "I'm either going to have to quit smoking or find another brand of cigars. These seem to rasp my throat lately."

"Hell's bells, General, I quit smoking two or three

times a year," Longarm said. "It's easy to quit. What's hard is to stay quit."

Grant's unhappy mood seemed to have passed as quickly as it had come on him. He chuckled as he replied, "So I'm told. Well, for no reason I can see, I feel better. I suppose it's because I got a lot of things off my chest and had a fine ride." He nodded toward the houses of Leadville, now just a short distance ahead of them. "I hate to have to let go the reins. Sovereign's a good horse. He wouldn't hold up alongside Butcher Boy, though."

"Maybe Senator Tabor'll feel better tomorrow, and you and him can have a ride together. He'd be able to tell you about the diggings a lot better than I could," Longarm said.

"I think I've enjoyed just driving and talking a lot more than I'd have enjoyed listening to Horace," Grant said. "You know, Longarm, it doesn't matter where I go, there's always people who want to show me their local sights. I've seen so many GAR memorials and historic churches and courthouses that I can't remember any of them."

"Not much reason why you should, that I can see."

Longarm shifted the Winchester from between his legs and leaned it against the buggy seat while he lighted a cheroot. Grant glanced at the rifle.

"I'm glad you didn't need to use that," he said. "It'd have spoiled a good afternoon." He paused before asking, "By the way, that man who tried to shoot me—did you ever find out anything more about him?"

"Not one single, solitary thing so far, General, about who he was or who he might be in cahoots with. I'll be talking to Mart Duggan, the city marshal, later on this evening, though. Maybe I'll have something to tell you tomorrow. But I wouldn't worry about him if I was you."

"I'm not worrying about him or whatever friends he might have. I've got too many other things on my mind." Grant shook his head and added, "And a whole evening ahead to think about them." They were driving along the streets of Leadville now, and Grant seemed to enjoy the way Sovereign passed the slower rigs. As they turned into Carbonate Avenue, he said, "We'll each be busy now taking care of our own problems, Longarm."

Longarm couldn't think of any answer to that, so he stayed quiet. The silence between the two men lasted until they reached the Tabor mansion and went inside. Longarm sensed that Grant was already beginning to think about the problems he'd mentioned, and that the brief comradeship that had sprung up so unexpectedly had come to an end. He returned Grant's nod when the general turned away and went into the mansion's main salon. Longarm went in the opposite direction, up the stairs. As he climbed them, Longarm decided he'd a lot rather be *protecting* Grant than *be* Grant.

You don't know how good you got it sometimes, old son, he told his image in the mirror while he poured himself a glass of Maryland rye. *All you got to worry about is keeping Grant from getting killed. But he's got to worry about what's going to happen to him if he don't do anything except just go on living. I guess being a big, famous man ain't such a much after all.*

Dinner was a hit-or-miss affair. Horace Tabor was feeling much better, but still remained in bed. Baby Doe kept Suzanne standing by to help her in case help was needed; they ate with Tabor, from trays brought up from the kitchen. Mrs. Morgan kept getting up from her place in the staff dining room to rush into the kitchen and make sure the trays going upstairs were properly prepared. Forbes divided his time between the staff dining room and keeping an eye on the service the kitchen maids were giving Grant, who ate in solitary splendor in the main dining room. Jean-Pierre was glowering because his talents were being wasted in such a household.

"How," he demanded of Longarm, with whom he was alone at the staff dinner table through most of the meal, "How can I exercise my skill on *oeufs mollets* for one? I, who am used to cooking for those who appreciate the finest?"

"Now, even if I knew what them 'erfs muleys' was,

I couldn't tell you that," Longarm replied. His voice showed the disgust he was feeling for the whole business of everybody running off in different directions and disturbing his meal. "Looks like you're going to have to save up that skill of yours until tomorrow night, and fix up something real special for the big dinner General Grant's having at the hotel."

Then, before the volatile chef could begin telling him what he'd planned for tomorrow night's dinner menu, Longarm got up, reached for his hat, and hurried outside.

Duggan's man was stationed where he was supposed to be, on the dark front porch of the house next door. From there, he could watch the Tabor house and grounds unobtrusively, without attracting attention.

"You likely won't have any trouble," Longarm told him. "Just keep an eye out for anybody who comes skulking around. If somebody shows up who's got no business in the neighborhood, drag 'em downtown and throw them in jail. I'll stop by there tonight and have a word with Mart after my other business is finished."

Longarm's "other business" opened the door and greet him with a smile. "I was wondering if you were going to forget me again," she told him. "It didn't occur to me until I saw you at the Tabor's reception that you were here to protect General Grant, and that your duty might keep you from coming to see me."

"Now, Vivian, you know I didn't forget you before," Longarm protested. "I've just been too busy. When I got a case on hand, it don't matter what I'd *rather* do; I got to tend to business first."

Vivian had started down the hall, but now she stopped and turned back to face Longarm. She was wearing a dressing gown that buttoned high around her throat and hung in a straight line from her shoulders. Only the bulge of her breasts broke the gown's severe downsweep. She said, "I hope you're not just dropping in for a minute or two, to say hello. In case you are, hello and goodbye. In case you're not, I had the cook fix a cold supper, because I really didn't know when to expect you."

"Now, there's not any call for you to be mad at me, Vivian. You know I wouldn't come here if I didn't have time to stay till you got tired of me."

"That's better," she purred, smiling. "What about supper? Are you hungry?"

"You look a lot better to me than food does, right now."

"You're improving every minute, Longarm." Vivian's smile widened. "That's what I was hoping you'd say."

She came to Longarm then, and offered her lips. He bent to meet them and they clung together in a long embrace. His hand roamed over her body, and told him that she had nothing on under the long silk gown. The sleek texture of its fabric was as excitingly smooth to Longarm's touch as the skin beneath it. Her nipples rose to his touch. She brought her hand up along his inner thigh and felt him beginning to bulge and swell.

"You're always ready, aren't you?" she whispered. "Maybe that's why I enjoy you so much. We share a lot of things, don't we?"

"Looks like it. And I don't see much reason for putting off going upstairs, do you?"

"No. I've put a tray of liquor in the bedroom, your Maryland rye and my brandy, if you want a drink."

"A drink's always a good way to start, I've found."

"As far as I'm concerned, we've already started," she replied. "And I'm not in any mood to stop." She led the way upstairs. In her bedroom, she said, "Have your drink, if you want one, while you're undressing. I'll go start the bath water."

Longarm poured himself a drink and lighted a cheroot. He took his mind off Vivian long enough to take his usual precautions in case trouble broke unexpectedly. He didn't look for any, but the habit was too ingrained for him to change it. He hung his gunbelt on the back of a chair that he carefully placed near the head of the bed, where his hand could sweep the Colt out instantly. Only then, while he drank the last of the rye, did he lever off his boots and shed the rest of his clothes.

Naked, he followed Vivian into the ornate bathroom. She was bending over at the edge of the marble tub, adjusting the flow of water from the tap. She hadn't yet taken off her gown, and the clinging silk outlined the twin swells of her buttocks and the deep crease between their cheeks. Longarm stepped up behind her and lifted the gown. He rose quickly and slipped his erect member between her thighs. Vivian gasped and stood up, her flesh closing around him. She began to move her hips back and forth, and he felt moisture seeping around him. Longarm slipped his hands under her gown and brought them up her body, seeking her breasts. Vivian leaned back against him when he clutched their round softness. Her head lolled back on his shoulder.

"It's going to take the tub a while to fill," she said softly. "There's no need for us to waste time waiting."

Vivian bent forward to let him into her from behind. Her fingers trembling with anticipation, she tucked him into place and squeezed her thighs together tightly while Longarm plunged between them. His first hard thrusts brought gasping sighs from her lips, and she bent further to let him go still deeper. Longarm grasped her hips to pull himself fully into her and, for a long moment, held her there, motionless. In the mirror that covered one wall of the room, he could see Vivian's face. Her eyelids were pressed tightly together by the grimace of pleasant pain that held her lips wide and pushed her cheeks high.

"I ain't hurting you, am I?" he asked.

"Yes, but in a way I like. There aren't many men who can fill a woman as completely as you do, Longarm."

As if to reinforce her statement, Vivian began to roll the muscles of her abdomen. Inside her, Longarm felt her movements as a series of undulating caresses. He moved his hips from side to side in response, and was sure that his erection swelled still more. For as long as they could endure it, they continued the small, almost painful movements, until Vivian gasped and brought her back up straight to end the cramping embrace.

"No more right now, Longarm. Look, the tub's going to run over when we get in unless I turn the water off."

Longarm released her and she pulled free, stepped into the tub, and stopped the faucets' flow. Longarm joined her and she moved to meet him, spreading her legs when they stood face to face, and cradling his thick, moistly slick length in her palms as he slid into her once more.

Vivian locked her hands around Longarm's neck and let herself fall backward, pulling him down into the warm water on top of her. They were almost weightless now, with the water supporting them. Longarm tried to drive into her, but the lack of resistance offered by the water slowed his thrusts. He gave up trying to stroke hard, and lapsed into a slow, deliberate rhythm. Vivian grasped him around the chest and planted her feet on the tub's bottom to give her the leverage she needed to turn them both over.

Her weight drove Longarm to the bottom of the tub. He braced himself with his arms straight behind him to keep his head above the water while Vivian, kneeling above him, rocked back and forth on his impaling shaft. Their weightlessness, suspended in the warm water, brought languor to their embrace. Without the urgency brought by quick motion, neither of them could build to a climax. After what seemed an endless time, Vivian slowed her gyrations and stopped.

"I could go on this way all night," she said. "But the water's going to get cold. Let's scrub a while, and go to bed."

"Suits me fine," Longarm agreed. "Except I hate to stop anything that feels as good as this does."

"It'll be even better when we start again," Vivian promised.

She stood up, water flowing off her in a thin sheet that brought a warm lustre to her skin, pink now instead of white. On her dark rosettes, there were sparkling drops that turned into jewels. Longarm stood and put his mouth to her nipples, but she twisted away and reached for the jar of salt that stood on the rim of the tub.

"Not now," she told him. "Just think how much more we're going to enjoy it later."

Later came sooner than it had when they'd rubbed one another down before. Vivian's lips brought Longarm erect quickly again when she kissed and caressed him after she'd rinsed away the salt, and when he felt the sensuous slipperiness of the salt granules dissolving under his calloused palms while he rubbed her breasts and stomach, he could feel her muscles tightening as well. He moved to her thighs, and when he rinsed their inner surfaces, he followed the rinsing with quick, flicking caresses that brought fresh beads of moisture flowing to the petalled edges of her inner lips.

When they emerged from the tub, their glowing bodies needed little drying. They tumbled into bed as Vivian gasped, "Hurry, Hurry! I'm just holding back until you get inside me!"

Longarm thrust into her and began stroking, felt her inner muscles grab him, and then let go as she surrendered, with her high, sharp scream, to the quaking orgasm she'd been postponing for so long. He needed more time, and did not stop. The steady rhythm of his deep lunges brought Vivian back to readiness again by the time he was ready. He didn't try to prolong their embrace; he'd been holding back too long. He peaked and let go, and as he jetted in quaking release, he heard Vivian's high-pitched cry burst from her throat.

They lay connected for a while, as he grew flaccid and her muscles relaxed in short, quivering shudders. When Vivian stirred under his weight, Longarm rolled away and stretched out beside her.

Vivian said, her voice a dreamy whisper, "Damn it, Longarm, I wish I'd met you twenty years ago."

"Not much use being sorry about something that never happened," he consoled her. "We might not even have liked each other then."

"I think we would have."

"Maybe so. But there ain't much wrong with the way we get along right now."

"Of course there isn't. But if I'd met you years ago, I've got a feeling that my life would've been a lot different."

"Now look here, Vivian, you're a real fine lady. You know what you want and ain't bashful about getting it. But you might not be the same way if you'd lived any different."

"Oh, you're right, of course, but—" She stopped short. When she spoke again, it was in a different tone. "Longarm, why didn't you tell me, when you were in Leadville that first time, that you'd be coming back as General Grant's bodyguard?"

"There wasn't much reason to talk about it then. If you'll recall, we didn't do a hell of a lot of talking about anything," he reminded her. Longarm was totally relaxed, bathed in the pleasant glow of a satisfied man. He didn't especially want to talk about Grant or Tabor or anything else connected with them.

"But if you'd told me, I wouldn't—" Again Vivian stopped short. After the briefest pause, she went on, "I wouldn't have thought you might not come to see me when you said you would."

"I'm here, ain't I?"

"Yes, very much so. And I know it. But you're not all here. Not yet. Not as much of you as I want to be here."

Vivian leaned over him. Her moist tongue traced a path down his throat. Her head moved lower, and when she spoke, her voice was muffled by the matted curls of Longarm's chest. "Is it too soon? Are you too tired?"

"You go on. You'll find out quick enough," he told her.

Vivian devoted herself to finding out. The warmth of her breath and the soft moisture of her tongue moving down the tautening muscles of his belly, and then the heat of her mouth around him, gave her the answers to her questions. Longarm looked at her kneeling beside him, her plump buttocks raised, the scar on one hip a dark patch of roughness in the otherwise unmarked expanse of her satiny skin. He reached out to stroke her and finger her gently. She threw a knee over his shoulder as an invitation to him to share the pleasure.

Passive lovemaking was not Longarm's way, though. He shared the lazy caresses Vivian was enjoying until he felt her lips grow more urgently demanding. Then he picked her up bodily and shifted her to lie beside him. Vivian looked at him, her swollen lips set in a small, puzzled pout, until she felt him going into her with a smooth, slow, powerful thrust that bent her spine into an arch of excitement. Her eyes closed dreamily, and she did not open them when Longarm knelt on the bed and grasped an ankle in each hand. He raised her legs high, and pulled her thighs to him, sending him into her in even deeper penetration. The backs of her knees rested on his shoulders, and her ankles were locked above his head; only her head and shoulders now rested on the bed.

Closing his strong hands on her hips, Longarm took command of Vivian's movements. Her body was swinging freely. He pulled her to him, at first slowly, then swiftly, while he twisted his hips from side to side. He rotated her hips between his hands while holding his own body still. He thrust into her strongly while he raised and lowered her body in time to his deep stroking. They'd both been almost ready before Longarm took control of her body, and the swiftness of his movements brought them to a spasm within moments. Vivian screamed and twisted and writhed in his hands as he drove into her while his own orgasm lasted. Then he let her go, and dropped to the soft feather mattress beside her quivering form.

"Oh, God!" Vivian sighed when her breathing began returning to its normal tempo. "I feel like I'd just been pleasured by twenty men, one right after another! I'm so sleepy I can just barely hold my eyes open, but I don't want to close them because I'm afraid that if I do, you won't be here when I wake up."

"I don't plan to go anyplace," he told her. "Not for

a while. And a little nap wouldn't hurt me, either. I'll just turn down the light and we'll both doze awhile."

He rolled out of bed and adjusted the wick of the lamp on the dresser until it cast no more than a dim glow in the spacious room. Vivian was already half asleep when he slipped back into bed beside her. She stirred, her eyes veiled, and snuggled up to Longarm, throwing an arm across his chest, her body pressing against him full-length.

"I'm glad you're going to stay awhile," Vivian sighed, her voice soft and heavy with sleepiness. "It feels good to cuddle up to you. And you sleep too, Longarm." She stopped and yawned hugely. Her voice was even more languid than it had been when she finally overcame the yawning spell. "You can sleep with me as long as you want to. You won't have to worrry . . ." her voice trailed off into silence. Longarm was sliding into sleep, too. He slid an arm under Vivian to hold her to him. The movement roused her and she said in a breathy whisper, "You don't have to worry about General Grant until tomorrow night."

Longarm heard her distantly through the haze of slumber that was descending over him. His thoughts formed slowly: *Now that ain't exactly right. Sounds like Vivian's expecting me to stay here with her tonight and all through tomorrow, too. And there just ain't any way for me to do that. If the senator's feeling up to snuff, him and the general might want to go someplace in the morning. Then there's that hen-party Baby Doe's having in the afternoon. And the general's big dinner at the hotel, too. And I got to catch Duggan before he goes home.*

Longarm tried to wake Vivian up and tell her all this, but when he opened his eyes and looked at her, she was asleep. He decided there would be plenty of time to tell her later. With a sigh of satisfaction, he closed his own eyes and, within seconds, was sleeping soundly himself.

Instinct born of long habit brought Longarm snapping

awake. Beside him, Vivian still slept peacefully. The night-scent of her perfumed body was heavy in Longarm's nostrils. Pleasant as it was, he rolled quietly out of bed and padded barefoot over the thick carpet to pour himself a wake-up drink. The lamp on the dresser was still burning low. With the shades drawn tightly down, there was no way for him to tell what time it was. He went to his vest and slid out his watch. The hour was six, his usual waking time.

Except today, that makes me late, he thought. *Duggan's left by now, and I sure don't aim to rile him by getting him up right after he's started sleeping good.*

Longarm pulled on his balbriggans and squeezed into his pants. As he moved and stirred the air, he realized that Vivian's perfume was clinging to his body, that he smelled almost as pretty as she did. He was tucking in the tail of his gray flannel shirt when Vivian moved and opened her eyes.

"You're not going so soon, are you, Longarm?" she asked.

"It ain't what I'd call soon. It's six in the morning."

"An hour or two won't matter, at this time of day."

"Vivian, honey, you know I'd stay here, if it was up to me."

"Or if it were up to me, either." Vivian sat up. She winced as she moved. With a rueful little smile, she said, "I suppose it's just as well that you've got a conscience. I seem to be a little bit stiff and sore this morning. Not that it'd matter, if you came back to bed."

"No, you know I can't. Now go stretch out in that fancy bathtub of yours. Soak awhile in good hot water."

"It won't be any fun without you."

"I'll be back, the first minute I'm free."

"When will that be?"

"I can't rightly say. Maybe after lunch, while Mrs. Tabor's entertaining the ladies. Or maybe not until tonight, after the general's dinner's over with."

"Whenever it is, I'll be waiting."

"Sure, but I've got to make tracks now." Longarm bent over Vivian when she held up her face for a goodbye kiss. He backed away quickly when her hands sought his crotch. "Not now. Later."

Hurrying downstairs, Longarm let himself out and walked briskly down Carbonate Avenue in the cool morning air—still carrying a hint of sulphur in it—to the Tabor mansion. Duggan's man was still sitting, bleary-eyed, on the porch of the house next door. Longarm stopped to ask him, "Anything happen last night?"

"Not one damn thing. For all the good I done here, I might as well have been at home in bed."

"Well, go on home now. Your job's all done."

Longarm crossed the bare ground between the two houses, and was just angling toward the Tabor mansion's back door when Grant came out of the stable. He was coatless, and had his customary cigar in his mouth.

"Oh, Longarm!" he called. "I'd like to have a word with you."

"Morning, General." Longarm veered to join Grant. "You're out a bit early. You and the senator going someplace?"

"Not this morning. Horace is still a little shaky after that attack of dyspepsia yesterday," Grant replied. "No, I just wanted to look in on Sovereign. I had in mind talking to you later on, but now's as good a time as any."

"Something you want me to do for you?" Longarm asked.

"As a matter of fact, there is." Grant cleared his throat. "I hope you'll take it the right way, Longarm. I talked about a few things yesterday that I hope you'll put out of your mind. It won't do me a bit of good if word gets around that I've got suspicions about the soundness of my son's business."

"Why, if you said anything at all besides talking about horses yesterday, I plumb disremember it," Longarm said, straight-faced.

Grant looked at him narrowly, then smiled. "I was pretty sure you'd say something like that, the way I sized you up. It's just between the two of us then."

"As far as I'm concerned, it is."

"Good." Grant started for the house. "Breakfast ought to be ready now, don't you think? After that fine ride we had yesterday, I've got a very healthy appetite this morning."

Chapter 9

Longarm kept close to his room through the morning. There was always the chance that Tabor and Grant might take a sudden notion to go somewhere, and he didn't intend to let them go unless he was along with them. Anytime Grant went out, he became a target. Longarm was sure of that now, and sure also that the general would be a target until the identity of the mysterious "senator" could be uncovered and whatever plot had been hatched was smashed. He mulled over, for perhaps the tenth time, the scanty bits and pieces he knew, but by the time noon arrived, he'd still made no progress.

When Longarm went into the staff dining room for lunch, he brushed past Suzanne, who was standing just inside the door. He wondered why the smile with which she greeted him suddenly twisted into an angry frown, and why she ignored his own greeting to her. During the meal, Suzanne said little to anyone. Most of the time, she glowered across the table at Longarm.

He dismissed her actions as being the unpredictable way of a woman, and gave up trying to make conversation. While eating, he decided that since he wouldn't be needed to watch for trouble while Leadville's womenfolk oohed and ahhed over Grant at Baby Doe's afternoon soirée, he'd steal the time to walk down to

Chestnut Street for a shave at the barbershop he'd noticed there. He was pretty sure Suzanne wouldn't be offering to shave him today.

Stretched out on the bed in his room, waiting for the soirée to free him, Longarm resumed gnawing at the puzzle he was faced with solving. He'd taken off his boots, his gunbelt was hung in its place at the head of the bed, and two pillows propped him up comfortably. He was sipping at his after-lunch glass of Maryland rye, a cheroot in his other hand, when Suzanne erupted into the room.

"Of all the low-down men I've ever known in this world," she blazed, "You're about the lowest! Longarm, how could you sit there across the table from me at lunch and look me in the eye and grin that brazen grin? Why, you're—"

"Wait up, Suzanne!" Longarm broke in. "Maybe you better start out by telling me what I've done that's got you so riled up."

"What have you done! You're asking me what you've done?" she retorted. "Don't add lying to everything else! You know damned well what you've done!"

"If I knew, I sure wouldn't be asking."

"Oh, you know! Sure you know! Just like I know, as well as if I'd been there watching! All you've got to do is smell of yourself!"

Longarm realized then that he'd gotten accustomed to the faint aroma of Vivian's perfume that still clung to his body. He'd washed all right, he thought, but not nearly well enough, apparently. But he'd found out that where women were concerned, it was fatal to admit to being guilty of anything of which they might accuse a man. Give them that satisfaction, and they'd dog a man about it the rest of his days.

He said, "All I can smell right now is this whiskey I've got here."

"I suppose you think I can't smell the perfume that other woman rubbed off on you while you were fucking her?" When Longarm calmly took another sip of his rye without answering her, Suzanne went on, "I didn't say a word the other night, when I waited and waited for you to come back. Even if I did stay up here until it was almost daylight, and you still hadn't shown up. And when—"

Longarm interrupted her before she could list his other failings. "Just hold up, now! I never did make you any promise I was going to get back here. The way things worked out, I had business downtown that took me longer than I'd figured. And I didn't even know you'd be here, either."

"I told you—"

"You said you wanted me to hurry back. For all I knew, you figured to listen for me to come in before you came up here."

"I suppose you were with that woman the other night, too!" Suzanne flung the accusation at him. "I wouldn't put much past you!"

"Whoa!" Longarm commanded. He was getting a bit riled himself, now. "I don't recall when you and me stood up in front of a preacher and said the words that'd give you the right to be telling me who to see and where to go."

"Well, we didn't, but—"

"Don't go butting, now. It don't signify."

"All right," Suzanne said reluctantly. "I'll admit I don't have any strings on you. But I thought—"

"You're butting me again, Suzanne," Longarm said sharply. "What you thought was likely different from what I thought. You might just remember it was you who come in to see me first, on that train up from Denver. I sure didn't send you any invitation. And I never invited you up to my room here, either. You came up of your own free will. I never sweet-talked you, or promised you a thing."

"It's that other woman! She's turned you against me! The one who uses that nasty perfume! Oh, what a mean brute you are, Longarm! I never want to see you again as long as I live!"

Whirling, Suzanne flounced out the door, slamming it behind her. Longarm shook his head as the echo of the slammed door died away. Then he got up to pour himself a fresh drink before resuming his interrupted thinking.

He'd already concluded that the senator to whom the letter written by the would-be assassin was addressed wasn't a U.S. senator. A U.S. senator, who spent a good part of his time in the East where Grant lived, would have found it easier to arrange for him to be killed *there*. No, it had to be a state senator, who'd been inspired by word of Grant's visit to the West to use local talent. Of which there was plenty, as Longarm knew.

Maybe I ought to've paid more mind to politics, Longarm told himself, lighting a fresh cheroot. *I don't even know how many senators are in the state senate. And the only one I can recall meeting face to face is that skinny one Vivian had in tow the other night.*

Tilting his glass to his lips, Longarm found it empty. He got up and refilled it, stepped idly to the window to look out, and saw a line of carriages lined up at the curb on Carbonate Avenue. As he watched, the line moved forward the length of a carriage.

That'll be the ladies getting here for the shindy, Longarm thought. Then a second thought struck him: *If I want a shave so I won't disgrace old Billy at the dinner tonight, I better get cracking.*

He got ready quickly. Before he left the house, he wanted to tell Tabor or Grant where he'd be for the next hour or so.

He caught Tabor just as he was entering the main salon, where the high-pitched chatter of voices indicated that the afternoon's event had already gotten under way.

"If it's all right with you, Senator," Longarm said, "I'm going downtown and get me a shave while you and the general are visiting with the ladies. I don't figure they're apt to have any plans to hurt him."

Tabor smiled, his drooping mustaches twitching. "No. I think you can trust the ladies of Leadville, Marshal. You don't have to worry about General Grant until tonight."

Longarm walked the short distance to Chestnut

Street, and found the barbershop he remembered. He relaxed a bit under the soothing influence of warm lather and hot towels, but his mind was still busy on his urgent problem.

Most of those senators are likely to be there tonight, he thought, as the bay rum the barber was patting on his face filled the air with its pungent aroma. *It's risky waiting so long, and chancy as all hell, but it's about the only way I can see to handle things. Old Silver Dollar Tabor didn't say but half of it. I don't have to worry about General Grant until tonight, but I sure got a lot—*

An alarm bell rang in Longarm's brain. He said aloud, "Somebody said that to me besides Tabor. Before he said it."

"Sir?" the barber asked.

"Nothing. Just talking to myself," Longarm said. Then as though the aroma of the bay rum were stimulating his thoughts, he remembered.

It was Vivian who'd said exactly what Tabor did; she'd made the remark while she was falling asleep the night before. And there wasn't any doubt in Longarm's mind that what she'd meant was that the time he'd need to worry about Grant was at the dinner. Which meant Vivian knew what he'd been busting his brain trying to figure out.

Longarm wasted no time. He stood up before the barber had begun to take off his cloth. Longarm ripped away the cloth, tossed it and a half-dollar to the barber, saying, "Keep the change, friend," and was out of the shop, hotfooting it down Chestnut Street, before he realized that he still had a towel tucked into his shirt collar. He tossed the towel aside, reflecting that the thirty-cent tip he'd given the man ought to pay for two or three new towels.

To save time, Longarm cut through the alleys down which Duggan had led him. He got to Carbonate Avenue and ran up the steps of Vivian Montgomery's house. He rang the bell and waited. When no one answered the door, he rang again, and then a third time, before trying the knob. The door was locked. He'd been sure it would be. He hurried to the back door, and knocked without getting a response. It was locked too. Longarm pressed his ear to the door and listened. He heard none of the small, accidental noises that identify an occupied house. For a moment, he thought about kicking in the door and searching the place, but dismissed the thought instantly. It was Vivian he wanted, not her empty house.

Because the Tabor house was closer than the police station, he went there first. The soirée was still going on, though he'd seen a carriage or two leaving while he was walking the short distance down Carbonate Avenue. Longarm went to the back door. Forbes was in the staff dining room, sitting with Mrs. Morgan. A teapot was on the table in front of them.

"Senator Tabor said you had a list of women invited to this blowout," he said to Forbes. "You got it handy?"

"In my pocket." Forbes produced the list, three pages of names. "Why?"

"I just wanted to check something out." Longarm took the list and scanned it quickly. Vivian's name wasn't on it. He handed the ruffled papers back to Forbes. "You got one for the general's dinner tonight, too?"

"Of course." Forbes reached into his breast pocket, but Longarm stopped him.

"I ain't got time to go over a lot of names right now. You remember how many state senators are on that list?"

"Why . . . eleven, I believe. You know Senator Tabor's running a special train up from Denver to bring most of the guests."

"I recall that. You remember whether there's a senator named Purvis on the list, Forbes?"

"Yes, of course he is. Senator Purvis is what you'd call a neighbor. He lives in Climax, you know."

"I know. Thanks, Forbes. Tell Senator Tabor not to worry if I don't get back in time to ride to the hotel with him and the general this evening. I'll be there to meet them. I've got some more business to tend to, right quick."

Although he knew it was too early, Longarm went

first to Duggan's office. As he'd expected would be the case, the city marshal hadn't come in yet. Longarm made a beeline for the U.S. Hotel. He went directly to Duggan's room and knocked.

Duggan responded with the speed of an old firehorse taking his place between the shafts the instant the alarm bell rings. He opened the door, sleep still in his eyes. He was wearing his underwear. "Longarm? What in hell's happened now?"

"It ain't happened yet, Mart. If I get a little bit of luck, it won't happen at all. Mind if I come in? I got a question or two you can maybe answer."

"Sure." Duggan opened the door wider. Longarm went in and closed the door. Duggan had gone to the tousled bed and was sitting on its side. He said, "Well? Fire away."

"You know a lady named Montgomery in town here? Lives up on Carbonate Avenue?"

"Sure. That is to say, I know her when I see her. I don't recollect that I was ever introduced to her," Duggan replied.

"What-all do you know about her? Or about her husband?"

"What husband? She's got no husband, Longarm."

"I know that," Longarm replied impatiently. "I mean *late* husband. She's a widow woman, I understand."

"Well, if she had a husband, he never got here to Leadville with her. She blew into town right when the boom begun, in '78. Hell, it wasn't too long after they changed the name of the place from Slabtown to Leadville. I wasn't even marshal then."

"Go on. I want to know everything you can remember about her."

"There just ain't much to remember, Longarm. She was pretty well-heeled, I guess. Bought up a few claims at first, but nothing big. Then she bought the old Meyers smelter when he died, dickered the deal out with his widow, I've been told. She's run it ever since. I guess Mrs. Montgomery's the only woman smelter operator in the country."

"That's fine as far as it goes, Mart. But what about

her? Who's she friends with? Where did she come from? What does she do when she's not running her smelter?"

Duggan's brow crinkled thoughtfully. "I don't believe she's 'specially friendly with much of anybody. If she is, I never heard any remarks on it. If you mean is she somebody's special woman, I'd say no and be real sure I'm right. In this town, you can't keep a thing like that quiet, and nobody seems much inclined to hide it. Like Silver Dollar, when he set Baby Doe up in that apartment in the Clarendon Hotel. He never did try to fool anybody that she wasn't his property. And that's when him and Augusta were still living together."

"Mart," Longarm said patiently, "we're talking about Vivian Montgomery, not Silver Dollar Tabor."

"Sure, I know that. Let's see. Where'd she come from, you asked. Damned if I ever heard. She knew something about mining and smelting, though. Knew enough to hire a smart manager and keep out of his way while he runs the place for her."

"This manager of hers—has he got a name?"

"Jesse Wilkes."

"Wilkes? Would that make him kin to Wilkes Purvis?"

"I can't say about that. If they're kinfolks, they sure don't show it. Senator Purvis comes to town right often, but I never heard he spent any time with Jesse. Or with Mrs. Montgomery, either."

"He was with her at Tabor's reception for the general the other night," Longarm said.

"Well, maybe they know each other. Maybe come from the same place, something like that," Duggan suggested.

"You could be right."

"Longarm, if you're so damn curious about Mrs. Montgomery, why don't you ask her what you want to know? I'll go over to her house with you and introduce you to her, if you want."

"I've met the lady, Mart. On the train Blackie Spencer's gang tried to hold up."

"Oh. Well, go ask her, then. I imagine she'd tell you."

"Sure, Mart. I'll try that." Longarm hauled his watch

out and looked at it. He'd spent a lot of time—or *wasted* a lot—since he'd started this new line of investigating. He didn't have too much more to waste before the dinner was due to begin. He told Duggan, "I've got to get going now, Mart. I'll look in on you later tonight, at your office."

Leaving the U.S. Hotel, he checked his watch again. There was just about time for him to make another try at finding Vivian home before he'd have to head for the Tabor Grand Hotel, if he intended to get there before Grant's dinner began. He walked briskly through the alleys, the shortest route he knew of to get to Carbonate Avenue. Even before he reached Vivian's house, he could tell he'd wasted his time once more. There were no lights showing at any of the windows.

Just the same, Longarm went on, and knocked at both front and back doors, as well as trying them to make sure they were indeed locked. He walked around the house once more, checking the windows, straining his ears to hear any sound of movement. The curtains at all the windows were exactly as they'd been on his earlier visit, drawn tight, and he could detect no noises from inside. Longarm gave up for the time being, and started back to town.

He reached Tabor's Grand Hotel just as Grant's guests were sitting down. Forbes was standing just inside the entrance to the main dining room, which opened off the lobby.

Longarm asked Tabor's factotum, "Everybody show up that was invited?"

"Not quite. There were five or six on my list who aren't here. That's why I'm waiting, to see if they might still arrive."

"Are any of them in that bunch of eleven state senators that you said were supposed to be here?"

"Three." Forbes ticked them off on his fingers. "Senator Purvis, Senator Williamson, and Senator Young. All of them sent acceptances of their invitations."

Longarm scratched his chin. The absence of the three could mean anything, or nothing. He surveyed the big dining room. A low platform had been set up across one end, on which the head table stood. Grant and Tabor were seated at the center of the long table, flanked by eight or ten men on each side. The other three tables were at floor level, and stood at right angles to the head table, extending the length of the long, narrow room. Swinging service doors with round glass panes in their upper sections were opposite the main entrance. The room was on the inside of the hotel; its walls, covered with flocked, embossed wallpaper and dotted with gaslights, had no windows. Half the guests faced the lobby doors, and the remainder faced the service doors. Longarm saw no faces he recognized among those facing him.

He asked Forbes, "How long do you aim to wait for the ones who ain't here yet?"

"Another five minutes or so. Then I'm going to the senator's office and wait until the dinner's over. It'll be late, I'm afraid. They'll sit over cigars and brandy for a while after they've eaten and heard the speeches the general and Senator Tabor will deliver."

"I'll ask a favor of you when you leave, Forbes." Longarm indicated the wide double door behind them. "Shut those doors and make sure they're locked."

"You're surely not expecting more trouble?" Forbes asked with a frown.

"Hell, Forbes, I'm not expecting anything. All I'm doing is hoping nothing's going to happen. But I don't want anybody sneaking in here from the lobby. I'm going to find me a chair and sit by those doors across the room."

Forbes nodded. Longarm circled around the back of the dining room. As he passed the swinging doors through which waiters were beginning to pass, balancing loaded trays, he got broken glimpses of the kitchen. It was a bustle of white-aproned cooks and their helpers. Jean-Pierre passed once, hurrying from the huge black ranges at the back of the kitchen to the low counter near the doors, where a squad of helpers loaded the waiters' trays. Several spare chairs stood along the wall. Longarm moved one near the center of the wall, close to the service doors, where he had a clear line of sight to the head table. He sat down to watch and wait.

It was an elaborate dinner. Trout with stuffed tomatoes followed the soup that was being served when Longarm sat down; the fish course gave way to chicken with side dishes of asparagus spears and fluffed potatoes, then a rack of lamb, carved at each table by a waiter and served with artichokes and creamed corn. By the time these dishes had been cleared and the salad course served, the sight and smell of food was making Longarm hungrier than he thought he deserved to be, when there was so much food all around him. In the hurrying around he'd done, he'd missed eating supper.

Longarm noticed that a special waiter had been assigned to serve Grant, and that the dishes he carried weren't those placed before the other diners. He remembered, then, what Jean-Pierre had told him about the general's refusal to eat any meat except well-done beef, and that Grant also refused to eat most vegetables. Apparently, part of the job of Tabor's chef was to see that Grant wasn't given any food except that which the general would eat.

Try as he might, Longarm couldn't silence his hunger pangs. By the time the salad plates had been removed and steaks with baked potatoes and green peas were flowing from the kitchen on the waiters' big trays, his stomach was protesting so loudly that he was sure its growls could be heard across the width of the dining room.

Longarm thought of Jean-Pierre, who could certainly be persuaded to fix him a quick snack. He glanced at the lobby doors, which he'd seen Forbes close and—he was sure—lock, as he'd told the factotum to do. The only other access to the dining room was through the kitchen. After a quick look around the tables to make sure the diners were engrossed in their steaks, Longarm pushed through the swinging door and entered the busy kitchen.

Almost all the steaks had been served. Only two or three of the waiters still stood at the serving counter, ready to pick up their trays as the kitchen helpers filled them. The other waiters were lined up against the wall near a second service counter where Longarm spotted Jean-Pierre, his high chef's hat towering above those who surrounded him. He started for the second counter. Just as he reached it, Jean-Pierre grabbed the towel that hung from his apron, and began flailing one of the kitchen helpers with it. The helper, who wore a starched white jacket above street trousers, was trying to ward off the chef's slaps with his upraised hands.

"What's wrong, Jean-Pierre?" Longarm asked. "This fellow get his thumb in the soup, or something?"

"Non, non Márechal!" Jean-Pierre replied. *"Cet cochon gâte le génoise aux fraises Lucullus!"*

"Whoa, Jean-Pierre!" Longarm said. "Talk English, if you want me to follow you." As a precaution, Longarm moved around the counter and stood beside the man Jean-Pierre had been slapping. The man started moving away.

"Stay right where you are," Longarm commanded. "If you ain't done anything but step on Jean-Pierre's toes, I won't bother you."

The man stopped his sidewise motion.

"This pig is spoil my *gâteau aux fraises Lucullus*," Jean-Pierre explained. "My beautiful *gâteau*, which I make especially to please General Grant, because I find out he like cakes." He waved a hand over the counter.

Longarm looked, and saw a row of cakes already cut for serving. From several of them, the sliced wedges had already been removed to the smaller dishes in which they would go to the table. He said to Jean-Pierre, "This what you call your 'gatoo'? It looks like plain strawberry shortcake to me."

"Non!" the chef explained. "It is to your shortcake what a plodding mule is to a fine racehorse! And this one spoils it by putting on more sugar! Too much sugar robs the delicate—"

Longarm interrupted Jean-Pierre's excited flow of words. "Wait, now. Start at the beginning and tell me what he done."

Jean-Pierre covered his eyes with his hand and took a few deep breaths. He looked at Longarm then and said, "I have cut from the *gâteau* a special large piece for the general. I put it here, so—" he indicated a plate holding an oversized piece of the cake— "Then I see this one—" pointing an accusing finger at the man standing beside Longarm—" "I see this one sprinkle more sugar on it. Too much sugar—"

Longarm cut the chef short again. "Just a minute. Did he know that piece of cake was one you put aside for General Grant?"

"But of course! I have tell him to be sure the other waiters do not pick it up in mistake."

Longarm frowned. "You said he was putting sugar on it?" He searched the service counter with his eyes. "Where'd he get it from? There's not any sugar bowl here."

Jean-Pierre shrugged. "How am I to know that? I see the sugar shining when he sift it on the *gâteau*. I know what I see, *Márechal*."

"I ain't doubting what you saw, Jean-Pierre," Longarm said. He turned to the kitchen helper. "Where'd you get the sugar?"

"I wasn't doing anything," the man replied. "He's lying."

Longarm studied the man. There was nothing outstanding about him. His face was square, he was cleanshaven, there were no kinks in his nose, no scars on his cheeks. Judging by his sideburns, his hair was a nondescript brown. His eyes were also brown, and now were narrowed into slits, pulling the corners of their lids into wrinkles that gave his face a worried look.

"You feel like telling me what it was you put on that cake?" Longarm asked him.

"I didn't put nothing on it! That Frenchie's lying, I tell you!"

"*Non!* I do not lie! I see him!" Jean-Pierre insisted.

Longarm waved the chef to silence. "What's your name and where'd you come from?" he asked the kitchen helper.

"Jack. Jack Smith. And I don't come from anyplace, ain't going anyplace. I'm drifting. I needed a job, and this was the best I could do."

Longarm looked around at the kitchen crew who, by now, had gathered to see what was going on. "Any of you know this fellow?" he asked of the group. "Somebody must've hired him."

A stout, long-mustached individual with a chef's hat as tall as that worn by Jean-Pierre said, "I am Rene Montfleury. It is my responsibility, the kitchen. I employed the man, and four others, for the banquet. We do this often, m'sieu."

"He give you the name he just claimed?" Longarm asked.

The head chef shrugged. "Who can recall? I suppose he did."

Longarm looked at the interested spectators. There were too many of them, he decided. He asked Montfleury, "You got a little room around here, where I can talk to this Jack Smith private? A storeroom, office, anyplace?"

"You can take him to the linen closet," the chef said. He pointed. "The door, there."

Longarm took Smith by the arm. "We'll have a little visit, just the two of us." He picked up the plate holding the piece of cake that had been set aside for Grant. "I'll just bring this with us so nothing'll happen to it."

There was a small table and a single chair in the linen closet; they took up the scanty space in the room's center that was not covered with deep shelves stacked with napkins and tablecloths. Longarm motioned Smith to the chair and put the plate on the table.

"You know who I am?" he asked Smith.

"No. But I heard the Frenchie call you 'marshal,' so I guess you're some kind of officer."

"I'm a deputy U.S. marshal. And I don't like to be lied to. Now tell me what it was you put on that piece of cake, and who told you to do it."

"I've already said I didn't put anything on it, so there couldn't't've been anyone tell me to do anything," Smith replied.

"I think you're lying," Longarm said levelly. "Jean-Pierre wouldn't need to make up what he told me."

Longarm lifted the plate and smelled the cake, but all his nose could detect was the scent of strawberries. He looked at it closely, but could see nothing unusual about it, none of the sparkling crystals Jean-Pierre had described.

"You tell me why I'd want to put anything on a piece of cake," Smith challenged as Longarm returned the plate to the table.

"Mainly because you knew that piece of cake was going to General Grant."

"What difference would it make who'd get it? There's nothing wrong with it. I didn't put anything on it," Smith insisted.

Longarm changed his tactics. "Where'd you say you're from?"

"Here and there. I told you, I'm just drifting. I ran out of money, needed a job. I've worked in kitchens before, so I asked here, and got taken on for tonight. I'll collect my pay and leave tomorrow."

"Not if you're in jail, you won't."

"Hell, you can't arrest me. I haven't done anything."

"I know one sure way to find out," Longarm said.

"How?"

"You eat this piece of cake. If it don't make you sick or kill you, I might take your word that you didn't doctor it up." Longarm handed the plate to Smith with one hand, and drew his Colt with the other.

Smith met Longarm's challenging gaze without flinching. He took the plate and lifted off the wedge of cake. Without hesitating, he took a bite, then another and another. He was on his fourth bite when his body began to quiver, then to convulse. The cake and plate fell from his hands. His body shook, his back arched, and he fell from the chair. Longarm bent over him. He felt for a pulse, and found one that first raced, then faltered and stopped. The man who'd called himself Smith was dead.

Chapter 10

His eyes still fixed on Smith's contorted body, Longarm straightened up. "Ain't but one thing kills that fast," he muttered. "Bound to've been cyanide. Damn it! I didn't figure he'd eat that damn cake and kill himself. He was supposed to stall, and then I'd've found a way to start him talking!"

Longarm stepped back from the corpse and stood there for a few moments, his brows knitted thoughtfully. He bent down again and quickly searched the dead man's pockets. As he'd suspected might be the case, they were completely empty. The man who'd called himself "Smith" hadn't carried money, a wallet, a knife, or a gun—not even a pocket handkerchief. He pulled up the corpse's shirtsleeves, looking for a tattoo that might help identify "Smith," but there were no such marks on either arm. It looked as though the dead man had told the truth when he'd said he came from nowhere and was bound for the same place.

Moving deliberately, because his mind was still working out his next steps, Longarm took a napkin from the nearest shelf and put the partly eaten wedge of cake in it. He even scraped up all the crumbs that had scattered when the cake dropped to the floor. He folded the napkin over and around the cake, and dropped the little packet into a coat pocket. By the time he finished, he'd mapped out his next moves.

Longarm stopped in the kitchen long enough to warn Jean-Pierre and the hotel chef not to let anyone go into the linen closet.

He found Tabor's office, where Forbes was working over a stack of papers piled on a desk, and said to the factotum, "I got to leave before the dinner's over with. I don't reckon anything else is going to happen, but you better send a bellboy or somebody from the hotel over to Mart Duggan's office to tell Mart to get over here. There's a body in the linen closet, off the kitchen. And tell him I'd appreciate it if he'll send a man along to see that the general gets home safe."

Forbes's eyes had grown wider as Longarm talked. He gasped, "What do you mean, Marshal, a body in the linen closet? What's happened to General Grant? And Senator Tabor?"

"I just can't take time to explain it all right now Forbes," Longarm replied. "General Grant and Senator Tabor are both all right. They don't even know anything's happened. And maybe it's just as well they don't, until I can tell them myself. Now go on and do what I asked you to. I'll be at the Tabor place just as soon as I can get there."

Longarm wasted no time in getting to Vivian Montgomery's house. Almost as soon as he turned onto Carbonate Avenue, he could tell this was one trip he hadn't wasted. From the open front door of the house, a rectangle of yellow lamplight streamed across the front porch, along the walkway, and out to the brick sidewalk. He called Vivian's name the instant he got inside, but there was no reply. Quickly, Longarm went through the big downstairs rooms. Living room, dining room, kitchen, sun porch, breakfast room, were all deserted and unlighted.

He hurried up the stairs and went into the bedroom. At first glance, he thought it was deserted, too. Then he saw Vivian, lying half-in and half-out of the double doors of the closet on one side of the room. He bent over her. She wasn't dead, as he'd thought she might be, but she was unconscious, and had a huge bump on her forehead. The skin over the swelling was livid.

Longarm lifted her to put her on the bed. Her feet got entangled with the clothes hanging on the closet rail, and in trying to free her, he managed to pull down not only a number of dresses and a coat or two, but several boxes that were on the shelf over the rail. The boxes tumbled down on his shoulders, their lids popping off, their contents spilling on the floor. He kicked them out of his way and laid Vivian on the bed.

In the bathroom, Longarm grabbed a towel from one of the racks and wet it. He went back to the bed and began bathing Vivian's face. She did not respond at once, and Longarm belatedly thought of smelling salts. He looked on her dressing table, but saw nothing helpful. Just as he stood up to go and rummage through the drawers to try to find some, Vivian began to stir. He sat down on the bed again, and resumed bathing her face with the wet towel. In a moment, her eyelids fluttered and her eyes opened.

"Longarm?" she asked, her voice small and blurred.

"It's me, all right. You just stay quiet. Looks to me like somebody fetched you a pretty good wallop."

"What—what're you doing here?"

"Never mind that, for right now. You keep this towel on your head. I'll go down and get you some brandy."

When he came back after picking up the tray that he'd seen in the living room bearing bottles and glasses, Vivian was sitting on the side of the bed. Her negligee was hiked up above her knees, and her feet were spread as though she'd tried to stand up. She looked at Longarm, her eyes wide with the brilliance and clarity that so often follows a concussion.

"I—I don't seem able to walk," she said. Her voice was still low, and Longarm had to strain to hear her.

"I don't wonder. You got a goose-egg on your head from whoever it was hit you. Now lay back down and be still."

Longarm poured brandy into one of the glasses on the tray, and wrapped her fingers around it. He guided the glass to her lips and she took a swallow. He held her hand and the glass until he felt her muscles tightening around it, then let go. Vivian had no trouble putting the glass to her lips and taking another sip of the liquor. Longarm stood up.

"You just stay the way you are until that brandy begins to take hold," he said. He poured himself a drink from the bottle of Maryland rye that still stood on the tray—from his last visit, he thought. Vivian was watching him.

"How did you get in?" she asked. Her words were very precisely enunciated; she was making an extra effort to speak clearly.

"No trick to that. Your front door was wide open."

"Where was I?" she asked, frowning.

"On the floor, right inside your closet there, where you must've dropped when you got hit." Longarm looked at the tangle of dresses and boxes on the bedroom floor just outside the closet. A gleam of silver caught his eye. He stepped over to the tangle and pushed aside the wisps of fabric that had hidden the gleaming object.

A pair of slippers with silver heels lay revealed.

Vivian's eyes had been slow in following Longarm's swift movements. She turned just in time to see him pick up the slippers.

"Oh, no!" she gasped. She struggled to get up. "Put them down, Longarm! Please!"

Longarm heard her, but didn't obey. He was turning the slippers in his hands. From their weight, he could tell that the heels were made of pure, solid silver.

Like almost everyone who'd come to Colorado Territory after 1870, and who'd been there more than a week, Longarm had heard the story that sprung to his mind within a few seconds after he'd picked up the shoes. He looked at Vivian. She was sitting erect now, her eyes wide—not with the aftermath of a concussion, but with consternation and fear. He held the slippers out to her.

"You ain't—ah, hell, that's just a yarn folks tell!" he said.

"No. It's not just a yarn, Longarm. I won't lie to you. I was—" Vivian stopped short, a rueful smile forming on her face. She shook her head and went on, "I was—and I guess I still am—Silverheels."

Longarm looked at her without speaking for a moment. Then he asked, "Honest to God, Vivian?"

"Honest to God," she nodded.

"You're the one they named the moutain after?"

"I'm the one."

There was the ring of truth in her tone. Still carrying the slippers, Longarm came and sat down beside her. "You mean that old story's true? You're not just joking me?"

Vivian drained the rest of the brandy from her glass before replying, "No. I wish I were just joking. But you've found out, and I don't think you'd be an easy man to lie to, Longarm, even if I wanted to. And I've got a feeling that you're the kind of man who might understand."

"You feel up to telling me about it?"

"Yes. More than that. Now that you know, I *want* to tell you about it." She stood up shakily, went to the dresser, and poured more brandy into her glass. Then she came back and sat down beside Longarm.

"I'm not asking you to tell me anything you don't want to," he said.

"I know that. But I want to tell you." Vivian's eyes were looking back into the past, now. She said, "It's very much like the story everybody's heard and repeated, Longarm, but I'll fill in a few gaps for you that the storytellers don't know.

"I came to Colorado—it wasn't even a territory, then, just a lot of little towns scattered along the east foothills. That was in '58, and I was fourteen—a wild fourteen, the way I see myself now. Overgrown, knowing too much, wanting too much. My father and mother came out here from Indiana, but Father died of a fever after we'd been here less than a month. Maybe I inherited something from Mother. She turned whore, at Clear Creek. I knew what she was doing, and why—she didn't have any other way to make a living for us—but it made me angry. I stayed angry until I ran away with Bob. He was just another miner, a prospector, and never had any luck. He got shot in a claim-jumping fight just a few months after we got to Tarryall. I wasn't going back to Mother, so I started whoring myself."

Vivian's voice did not falter, but went on, calm, matter-of-fact, without emotion. "I said I was wild, and I was. I'd started fucking when I was twelve, and the older I got, the more I enjoyed it. But you know that, don't you? So I followed the big strikes in South Park, and there were a lot of them. There was plenty of money, or gold dust and nuggets, and the men wanted women so badly they'd pay almost anything for one. Then—well, you've heard the old stories, and they're pretty close to being true—there was this prospector in Alma, who thought he'd fallen in love with me, and I guess he had. He made me those slippers, and my God, I was proud of them! I wore them all the time, and people began calling me Silverheels."

She looked at the slippers, which Longarm still held and smiled bitterly. "Silverheels. It was as good a name as any—I'd change my name every time I changed camps. But the rest of what happened is pretty much like the story goes. I was in Alma when the big smallpox epidemic started killing the miners. It happened just the way they tell the story today. I stayed on after all the other girls left. Of course, most of the men ran too, those who weren't too sick to move. And I looked after the ones who'd stayed, as best I could."

Vivian paused long enough to drink the brandy that remained in her glass. When she spoke again, her voice was different; it was harsh, almost hard. "There's one part of what happened that the stories don't mention. Almost all the miners who were sick died. And whenever one of them died, I thought I was entitled to his poke and whatever else he had. So I took their gold, money, watches, rings—anything valuable. By God, Longarm, I'd earned it!"

Longarm said soothingly, "Nobody in his right mind would argue against that, Vivian. Maybe that's why it always gets left out of the story . . . if anybody even knows about it."

"I was lucky in two ways," Vivian said thoughtfully. "One was with the smallpox. I had one of the first cases, but it was just a light one. Maybe it was because I was so young, but I wasn't really sick. Just a few days. And only one small scar." She put a finger on the small, round indentation on her forehead.

"You got another scar I wondered about." Longarm touched her hip. "This one here. I figured out what it was, I guess, but it didn't make much sense, a lady like you."

"Oh, you guessed right, I'm sure. It's where I had a tattoo taken off. As long as I had it, I was afraid somebody'd see it."

"You said you were lucky two ways."

"Yes. The other way was that I left Alma a rich girl. I had all the pokes I'd taken from the bodies of the miners who died."

"That was the grubstake that got you started here, wasn't it?" Longarm asked.

"Yes. Oh, I didn't come to Leadville right away. There wasn't any such place then, of course, and Denver wasn't much, either. I was afraid to stay in Denver, anyway. I lived in fear of somebody recognizing me and calling me a thief. I tried to find my mother, but she'd vanished. I don't know what became of her. It's been more than twenty years—close to twenty-five—so I'm sure she must be dead by now. But I went back East. Went to school, and got some of my rough edges smoothed down. I learned a little bit about living, too. But after you've once lived in the Rockies, they're always calling you, I guess. So I came back. To Denver, first. But I was still afraid someone would recognize me as Silverheels. And there was that damned mountain. And the legend had begun to grow by then. I didn't feel comfortable in Denver."

"There's part of the story I've heard about Silverheels that you didn't include," Longarm said. "The way it was told to me when I first hit the territory, there's a woman who goes to Alma, or what's left of it, every year and puts flowers on the graves of the miners who died during the smallpox epidemic. Is that you, Vivian?"

She shook her head. "No. It might be kin of one of the men who died, or maybe one of the whores who had a steady man. A lot of us did, you know. The nearest I ever came to that was the man who made my slippers."

Longarm shook his head. "Well, that's sure one hell of a yarn."

"And it happens to be a true one, for a change. All of it, including the loot I took off the dead men's bodies."

"God A'mighty!" Longarm exclaimed. "I got so shook up finding you laying on the floor, then listening to that story of yours, that I'm overlooking things!"

"What? What's happened?" Vivian asked.

"That's what you better tell me, Vivian. Who knocked you on the head and left you laying there? And how'd you know somebody was going to try to poison General Grant tonight?"

"Oh, no! They didn't! Not after—" Vivian stopped, her eyes wide open, her face a mask of horror as she realized what she'd given away.

"I think I got most of it figured out," Longarm told her. "It'd help me some if you'll sort of fill in what I'm not right sure about."

She shook her head. "I'm not sure about anything right now, Longarm. And with General Grant dead—"

"Who said he's dead?"

"You said he'd been poisoned."

"No, I said somebody *tried* to poison him. The one who tried is the one who's dead. Grant's in good shape. He don't even know anything about it yet. I'm betting you know more than he does—and more than I do, too," Longarm added.

Vivian waited, trying to meet Longarm's piercing stare. After several moments, she finally succeeded. Her face was pale, her eyes worried. She said, "I've told you I wouldn't lie to you. I'm not going to start now."

"I appreciate that, Vivian." Longarm's tone was as sober as hers. "Senator Wilkes Purvis is a good place to start. You mentioned that you left Denver because you were always afraid somebody'd recognize you as Silverheels. Purvis did just that, didn't he?"

"How did you know?"

"I didn't. I guessed. Mainly because of what you've just told me, but I guessed even before then. Not the Silverheels part, but that Purvis had some kind of harness on you."

"I still don't see how."

"Maybe you don't recall it. Last night you dozed off, then you woke up when I said something about having to look after the general. And you might've been talking in your sleep, but you told me I didn't need to worry about Grant until tonight. I was so sleepy I didn't remember you'd said it until today. Then, after this try at poisoning the general tonight, I started tying all of it together."

"That's why you came to my house, here? To question me?"

"That's why. It didn't strike me that you and poisoning somebody went together very good."

"It doesn't." Vivian fell silent again. Longarm sat waiting patiently, and at last she said, "You know so much now, it'd be silly of me not to tell you the rest of it."

"Go on," he encouraged her.

"You're right about Wilkes Purvis recognizing me. And I was scared, Longarm. I've lived well, here in Leadville, and I didn't want to be pointed out as Silverheels, the whore with the heart of gold that turned out to be brass—the whore who robbed dead men. I wanted to keep what I've got. I turned coward."

"That ain't being a coward; it's being sensible."

"No. I was afraid. So afraid that, when Purvis wanted money, I gave it to him. But when he came to me with this scheme to kill Grant, I balked like a stubborn mule. His idea was for me to give Grant the poison at Baby

205

Doe's party. That's why I stayed away. But Wilkes caught me here. He must've found out that I didn't go to Tabor's today."

"He had somebody spying on you, most likely."

"I guess he did. I should have realized sooner that he'd be having me watched. But he came here in the middle of the afternoon. He was like a wild man, ranting, threatening. Finally, he tied me up, here in the bedroom. I thought I heard someone knocking this afternoon, once or twice—"

Longarm interrupted her long enough to say, "That was me."

She nodded. "I didn't know, of course; I wasn't even sure I heard someone. Then I finally got free, just as Wilkes came back. We had a fight, but he hit me with a silver vase he grabbed off my dresser. And the next thing I knew, you were here."

"Where's Purvis now?"

"I don't know. He keeps a room at the Clarendon Hotel, but he also has some kind of hideaway here in Leadville. I haven't any idea where it is."

"Vivian, have you got any idea why Purvis is so set on seeing Grant dead?" Longarm asked.

She shook her head. "No. But that's all he's been able to talk about since he first heard Grant was going to be in Leadville. And he's sworn to me that he won't give up."

"He'll have to give up pretty soon," Longarm said grimly. "He's lost two killers now. He can't have too many more on hand."

Vivian frowned, "Don't be too certain. When I told Wilkes that I wouldn't poison Grant, after he got over being angry, he said it didn't matter whether I did or not, he had somebody else ready to do the job. And the other day, after you'd shot the first man to try, he told me he's got another gunman—one who'll be ordered to kill you first if he has to, to get Grant."

"Well, maybe this new hired gun won't find his job all that easy. Might be, he won't even get here in time. The general's only going to be in Leadville one more day, you know."

Vivian shook her head. "He'll be here in time, Longarm. When Wilkes came back tonight, while we were arguing before he knocked me out, he said the gunman he'd sent for is due in tonight, on the midnight train from Denver."

"Purvis didn't mention this gunman's name, did he?" Longarm asked.

"He certainly did. He bragged about it. His name's Frank Jenks."

"Jenks? Hell, I know who he is," Longarm said with a grim scowl. "Purvis wasn't lying to you, Vivian. Jenks is good with a gun, and he's a killer. Smart enough not to've got caught up with yet. He's got a nickname: Hi Jenks." He stood up.

"You're not going, are you?" Vivian asked. "I—I'd rather not be left here alone."

"It can't be helped," Longarm told her. "I've got a few things to take care of, before I meet that midnight train."

As he turned onto Pine Street on his way to Mart Duggan's office, Longarm looked at his watch. He had three-quarters of an hour in which to lay his trap. It was a short enough time in which to work, but there had been occasions in Longarm's life when three-quarters of an hour had added up to an eternity.

Duggan sat at his desk. Each time Longarm saw him in his office, shoving papers from one stack to another, the Leadville city marshal reminded him more and more of Billy Vail and his endless battle against red tape. Longarm had his own ideas about where those papers belonged. If he had his way, they'd be hung on the hook in the outhouse, where they'd have some use, instead of cluttering up the job of upholding the law. Duggan looked up and shook his head when Longarm entered.

"I'm not right sure I'm glad to see you," he said. "Every time you come in here, you've got to have one or two of my men pulled off their beats for some job you want done, and it's playing hell with my routine."

Duggan could have been serious or joking; Longarm

couldn't tell which. He decided to take the gibe as a joke. He said, "Well, Mart, I figure I'm helping you keep down Leadville's crime rate just about as much as you're helping me. The way I look at it, it's pretty much an even swap."

Duggan grinned, "I suppose you could say that. What's on your mind, that fellow you spooked into swallowing a dose of cyanide at Tabor's hotel tonight? If it is, I haven't got any more of a line on who he is or where he crawled out from than I have on the one you shot at Jeff Whinney's place."

"It *was* cyanide he was using, was it?" Longarm asked. "I had a hunch it was, the way he folded up so quick, but I couldn't be sure."

"Oh, it was cyanide. There's a lot of it used out at the smelters. The whores that hit bottom swallow it enough for us to recognize it when we see it."

Longarm took the napkin-wrapped piece of cake out of his coat pocket and dropped it into Duggan's overflowing wastebasket. "I guess I won't need this, then. It's what's left of that piece of cake he was fixing to send out to General Grant. Now that you've put a name to the poison, and the man's been wrote down as a suicide you won't need it to prove anything with."

"You've got some fresh scheme cooked up," Duggan said, his eyes narrowing suspiciously. "You might as well trot it out. But I can tell you right now, before I hear what it is, I don't want any part of it."

"Don't be too damn sure." Longarm sat down in the spare chair that stood across from Duggan's desk. "You heard about a hired gunman name of Hi Jenks, I guess?"

"I sure as hell have. He's mean and he's good. Supposed to be the best quick shot in Colorado." Duggan slapped one of the stacks of paper on his desk. "I've got about eight wants on him here, from Durango all the way across to Julesburg."

"He's coming to town in about half an hour. He'll be gunning for Grant, if I don't stop him."

"I guess you've got some kind of scheme worked out?"

"I got a sort of one. But——"

"I know," Duggan cut in. "You're going to need my whole damn force to leave their jobs and help you with yours."

Longarm made himself busy for a moment, lighting a cheroot, to give Duggan time to cool off. When the cigar was drawing to his satisfaction, he said, "Well, I *could* use a little bit of help. Not just with Hi Jenks—I got something all figured out for him. But the man I'm really out for is the one who's so set on killing the general. You don't want Grant to get smoked up in Leadville, and I don't want him gunned anyplace in the state. But this fellow I'm after is going to keep on trying, unless he's stopped cold and quick."

"How many of my men am I going to have to pull off their beats this time?" Duggan asked.

"Only about three. They won't be off their beats but about ten minutes, and I need to use your private holdover. Not for very long, only an hour ro two. Unless you got somebody already in it, that is."

"Jesus!" Duggan exclaimed. "You're not asking for a whole lot, are you?" He frowned and looked narrowly at Longarm. "And what makes you think I've got a private holdover?"

"Because everybody in charge of keeping the law in a town like this has got to have one." Longarm stared levelly at Duggan across the desk. "You need a place that ain't public and official, like the jail is, where you can tuck away a real bad crook so his cronies and his lawyers can't find him while you're digging up the evidence you need to bring him up in court so he can be put away legal."

"All right," Duggan said. "Suppose I do have?"

"Why, I don't hold it against you, Mart. Sure, I know it ain't according to what the shysters call due process, but I never saw a real bad outlaw yet that paid any mind to due process when he went out to rob or kill somebody. The way I look at it, you don't put out a bonfire by spitting on it."

"What about these two or three men you want? What're they supposed to do?"

"See that nobody gets near the Denver & Rio Grande depot when the midnight train from Denver pulls in. Nobody but me, that is."

"Midnight!" Duggan exploded. He looked at the Regulator clock that hung, its pendulum swinging, on the wall opposite his desk. "Damn it, Longarm, that's only a little more than fifteen minutes from now!"

"Well, that's all the time I need, Mart. It's not more than a three-minute walk to the station."

"It's cutting things too close for comfort," Duggan snapped. He kicked his chair away as he rose and strode to the door. "Flood!" he shouted, then turned back to Longarm. "You'd better tell me what you've got in mind. I don't like working in the dark."

"Oh, I'm not scheming up anything real fancy, Mart. I just aim to cut Hi Jenks off at the depot and put him on ice in your holdover. That'll get him out of the way and give us time to catch up to whoever hired him."

"Jenks won't tell you that. I've heard enough about him to know he won't talk. Besides—"

Longarm said coolly, "If my scheme works out right, he won't *have* to talk."

"I've got a feeling you're holding something back from me," Duggan said. "When you started out, I got the idea you were just going to face Jenks down. Now you're talking about stowing him away."

"You know, Mart, a plan's not much good if you can't switch it around to fit what you need it for. Now—" He stopped as Flood appeared in the doorway.

"What's the matter, Mart?" Flood asked Duggan.

"You're going along with us on a job." Duggan replied. "Leave your turnkey in charge. Longarm's got something he needs a hand with, so we'll give it to him. We need one more man, but we'll pick up whoever we see on the Chestnut or Harrison Street beats, on our way to the depot."

Flood nodded and disappeared. Duggan turned back to Longarm. His jaw dropped when he saw Longarm standing beside the coattree. He'd hung up his coat and was unbuckling his gunbelt.

"What in the hell are you doing?" Duggan asked.

"You act like you're getting ready to brace Hi Jenks without a gun!"

"That's sort of what I had in mind," Longarm admitted. He took off his gunbelt and hung it on the coattree over his coat. "I guess it'll be safe here, won't it?"

"A damn sight safer than you'll be, going up against a man like Jenks without that Colt you just put aside. Why, damn it, Jenks will recognize you and draw on sight!"

"I don't think he'll recognize me, Mart. I never had the pleasure of taking Jenks in. He won't know me from Daniel Webster."

"Every outlaw in the state knows what you look like," Duggan pointed out.

"Maybe, from somebody describing me to them. But they look for me to be wearing my Colt. If I ain't got it on, I'll look just like anybody else."

Duggan looked Longarm's imposing figure up and down. He was obviously skeptical. "It's too much risk, Longarm. Put your gunbelt back on."

"I can't do that, Mart. My scheme won't work if I face Jenks down. Now, from what I've heard about him, Jenks brags that he won't throw down on any man who ain't carrying iron. I don't want to risk him spraying lead all over the place, maybe killing one of your men, or some of Leadville's good citizens. The easy way to keep that from happening is to let Jenks see right off that I ain't got a gunbelt on."

"How are you going to get him out of the depot and to the holdover, then?"

"Let's just eat the apple one bite at a time, Mart. You just get ahold of a hack and have it waiting. I don't imagine you'll find it hard to borrow one from a cabbie outside the depot, will you?"

"No, that'll be easy," Duggan said.

"And you'll have your men on both sides of the station, to keep everybody—and I mean anybody at all—from coming in?"

"Leave it to me. We'll just about have time to clear the place out and set my deputies up outside, if we leave right now. What the hell's keeping Flood?"

Duggan's deputy answered the question by appearing at the door, with his gunbelt strapped on. The three men walked down Pine Street toward the depot. Flood spotted one of the deputy marshals on patrol before they reached State Street, and whistled the man over to join them. Just as they crossed Chestnut, Duggan saw another of his uniformed deputies and added him to the group without consulting Longarm. As they covered the rest of the short distance to the station, Longarm explained to the newcomers exactly what they'd be expected to do. Then, walking beside Duggan, he talked with him for a moment while they covered the rest of the short distance to the depot.

Distantly, they heard the whistle of the approaching train.

Longarm said, "It's running a minute or two early. Mart, you and your boys are going to have to hustle."

"I told you we were cutting it too fine," Duggan complained. "But we'll manage to get everything done in time."

Mere minutes before the incoming train huffed and hissed to a stop at the depot platform, Duggan's deputies had cleared the station and taken up their posts to bar any latecomers from entering the area. Longarm took his place just inside the station door, where he was sure he'd be seen plainly by those getting off the train. He counted it a stroke of luck that only three passengers alighted. Two of them carried valises; they paid no attention to the vacant platform, but hustled off toward the exit.

It was the third passenger who interested Longarm. Most of his assignments during the past few years had taken him outside of Colorado, and he hadn't encountered Jenks since the gunman had begun to make himself a name in the area. He was sure the third man off the train was Jenks. Longarm had read enough descriptions of the outlaw on wanted fliers to be sure of his identity.

Jenks was about as wide as he was tall, and in height, he almost matched Longarm. Sandy red sideburns dropped down his cheeks below his hat, and swept forward along his jaw to merge with a bushy reddish mustache. His chin was clean-shaven and jutted forward. What spoiled the gunman's appearance were his eyes. They were set deep between high cheek bones and beetling brows—opaque blue-white eyes, like those on a pig.

He had on a dark checked shirt under a waist-length jacket, and his plain brown covert cloth trousers were tucked into the tops of Texas-style high-heeled boots, adorned with fancy stitching. Low on his right hip, Jenks carried a Schofield model Smith & Wesson in a ten-loop cartridge belt. Longarm couldn't tell whether the revolver was the .41 Schofield or the .44, but guessed it was the heavier caliber.

Jenks walked toward the station, and Longarm opened the door and went out to the platform to meet him. He wanted the bright light from inside the depot to be at his back and in Jenk's eyes when they came together. For all Longarm knew, Jenks might have a pretty good idea of Longarm's appearance. Jenks stopped when he saw Longarm approaching.

"I guess you're the man I'm looking for," Longarm said, when the distance between them had narrowed to less than a yard.

"Maybe. Except you don't fit the description of the one I was told was going to be here to meet me," Jenks growled suspiciously.

Longarm noticed that the outlaw's eyes had dropped to look for a gunbelt, and was glad he'd taken his Colt off, even if he did feel naked without it, right this minute. He said easily, "I came in to get you. The boss don't want anybody to see you and him together."

"Hmph," Jenks grunted. "How the hell do you know you're talking to the right man, then?"

"You were described to me clear enough," Longarm replied. "And I don't guess there's many people in the state who don't know what Hi Jenks looks like."

Jenks seemed pleased. He asked. "Heard about me, eh?"

"I sure have. I been hoping I'd get a chance to meet up with you for a long time."

"Well, I guess if you know enough to recognize me, you must be all right. Only where's Purvis?"

"He's right outside, in a closed hack. You got a bag of some kind?"

"No. Just what I'm wearing's all I need."

"We might as well go, then," Longarm suggested.

"Just a minute." Jenks moved up to Longarm and poked a hand through the open lapel of his vest. He felt for a gun in Longarm's belt, then ran his hand down his arms, feeling for a sleeve gun, and when his fingers found no bulging metal shapes, the outlaw nodded his satisfaction.

"All right," he said, "let's go."

Longarm was careful to walk beside Jenks and not to let the outlaw get behind him. He spotted the right carriage at once—a closed hack with Duggan in the high driver's seat. He opened the door of the vehicle. Duggan had pulled the shades across both windows, and the hack's interior was pitch black to the eyes of anybody who'd just come from the lighted station platform.

Jenks put a booted foot in the stirrup-step and began to hoist his weight into the carriage. Longarm slid his hand along his watch chain and lifted out the derringer that was clipped to the end of the chain opposite his watch. At the same time, he planted his shoulder under Jenks's butt and gave the outlaw a combined lift and push that sent him pitching forward on his face to the floor of the hack. Instinctively, Jenks put out both hands to catch himself.

Before Jenks hit the floor, Longarm had vaulted into the carriage. He planted a foot on Jenks's backbone and pressed the cold muzzle of the derringer into the outlaw's ear. With his free hand, Longarm slid Jenks's revolver out of the sprawled man's holster.

"If I even feel you start to move," Longarm said, "You're going to feel what it's like to get your head blown off."

Jenks did not move. He did talk, though. "You son of a bitch! There's not a man anyplace who treats Hi Jenks like this and lives to brag about it!"

"Shut up!" Longarm snapped. "The next words you say are going to be your last ones!"

At a sedate pace, the hack rattled over Leadville's slag-paved streets for a few minutes. Then gravel grated under the wheels for a short time. The carriage stopped. Longarm prodded Jenks with his bootheel.

"We're where we're going," he told the gunman. "Now keep your hands down and in front of you when I let you out of this hack, and march right straight ahead of me, or I'll finish you off with your own gun."

Jenks behaved himself after Longarm had stepped out of the hack and commanded him to come out backward. The Leadville night was as bright as day to their eyes, accustomed to the coal-black interior of the shuttered carriage. They were standing in front of a nondescript house that might have been on any street in the town. Its windows were dark, its door closed. There were no houses close to it on either side. Longarm nodded to Duggan as he slammed the door of the hack shut, and Duggan geed the horse. The hack rolled away, leaving Longarm and Jenks standing alone.

"Inside," Longarm said curtly. At the same time, he prodded Jenks with the outlaw's own pistol.

Jenks marched ahead of Longarm to the door of the house. Keeping the pressure of the Smith & Wesson's muzzle in the small of Jenks's back, Longarm took a key out of his vest pocket and unlocked the door. He jabbed the pistol into Jenks's short ribs, and the gunman stepped inside.

Longarm kicked the door shut and lighted a match. The flame showed a lamp on a table. Without taking the pressure of the gun's muzzle from Jenks, he managed to get the lamp's chimney off and its wick lighted. The light revealed a barren room, uncarpeted, without curtains, furnished only with the table on which the lamp stood, two straight chairs, and a cot. Longarm prodded Jenks in the direction of one of the chairs.

Jenks backed rigidly onto the chair. Longarm could see that the outlaw was just watching for a chance to jump him.

"Don't go getting ideas," he warned. "You've got no edge left, Jenks."

"What the hell kind of deal did I get into?" Jenks demanded. "And just who are you, anyhow?"

"It don't matter who I am. All you need to know is that I'm the one in charge here."

"As long as you hold that gun, you are." Jenks frowned. "Damn it, I went over you good, too. Where'd you have that derringer hid? In your boot?"

"No, up my ass," Longarm told him. "I guess there's a few tricks you don't know, Jenks."

While he talked, Longarm was flickering his eyes around the room in search of the rope that Duggan had told him would be there. He'd begun to think there was none, and was wishing he'd accepted the city marshal's offer of a pair of handcuffs, when his eyes finally adjusted to the dim light enough for him to see the coil sticking out from the shadow cast by the cot. Keeping his eye on Jenks, and holding the outlaw's gun in readiness to discourage its owner from getting ideas, Longarm edged around until he could hook a toe in the coil of rope and move it out to where he could reach it.

Longarm was behind Jenks's back now, and this made the gunman edgy. He kept turning his head as much as he dared, trying to see what was going on in back of him. If he'd been able to see Longarm, he'd have known that his captor was forming a running knot in the rope, using only one hand, keeping the Smith & Wesson ready in the other. Longarm finally got the knot tied to his satisfaction and stepped up behind Jenks.

"Just take it easy for a minute, now," he told the outlaw. "All I'm going to do is drop a loop around you so I don't have to worry about you jumping me."

He let the loop fall over Jenks's shoulders and pulled it tight, pinioning the gunman's arms. He wrapped two or three turns around Jenks's chest to bind him to the chair, and tied off the end. Then he came around in front of the outlaw.

Jenks was fuming. He spat, "What in the fucking hell's the idea here? Where's that fellow Purvis? I want to talk to him! We've got a few things to clear up between us."

"Why, I'd imagine Senator Purvis is resting easy in his bed over at the Clarendon Hotel right now," Longarm replied. "And you're wrong about having anything to settle up with him. He don't want to have any part of you anymore."

"Like hell! He paid me a pisspot full of money to come over here and get rid of General Grant for him. He'll owe me another potful when I do the job. Now, you get him over here quick, or—"

"Or what?" Longarm demanded tauntingly. "You fell out of the catbird seat back there at the depot, Jenks. I'm the one sitting in it now."

"You still ain't told me who you are."

"Now, I haven't at that. You ever stop to think that might be because you don't need to know? Knowing things won't do you much good, where you're going."

"Where's that?" Jenks demanded.

"Six feet under," Longarm replied, "just as soon as I take care of the job Purvis decided you weren't fit to do, and collect that potful of money you mentioned a minute ago."

"You're telling me Purvis has hired you to do the job on Grant that he got me here for?" Jenks asked incredulously.

"That's about the way it sizes up. And I've got it all set, too. Hell, I've been working on it the past two days, ever since Purvis decided he didn't need you."

"Why that double-crossing bastard!" Jenks blurted. "He can't treat Hi Jenks this way! I'll find that son of a bitch after I get out of here and cut his balls off and shove 'em down his gullet!"

"Hi, I've got some bad news for you," Longarm said, shaking his head. "You ain't *going* to get out of here. Not alive. Now, you been owlhooting long enough to know that Senator Purvis can't afford to let you loose, with you knowing what you do about him. No, Hi. After I get rid of Grant for him, I'll get rid of you too. Then the senator can go to bed in that fancy room of his at the Clarendon Hotel and just sleep like a baby, because neither the general nor you is going to be bothering him again."

Chapter 11

For the past half-hour, since Longarm had told Jenks that death on Wilkes Purvis's orders waited for him, a silence thick enough to cut with a dull knife had grown between the two men. Longarm had settled down on the cot, behind Jenks's back. Tied in the chair as he was, the gunman could see the cot only by straining his neck painfully. He looked around once or twice, and each time he saw Longarm taking his ease, holding the Smith & Wesson in his hand, while he lounged in whatever comfort the cot provided.

If Longarm had any worries at all, they didn't show. He sprawled on the cot, with one leg hanging over the side to keep a foot on the floor. He had just lighted a cheroot, and was puffing a cloud of silver-blue smoke into the still air of the bare little room, when both he and Jenks heard the scratching. Longarm acted as though he hadn't heard anything, but Jenks tensed. He twisted his neck around to see if Longarm had noticed the faint, almost inaudible sound coming from the front of the house, but Longarm was lounging back, his eyes fixed on the smoke cloud.

Once again, the faint scratching sounded. Jenks looked at Longarm as he had before, and still saw no sign that he'd heard the noise. A few minutes passed before the sound was repeated for the third time. This time, Jenks couldn't stay silent.

"There's somebody prowling around outside," he said, twisting his neck around uncomfortably.

"What makes you think so?"

"Didn't you hear them noises?"

"Your nerves are all on edge, Jenks. I didn't hear anything."

"Damn it, I did! There's somebody sneaking around out there!"

Longarm took his time getting up. He said, "Well, I still say there ain't, but if it'll make you feel better, I'll go take a look around outside." Longarm took his time getting off the cot. He stood up, twirling Jenks's Smith & Wesson around his forefinger by the trigger guard. "You'll plague me from now on, if I don't go look, it seems like."

Longarm went outside, where Duggan was waiting. The Leadville marshal pointed to the revolver. "What's wrong? You think I was somebody else? I signaled just like you told me to."

"Oh, I knew it was you, Mart. I just wasn't about to leave Jenks's gun where he could try to get to it."

"How's things going?" Duggan asked.

"I got him started talking some. Not enough yet. He's a close-mouthed bastard. How about you? Did you check up on those men I asked you to?"

"Sure. That wasn't any job. All the senators from Denver who came up on that special train are staying at Tabor's Grand Hotel. I guess he's giving them rooms free. Senator Purvis is the only one who ain't at the Grand. He's at the Clarendon, where he always stops."

"All of them are safe in bed by now, I guess?" Longarm asked.

"Not exactly. Two of them went over to Molly Price's parlor house a little while after the dinner finished up, and another one went to Carrie Sunnel's. Late as it is now, I'd guess they've settled in with the girls for the rest of the night."

"How about Purvis?"

"He didn't get in at the Clarendeon till about half an hour ago. By now, he's probably settled in, too."

"You made sure Grant and Tabor got home from the dinner safe?"

"Safe and sound, Longarm. I had a man riding shotgun on them, keeping out of their way, like you asked me to."

"All right, Mart. Thanks for your help. I guess I can handle things by myself from here on out," Longarm said.

"You sure?"

"I'm sure."

"Fine." Duggan pushed a relieved breath through his brushy mustache. "I'll go on about my regular business, then."

Longarm watched the town marshal's broad back as Duggan walked away. He started for the house, stopped short of the door, and broke Jenks's Smith & Wesson. He lifted the cartridges from its cylinder and slid them into a pocket, then went on inside.

As far as he could tell, Jenks hadn't moved. He said to the gunman, "Just like I told you, there wasn't hide nor hair of anything or anybody out there."

"Well, I damn sure heard something," Jenks insisted.

"Rats, maybe. There's plenty of them in Leadville."

"It could've been," Jenks agreed. There was no conviction in his voice, though. Then he said, "Not all the rats around here go on four legs, either."

"Meaning me?"

"Take it if it fits. It's a hell of a note, whatever your name is. Here we are, you and me, in the same line, and you go selling me out."

"I didn't sell you out, Jenks. Purvis did."

"He bought you, didn't he? That's got to mean you sold."

"Well, if you look at it that way, you sold to him too."

"That's different. The job was open when I hired out to Purvis. When you took it on, it was mine, by rights."

"If I hadn't taken it, somebody else would've," Longarm said equably. "There's no call for you to have hard feelings."

"Hmph," Jenks grunted. "Maybe you got something."

Longarm laid Jenks's gun on the table beside the lamp. He went to the cot and lay down. He'd barely settled himself when Jenks twisted his head around and said, "You got anything to eat in this place? My belly thinks my throat's been cut. I had a pickup bite off the free lunch at a saloon where I stopped before I got on that damn jerkwater train in Denver, but that was a hell of along time ago."

"You'll just have to tell your belly to shut up, then," Longarm said. He put as much sympathy into his voice as he could force himself to. "There's nothing to eat here."

"I'd settle for a drink, if there's a bottle around," Jenks suggested. "Damn it, you oughta go that far with me, seeing as we're in the same line."

"There's no bottle, either," Longarm replied. "But I won't argue with you about a drink, Jenks. I'd enjoy one myself, right abut now. It's been a long night, and going to be longer."

Jenks did not reply, and silence settled over the room for a few minutes. Then the outlaw said, "The more I think about a drink, the better I like the idea. There ought to be someplace a man could find a bottle, close by."

Longarm took his time in replying. "There's a saloon a little way from here. Only I got my orders to keep an eye on you till somebody comes to take over."

"Purvis?" Jenks asked.

"You know better than that. He won't come within a mile of this place." Longarm snorted with disgust. "You ought to know his style, you've hired your gun enough times. The senator don't give me the time of day when we pass on the street, but I'm good enough to do the kind of jobs he ain't got enough sand in his craw to handle."

"Yeah," Jenks agreed. "Lily-white hands, snotty way. I know his kind." The gunman's little pig eyes slitted as he grinned at Longarm. "You don't sound like you got much use for the senator, either."

"He's paying me," Longarm replied curtly. "Don't look for me to badmouth him. That might be your way, but it ain't mine."

"You better watch him, though," Jenks warned. "Purvis has double-crossed me. What makes you think he won't cross you?"

"Oh, I guess he would, if I gave him a chance—which I don't aim to do. But I've done work for him before, and he didn't know anything about you, only your reputation. I guess when he got to thinking things over, he figured he could trust me more than he could you."

"That's no reason," Jenks snorted. "I'd give a lot to have him in my gunsights right now."

"If you're offering, Jenks, I ain't taking," Longarm snapped. "Now shut up. I got a hard day coming up. I want to rest."

There was silence in the room for a short while, then Jenks tried again. He said, "Listen, my belly's griping me real bad. I got to put something in it."

"I told you, there's no food on the place."

"I'm not thinking about eating. I want a drink. You said there's a saloon close by. I'll pay for the bottle, if you'll go get it."

"You're not pulling the wool over my eyes," Longarm snorted. "All you want is to get me out of here so you can work yourself free."

"If the saloon's as near as you say it is, you wouldn't be away long enough for me to do that."

Longarm knew pretty well how much time it would take a desperate and determined man to free himself from the kind of running knot he'd used when he tied the gunman to the chair. He made no reply; he was wondering whether the seeds of the ideas he wanted Jenks to believe were his own had planted deeply enough to root. At the same time, he didn't want to risk rushing things. The longer Jenks was held captive, the more eager he became to get away, and the less cautious he'd be when he was free.

Jenks resumed his efforts. "Listen, my belly's giving me fits. I honest to God need that whiskey. Damn it, if I was in your place, I'd sure as hell treat you better than you're treating me."

Letting Jenks see his reluctance, Longarm finally moved. He swung his legs off the cot and stood up. Facing Jenks, he said, "I guess you got a right to a last drink or two. It ain't any more than the hangman would do for you, before he started you walking toward the rope. All right, I'll go get a bottle. I could use a drink myself."

"There's money in my pants pocket," the gunman offered.

"I don't need your damned money; I'll buy the whiskey."

Straightening his hat, Longarm started for the door. He was careful to keep his eyes on Jenks, to give himself an excuse for not noticing the Smith & Wesson that still lay on the table beside the lamp. At the door, he turned back to give Jenks a final look.

"Don't try to get loose now," he warned. "It wouldn't do you any good. This place is only going to be out of my sight for two or three minutes."

"Just bring back a bottle of good whiskey." Jenks's pig eyes crinkled up in what he meant to be a disarming grin. "All I want is a drink or so to stop my belly from growling."

Longarm locked the door behind him with a click loud enough for Jenks to hear. There were plenty of windows the gunman could use. He ran quickly around the house and ducked into the outhouse behind the dwelling. In this isolated location, Duggan's private holdover had no connection with Leadville's rudimentary sewers, which served only the mansions on Carbonate Avenue, the whorehouses below them on Main Street, and the three business streets. By looking through the star cut in the outhouse door, Longarm could see both sides of the house, and its back.

He'd figured it would take Jenks about five minutes to muscle out of the ropes tying him to the chair, but the outlaw took almost twice that long. He came out the backdoor and went to the corner of the house, where he stood studying the area around it for several moments. Longarm was just beginning to think the gunman intended to wait, with the idea of evening the score when he returned with the whiskey, but at last Jenks started toward town. The tall, wide facade of Tabor's Grand Opera House, and the almost equally high roof of the Clarendon Hotel next to it were enough to show anybody with eyes where Leadville's center lay.

Longarm gave Jenks a good start before following. He cut across the gravel road and dodged up the street that ran parallel to the one chosen by Jenks. The always bright Leadville sky made trailing the man by following after him on the same street much too risky.

Secure in the feeling that he knew Jenks's destination, Longarm moved at the fastest walk he could manage. He headed for Pine Street and Duggan's office; he was certain Jenks's first move after ridding himself of his bonds had been to reload the Smith & Wesson from the spare cartridges he carried in his belt loops. Before he encountered the gunman again, Longarm intended to have his own Colt belted on and ready.

Mart Duggan wasn't in his office, which didn't displease Longarm a bit. He had no time to spend discussing things right then. He was working on a slender margin of time. He'd allowed himself very little leeway —certainly not enough to waste precious moments bringing Duggan up to date and perhaps having to argue with him about the way he'd worked to stop the plot to assassinate Grant. The Regulator clock on Duggan's office wall was striking three when Longarm buckled his cross-draw rig and shrugged on his coat. The metallic overtones of the clock's chimes were still hanging in the air as he left the office and began hurrying toward Harrison Avenue.

There were still night owls on the street, though most of them were making their bleary-eyed way home from the gambling halls and saloons on State Street and the parlor houses on Main or the cribs along Tiger Alley. Longarm dodged pedestrians all the way down Harrison until he reached the Clarendon Hotel, standing in the shadow of Tabor's Opera House. He pushed through the carved doors into the main lobby. There were a few diehards in the bar, but only a few, judging by the thin trickle of talk that reached the lobby, which, at this hour, was deserted. There wasn't even a clerk standing beside the registration desk.

Longarm went to the desk; he didn't know the number of Wilkes Purvis's room, and he was about to pound on the call button when he saw feet sticking out from behind the long counter. He went around the end and saw a man stretched out on the floor. Blood trickled from a cut on his head. Longarm felt for a pulse and found one. He hoisted the recumbent form up and slapped the man's cheeks as gently as he could. The unconscious man's eyelids fluttered and his eyes opened. He stared blankly at Longarm.

"Wh-where'd he go?" the man stammered. He was having trouble in focusing his eyes, and his voice was thick.

"Who?"

"Man with a gun. He—"

"You the desk clerk?" Longarm asked impatiently.

"Y-y-yes. Who're y-you?"

"U.S. marshal. Where'd the man with the gun go?"

"He—he hit me," the clerk stammered.

"You ain't hurt bad. Where'd the man with the gun go?"

"Up-upstairs, I g-guess. He asked—asked which room—Senator Purvis—is in." The clerk's words came with agonizing slowness.

"Which room is the senator in?" Longarm asked. "Hurry up, man!"

"T-t-two t-t-t-twelve."

A shot, almost drowning the clerk's words, rolled echoing down the stairwell. Longarm let go of the clerk and ran for the stairs. He drew his Colt as he reached the first step, then he took the wide steps three at a time, skidded around the landing, and mounted to the second floor.

Down a long, carpeted hall, light spilled from the open door of a room. Longarm raced for it, knowing he'd missed his chance. Jenks had bolted right after he'd shot.

He reached the opened door and looked into the room. Senator Wilkes Purvis lay on the floor, his bare feet and matchstick thin legs protruding from below his rumpled nightshirt. The white linen fabric of the nightshirt was drenched with blood.

Longarm bent over Purvis. The senator's long, thin face was ghastly pale, but his eyes were open. He recognized Longarm, and his lips began twitching. Longarm brought an ear down close to Purvis's mouth.

"Shot me," Purvis was saying in a reedy voice. "Wasn't supposed to shoot me."

"Jenks?" Longarm asked.

Purvis nodded, a single weak inclination of his lolling head.

"Why?" Longarm pressed.

"Don't know why," Purvis wheezed. "He was supposed—to get—Grant."

"Why were you so set on killing Grant?" There was urgency in Longarm's voice. He'd seen many men in Purvis's condition, and he knew the senator wasn't going to last much longer.

"Grant's—a—dirty, red-handed—killer," Purvis gasped. His voice grew weaker with each word. "Killed —killed my—"

Purvis's body twitched and his jaw went slack. A gust of sound, no louder than a cork being pulled from a bottle, came from his open mouth. His eyes stared sightlessly up at Longarm.

Longarm stood up. Only a part of his night's work had ended with Purvis's death. Hi Jenks was too dangerous a man, wanted in too many places for too many other killings to be allowed to get away. Stepping into the hall, Longarm looked along its narrow length. Doors were beginning to pop open, with tousled heads emerging from them. Questions were thrown at Longarm, but he ignored them. At the end of the hall, an open door showed the bright night sky. Longarm hurried down the hall, waving aside the questions of those roused by the shot, and reached the door.

Outside, a small landing jutted from the wall. Longarm stepped out, and found himself in the center of a stairway that ran up the outside wall of the hotel, from the ground to the third floor. Leadville's last houses ended almost below his feet, as the minehead shacks and smelters took over. Most of the town was hidden by the bulk of the hotel; only a small portion of Harrison Avenue was visible to the south.

In the east, the lights of minehead buildings and the glare of smelter furnaces slanted up both sides of Strayhorse Gulch. South of the gulch, Carbonate Hill was dotted even more thickly with mine and smelter structures. Past Carbonate Hill, Iron Hill jutted in dark profile, and beyond them, the conical tip of Fryer Hill rose above both. The railroad spur that ran around the flanks of Carbonate and Iron Hills, halfway up the side of California Gulch, showed as a narrow streak, bright as the silver hauled over it by the trains that ran from the smelters.

One short street jutted like a finger from the town before it turned into a winding road that looped along Carbonate Hill, dodging smelter furnaces and minehead shacks in a torturous maze of curves from which short extensions led to the buildings the main road bypassed. The road was deserted; there would be little surface activity on Carbonate Hill, or at any of the other diggings, until the shifts changed. Both miners and smelter workers put in a twelve-hour shift; the day and night shifts changed at six o'clock in the morning and evening. In the minehead shacks, one man stood by the hoists. In the smelters, the men stayed around the furnaces except for the slag car crews who trundled the red-hot smelter wastes in deep-bellied cars that ran on narrow, temporary tracks to the dumps.

In that bare landscape, a moving man stood out, especially a man running. Even though the distance was too great for Longarm to see his features, the one man running along the road that zigzagged across the side of Carbonate Hill could only be Hi Jenks. While Longarm watched him, Jenks left the road and started down the slope at an oblique angle in the direction of the railroad tracks.

Longarm's bootheels clattered on the narrow wooden stairs as he dashed down them to the ground and ran after the fleeing killer.

Though the perennial twilight that passed for darkness in Leadville had made it possible for Longarm to locate the running figure of Jenks and start chasing him, the absence of darkness made pursuit more difficult. Normally, Longarm would have noted Jenks's location and the direction he was taking, and would then have headed straight for the place where he'd last seen the fugitive, and taken up his trail from there. Leadville's bright nights made that course of action impractical. Long before he could get close to Jenks, the gunman would see him following.

While watching from above, Longarm had gotten a clear view of the area toward which Jenks was heading. To judge by the angle the gunman had taken in his flight after leaving the road, Longarm felt sure he was heading for the railroad spur. Jenks had gotten the same view of the terrain that Longarm had seen from the stair landing, and to the fleeing man, the railroad must have seemed his best chance for a safe, quick escape. More than a few outlaws, running ahead of their pursuers, had managed to find and follow a railroad track, hop aboard a train, and outdistance those who were chasing them on foot.

Longarm had gotten only a short look at the slopes west of Leadville, but even that quick glimpse had left most of the landmarks imprinted on his trained memory. He ran out to the end of the street and followed the road for a short distance, then cut south, taking a course that would enable him to intercept Jenks before the outlaw reached the railroad line.

Along the tracks on both sides, the minehead shacks and smelter furnaces were thicker than elsewhere on the hill. It occurred to Longarm as he jogged along that the very density of the structures might have drawn Jenks in that direction as much as the railroad. Along the tracks, he'd have more cover than higher on the hillside, where there were fewer buildings, spaced farther apart.

Jenks had a head start of between five and ten minutes, and Longarm had not seen him since he'd run down the stairs from the second floor landing. Then, Jenks had just turned off the road and begun to work downslope. Longarm reached the first of the minehead shacks and stopped to look around. The square, squat buildings looked as though most of them had been built from the same raw lumber and the same set of plans.

Many of them were windowless; none were more than four walls, with a peaked roof just high enough to clear the big wheel of the hoist. They stood in no apparent order, one on each claim. The state's mining laws limited mountainside claims to an area one hundred feet long by fifty feet wide, and though many claims had been consolidated and others abandoned, there were still enough minehead shacks standing close enough together to limit Longarm's vision.

There were far fewer smelters, and most of those dotting Carbonate Hill were old and small, built during the first days of the Leadville boom. The biggest smelters had not been built until later, after Eastern capitalists had verified that the black deposits, which, when melted down into dirty brown carbonate-yielding silver, had enough of the metal to justify their investments. The Carbonate Hill smelters, and those on Iron Hill just to the east, were for the most part one or two stackers, but the fires in their open furnaces combined and merged to turn night into semitwilight on the two hillsides, and to load the air with drifting, sulfur-filled fumes.

Longarm strained his eyes, looking between the buildings, always finding the clear spaces that separated two of the shacks closed by another one- or two- that stood farther away. Between the structures—minehead shacks and smelters—the earth was scarred and gouged and raw, dotted with old slag heaps. Here and there, their plumes of smoke rose beside smelters that still dumped their slag beside their furnaces, and everywhere the dirt was piled in windrowed lines or in humped hillocks; this was the debris removed when the surface soil was stripped away to uncover the ore below it.

It had been this way since the first gold-seekers had passed. They'd found no gold for all their digging and gouging, and neither knew nor perhaps cared that the ugly black dirt they uncovered and spurned as worthless contained silver in deposits of a richness beyond their most fevered dreams of wealth. Following the gold-seekers, the silver miners had completed the gouging, and the fuel-hungry smelters had devoured such trees as had survived the digging. The land Longarm scanned as he looked for the running fugitive might have been the surface of the moon, or of a planet to which men had come, stayed long enough to throw up crude buildings and strip the soil of vegetation, and then departed.

Across such a barren landscape, no man could move far without being seen. Longarm saw Jenks as the gunman dodged between two minehead shacks. The outlaw was still moving downslope, as nearly as Longarm could tell during the brief glimpse he'd gotten when Jenks crossed the opening between the two buildings and vanished behind one of them. Even that brief sighting was enough, though, to assure Longarm that the running man he'd seen from the stairs of the Clarendon Hotel was the one he was after. He took a fresh breath and started again, working his own way between the minehead shacks, at an angle that should let him intercept his quarry before the fugitive reached the railroad tracks.

Hi Jenks had apparently seen Longarm, too. His first warning that he'd been spotted came within minutes. He stepped from behind a shack, and a bullet slammed into the dirt in front of him, sending up a small geyser of earth close enough to dust the toes of his boots. At the same time that he saw the spurt of dirt, Longarm heard the shot. He dodged back behind the shack and dropped to his knees before sweeping his hat off his head and peering cautiously around the corner of the structure. Jenks's near miss was, he knew instantly, an accident of trajectory; the gunman had misjudged the slant of the hillside when he snapshotted, and the bullet had dropped too low.

Besides, Longarm thought as he risked exposing himself for another quick peek around the building, *the damned fool ought to know he's out of handgun range. He'd be better off saving his shells instead of wasting them, but every shot he wastes tilts the odds my way a little more. He had ten cartridges in that belt, and used one on Purvis. Now he's only got eight chances. And now I've got him spotted, and I know which way he's headed.*

Longarm's quick look showed nothing, but drew no fire from Jenks. Either the gunman hadn't been looking when Longarm exposed his head, or had already moved on. Longarm decided to gamble on Jenks's having moved. In the outlaw's place, he'd have been running again the instant he'd seen that his shot had missed.

Trying to get in front of Jenks and cut him off, Longarm made a quick run in the direction he judged was about parallel to that being taken by the gunfighter. Holding to a straight line was hard to do when dodging between buildings that stood hit-or-miss on the claims, no two of them squared at the same angle.

Ahead of him, Longarm saw a small smelter, a onestacker. It covered two or three times as much area as one of the shacks, and had a cleared space around it where old, hardened slag thrust jagged chunks up from the earth. He stopped behind a shack at the edge of the cleared ground, and set himself to wait and watch.

Minutes ticked past, and Jenks did not show. Longarm began to get edgy. For all he knew, Jenks might be circling around to take him from behind, or he could be holed up, as was Longarm himself, waiting for a movement that would expose a target.

Longarm tried to put himself in Jenks's place and figure out what he'd do if he were running over an area strange to him, trying to reach the only familiar feature that promised an easy escape, such as a railroad line.

Damned if I'd wait around for whoever's after me. Wait long enough to make one try at stopping them, maybe. But not any longer. Was it me hightailing, I'd keep on moving and let whoever was chasing me catch up, if they could.

He took up the chase again. On the off-chance that Jenks might be holed up at the edge of the cleared space around the smelter. Longarm crossed the bare ground at a dead run, keeping his ass down and zigzagging until he reached the nearest minehead shack beyond the smelter. During his dash across the clearing, he drew no shots. He did not linger behind the shack, but kept going, trying to keep to the line he'd set for himself.

Concentrating on keeping moving in his chosen direction, Longarm dodged in and out between the shacks. He'd just left the cover of one and was making for the next one ahead of him when, out of the corner of his eye, he saw movement. He was in mid-stride when the flicker caught his eye, a dozen yards distant, between two shacks.

A shot sounded as Longarm stopped quickly and turned, drawing. Jenks stood in a narrow clear space not more than a dozen yards distant. Longarm snapshotted just as Jenks dove for cover. His shot shaved the outlaw's bootheels as Jenks disappeared.

Longarm ran toward the shack that now sheltered Jenks. He saw the muzzle of the outlaw's pistol moving from behind the corner of the shack. Jenks was cagy. He thrust the gun in front of him, exposing a cheek and one eye in a flash as he tried to spot Longarm. His movement was too fast even for Longarm's cat-quick reflexes. Longarm's slug, which would have caught Jenks between the eyes if the outlaw had shown his full face, whistled harmlessly past the corner of the shack.

Jenks returned Longarm's shot, but by the time the gunman fired, Longarm had hit the ground and was rolling to the cover of the shack he'd just left. The lead from the Smith & Wesson cut through empty air above Longarm's moving body, and he was behind the mine building before Jenks could trigger a second shot.

Longarm changed tactics. He reversed directions, weaving in and out between the shacks, circling around the bare area that surrounded the smelter, until the long, sheet-metal building that housed the four furnaces was between him and Jenks. Then, with the outlaw's line of sight blocked by the smelter, Longarm ran in the straightest possible line to the last shack at the edge of the smelter area. It stood only a score of feet from the cut through which the railroad tracks ran.

Shielded by the shack, Longarm watched the clear space between the smelter and the tracks. He reloaded his Colt by touch while he waited for Jenks to show himself again.

For several minutes, Jenks did not reappear. When Longarm saw him next, the gunman had worked his way around the half-circle of the clear land surrounding the smelter, and was ducking behind a shack at its edge. Like the buildings behind which Longarm waited, the one Jenks had chosen was the last shelter between the diggings and smelters and the railroad cut.

Longarm wished for his Winchester, standing in a corner of his bedroom at the Tabor mansion. The rifle's greater range and muzzle velocity would have sent slugs tearing through the raw planks of the building behind which Jenks had taken cover. With the rifle, the gunman could have been forced from cover; the Colt did not have the long-range accuracy to do the job.

Looks like I got to close in on him, Longarm told himself.

He looked for cover along the railroad bank, but there was none. The only outside possibility was the dead-end, a stack of railroad ties with a mound of dirt heaped up behind them, which stopped the slag cars when they were shoved down the slope to dump their loads of molten slag into a gondola car on the siding below the high embankment.

If I don't move, Jenks will, Longarm thought. *And he knows he's down to six shells now.*

Longarm took a calculated risk. He broke cover in a running zigzag, great strides of his pumping legs driving him over the hard ground toward the dead-end. Just as he started his run, he heard the distant whistle of a train.

Jenks was smart enough to wait until Longarm had covered half the distance to the dead-end. Then he fired, an aimed shot this time. His round plucked at Longarm's coat and ripped through its fabric, but did not touch flesh. Longarm dove and rolled again. Jenks made another try, but he was anxious after his aimed shot had missed, and his snapshotted slug was wild by a foot.

Longarm reached the dead-end and crouched behind it. He knew Jenks had only four shells left, and could not afford to waste them on long-range, random sniping. The dead-end was closer to the shack sheltering the outlaw, but not close enough for pinpoint shooting with a handgun. Longarm raised himself up and let off a shot; Jenks saw his movement in time to fall back behind the shack where he'd taken cover. Longarm heard his bullet rip into the wood of the shack's walls. The train's whistle sounded again—a long, mournful blast, closer than before.

Longarm sensed that his chase was drawing to an end. He opened the Colt's loading gate and took out the single empty shell the cylinder contained. From his coat pocket he took a fresh shell and inserted it, then added another to fill the empty chamber on which the hammer normally rested.

Once more, the locomotive's whistle cut the air, and Longarm leaned out over the embankment. Fifteen feet below him, the rails were beginning to sing. Up the cut, from the direction of Iron Hill, he could see the puffs of smoke as the train entered the long curve around the slope of Carbonate Hill.

Longarm was ready when the first gondola cars came into sight. Smoke from their cargo of molten slag from the smelters on Iron Hill and Fryers Hill rose in wisps above the open cars. Crouched behind the low embankment, Longarm scuffed the hard earth under his bootsoles to insure a firm footing when Jenks broke cover. The train ground closer.

When the first gondola car came abreast of the shack behind which Jenks was sheltered, Longarm stood up. Jenks would be running when he emerged, and shots taken on the run go wild more often than they connect.

Jenks took Longarm's implied challenge. He broke cover shooting. Longarm stood without flinching as Jenk's first shot plunked into the dead-end. The outlaw was running at full speed for the railroad cut. Longarm fired, and Jenks faltered, but did not stop. Twenty feet separated him from the edge of the embankment. He fired as soon as he'd recovered his stride. The slug grazed Longarm's thigh.

Longarm winced as the hot lead seared his skin, but he held his sights firmly on Jenks. He aimed as calmly as though he was shooting vermin. The heavy slug took Jenks squarely. Longarm saw the outlaw stumble and almost go down, but Jenks refused to fall. His legs kept pumping until he reached the edge of the embankment.

Just as he mustered a final burst of strength and launched himself in a jump designed to put him in one of the gondola cars rolling slowly below him, Longarm fired again.

Jenks was in midair when Longarm's bullet caught him. His body doubled up as he fell. Longarm could not tell whether the gunman was alive or dead when he landed on the load of molten slag the gondola carried.

Whether he was alive or not, Jenks died the instant his body touched the searingly hot slag. His clothing smoked for a fraction of a second before bursting into a flicker of flame which outlined the outlaw's sprawled body. Then the intense heat began to calcine flesh and bone. The process took so little time that when the car passed below him, Longarm, looking down, could see only a flaming lump of charcoal where Jenks had lain. Before the gondola car was out of sight, the charcoal had burned away to fine, white powder that rose into the air on the updraft from the hot slag.

Longarm waited until the engine pushing the train passed; it was a short, easy leap down to the top of the cab. He swung into the cab as the engineer was reaching for the brake lever with one hand and easing off the throttle with the other.

"Didn't I see a man fall or jump on one of those slag cars?" the engineer asked Longarm.

"You did. But there's no need to stop. He's fried away by now. He was likely dead before he hit anyhow," Longarm replied.

"I've got to stop and put you off, just the same," the engineer said. "No unauthorized passengers on work trains, mister."

Longarm took out his wallet and opened it to show his badge. "Is this good enough to authorize me?"

"Well—" the engineer studied the badge— "U.S. marshal? I guess it does. Now what about that fellow who fell in that gondola?"

"Nothing you can do for him, is there?" Longarm asked.

"No. But the rule book says—"

"I know what it says," Longarm interrupted. "The fellow you saw just fried a little quicker than he would have if he'd been sent to hell by the hangman. I'd advise you to forget you saw him."

For a moment, the engineer seemed inclined to argue, but after a second look at Longarm's stern face, he said, "That's good advice, Marshal. I'll take it."

From the railroad yards, Longarm walked the short distance to Mart Duggan's office. Duggan was awake this time.

"Where the hell have you been?" he asked. "I looked for you at my holdover, but you and Jenks were both gone. I've had my men looking all over town for him. From the description I got from the night clerk at the Clarendon, Jenks is the man we want for killing Senator Purvis."

"It won't do you much good to want him," Longarm said "Hi Jenks is dead."

"You killed him?"

"I ain't right sure. He had a couple of my slugs in him, but they might not have done the job."

Duggan's bewilderment showed on his face. "Say that again, will you? Either you left out something or I'm losing my hearing."

"Jenks fell on a load of hot slag and sort of melted down. You don't have to worry about burying him."

For a moment, Duggan sat in silent thought. Then he said, "You know, Longarm, if you weren't carrying your badge, I just might have to arrest you on a charge of incitement to commit murder. You're not the man to let a prisoner like Jenks get away from you, not unless it suits some scheme you've hatched up."

"Don't figure on charging me with anything you can't prove, Mart," Longarm said with a grim smile. "Hi Jenks killed Purvis. Just let it rest at that. Now, I'm a little bit frazzled at the edges, after tramping over half of Carbonate Hill. I'll be dropping in again before I go back to Denver."

Longarm was tempted to stop at the first saloon he passed, but he knew he'd get a better grade of Maryland rye when he got to where he was going.

Vivian opened the door before he could knock. She threw her arms around him and buried her face in his chest.

"I saw you coming across the street," she said. "I've been watching for you—well, for hours and hours. I've been so worried and upset that I couldn't rest or go to sleep."

"There's not any need to be upset now," Longarm told her. He touched the red lump that still showed on her forehead. "That'll go away, too. Just like Purvis has."

"Wilkes has gone? Where?"

"To wherever Hi Jenks's bullet sent him. I'd say that's most likely to hell."

"You mean he's dead?"

"Him and Jenks both. Jenks got real mad at Purvis when I told him how Purvis had double-crossed him. So he busted away from me and shot Purvis. A while later, I caught up with Jenks."

"And killed him?"

"There wasn't any way I could take him alive."

Vivian stood back at arm's length and stared at Longarm. "You mean all that has happened since you left here? Nine or ten hours? My God, Longarm, you must be exhausted! And here I am, keeping you standing in the hall!" She took his hand and led him into the living room. "You sit down right now, and I'll pour you a drink."

While she poured Maryland rye into a glass, a puzzled frown formed on her face. She took the glass of whiskey to Longarm, and sat on the sofa beside him.

Longarm was lighting a cheroot. He took the whiskey and sipped it, smiling when its smooth bite trickled over his tongue.

Vivian said hesitantly, "Longarm, you told me when you left that you were going to meet a train. That was the one the killer Wilkes Purvis was looking for came in on, wasn't it?"

"Sure. That's why I met it."

"And you said the gunman killed Wilkes." Her frown deepened. "Then, just a minute ago, you said the killer found out that Wilkes had double-crossed him, and that's why he killed Wilkes. But you were after Wilkes because he was trying to assassinate General Grant."

"Only Jenks got loose and got to Purvis first," Longarm said.

Vivian nodded slowly. "I think I understand. It wouldn't have looked good for a deputy U.S. marshal to shoot a member of the territorial senate. And you didn't really have any evidence to bring Wilkes Purvis to trial on, did you?"

Longarm took another leisurely sip of the rye before he answered her: "Now, Vivian, the best thing you can do is just put all that trouble you had with Purvis out of your head. It's all over and done with. He won't bother you again." Longarm puffed his cheroot and, through the smoke, said, "Nor the general, either. But that's past, and there ain't any use in fretting over something that's finished." He held out his glass. "Now why don't you pour me another swallow? And I don't want to go waking up everybody at Tabor's house, coming in at this time of morning. But I do feel like I'd enjoy a nice bath, if the water's hot."

Ulysses S. Grant, ex-president and general of the army, stood on the observation platform of Silver Dollar Tabor's private railroad car and waved to the crowd that had assembled in the Denver depot to see him off on his return to Washington. He'd just shaken hands for the last time with his host and hostess, and the Limited was almost ready to pull out. Looking down, Grant saw Longarm standing beside Billy Vail in the front row of the crowd. He motioned for Longarm to come closer.

Longarm stepped up to the observation platform. Grant leaned over the polished brass railing and extended his hand. Longarm reached up and shook it.

Grant said, "Longarm, I may never see you again, unless you come East. If you do, drop in at my place on Long Island. Anybody can tell you where it is. I'll promise you a ride behind a horse that's at least as good as Sovereign. And thank you for making my visit here safe."

"I just did my job, General," Longarm replied. "But it's nice of you to invite me. Maybe I'll take you up on it someday."

With a final warning toot, the Limited began to inch forward. Longarm stepped back, and Grant continued waving to the crowd until the train was out of sight.

"Well," Billy Vail said, "you've spent some time in the gilded halls of the richest man in Colorado now, hobnobbing with one of the most famous men in America." When Longarm didn't answer, Vail went on, "How'd you enjoy living like a millionaire, eating all that fancy, rich food and guzzling the best liquor, in a big mansion with servants to jump any time you call froggie?"

Longarm took the time to light a fresh cheroot before replying.

"I tell you, Billy," he said slowly, "I guess it's fine for those who like it. But I figure I can get along pretty good as long as I get a shot of Maryland rye now and again, and have a plate of steak and potatoes for supper, and go home to a place I don't rattle around in." He puffed at the cigar and blew out a cloud of fragrant blue smoke. "And I'll tell you something else. Now that I've seen them up close, what you call those 'gilded halls' ain't such a much as you might think they'd be."

SPECIAL PREVIEW

Here are the opening scenes
from

LONGARM ON THE DEVIL'S TRAIL

fifteenth novel in the bold new
LONGARM series from Jove

Chapter 1

Longarm was feeling wary. He was not lost in the wilds of some bleak canyon or fleeing before the guns of outraged outlaws he had come upon too quickly. Instead, he was deep within the carpeted, oak-paneled reaches of the Windsor Hotel, Denver's finest, sitting at a small table, enjoying a friendly, though expensive, game of draw poker.

He was wary because of the hand he had just been dealt. It was not the poverty of his cards, but his feeling that this hand was the result not of luck, but of pure and calculated design. He had been winning steadily but modestly up until this moment, and as a result, the game had seemed eminently agreeable to him, a welcome respite while he waited for more exciting employment from his chief, Marshal Billy Vail.

A pair of tens, the rest garbage of varying suits, stared up at him from his hand. As the betting continued, Longarm shrugged, pushed his coins forward to stay in, discarded, and asked the dealer for three cards. They were dealt to him neatly, expertly, the fingers moving with a speed that defied the eyes, even eyes that were as sharp as Longarm's.

Longarm realized suddenly that he was in the hands of a real professional. Only it was not Longarm the dealer was after. He was certain of that as he saw the growing delight mirrored in the face of the player to his right, a young man from the East who had shown himself throughout the evening to be an inconsiderate, blustering rake with more money than sense.

He had attached himself to Longarm at the bar. His name was Charles Richter, and he had insisted on relating to Longarm, over and over, the reason for his trek West: he was going to claim his inheritance, a gold-filled valley somewhere in the Arizona Territory. It was a wild tale, obviously fueled by the copious amounts of bourbon the fellow consumed, and the only thing that saved the evening for Longarm was the presence of the wastrel's "sister," as the young man called her. He had done so with a broad, completely unnecessary wink, since it was obvious to Longarm and anyone who saw them together for any length of time that their relationship was anything but familial.

Her name was Lydia, and she sat now in the corner, a drink she had been nursing the entire evening in her hand, waiting for Charles to leave the game and retire with her. They were an impressive-looking pair. Charles was handsome. A pencil-thin mustache graced his pale, ascetic face. His cheekbones were pronounced, his chin square, his eyes cold and calculating. It was his mouth that betrayed him. It was in turn weak, sullen, gleeful—a perfect barometer of his shallow moods.

Lydia, almost as tall as Longarm, was tightly bound in a long, wasp-waisted maroon dress that revealed a figure already ripe. Lace at her long throat and her cuffs only accentuated the fine, long-limbed beauty she possessed. Her mouth was passionate, her lustrous green eyes hypnotic in their intensity. Her auburn hair was just barely proper as it hung in tight ringlets almost to her shoulders.

She was of that universal type that was always attracted to men of wealth and breeding, as moths are attracted to a flame. Only somehow, Longarm detected something more substantial in this woman.

The cards the dealer had just dealt him after his discard were no better than those he had discarded. With a sigh, he dropped his hand facedown on the table and leaned back to watch, puffing contentedly on his cheroot. He had smoked too many of these this evening, and had had too many glasses of rye, but he was bored—for Longarm, an unusual condition.

The old gentleman across the table from Longarm followed his example, and that left only Charles Richter and the dealer still playing. The dealer was a stranger to Longarm, a man who had only recently checked into the Windsor. He was graying about the temples, and had a slack face with watery, imprecise eyes. Throughout the game, he had been a jolly fellow, losing almost contentedly as he regaled his fellow players with accounts of his early years on the Mississippi. He had been a steamboat deckhand, as he told it.

Longarm watched him raise Charles; the dealer's eyes were suddenly gleaming, and Longarm realized at once that the fellow—his name was Rufus Willoughby—had been on the Mississippi, all right—but not as a deckhand. Longarm was convinced he was watching a riverboat gambler working on dry land.

The size of the pot was suddenly quieting the room. Longarm saw two players at another table get up and come over to watch. Charles Richter, obviously certain he had an unbeatable hand, was raising insistently, unwilling to allow his opponent to call him.

"Now listen, young man," Willoughby drawled softly, his accent recalling the slower pace of an earlier South, "I presume you have a fine hand there, but I caution you that I have excellent cards myself."

The warning was calculated to make the young man even bolder, and it worked. He smiled, reached into his vest pocket, and pulled out a large, crammed billfold. Counting swiftly, he met the other's bet of nine hundred dollars, then upped him another thousand. Lydia got up from her seat and, with a slight frown on her patrician face, approached the table.

"Charlie?" she asked softly, "Are you sure? . . . "

"Shut up," Charlie snapped, without looking at her. "I've got into a square game at last! A good player always wins in a fair game!"

"Why, that's certainly true," said Willoughby, reaching for his own billfold. "And since we're two honest men and this game is as honest as a schoolmarm, I'll just match your bet—" He started counting out neat, crisp bills, "—and raise you another thousand."

By then, this was the only game in progress. The table was ringed with spectators. A collective gasp went up as Willoughby starting counting out the thousand. Glancing up at Lydia, Longarm saw that the girl's face was as white as the lace at her throat. Tiny beads of perspiration were standing out on her brow.

"Charlie!" she said, leaning closer. "This is all we've got!"

"Not for long," he chuckled happily, obviously convinced that he had his opponent just where he wanted him. "Now stand back, woman, and let a real cardplayer show you how it's done." He regarded Willoughby with mocking eyes. "Another thousand, you say? I'll match that—and then some!"

Charlie's billfold was noticeably slimmer now, but he began counting out the thousand with almost indecent eagerness. Longarm glanced back up at the woman, and saw that her dismay had turned to fury. She straightened as Charlie counted out his remaining bills, then turned and stalked from the room. Charlie paid no attention as he gathered together the money and pushed it forward into the pot.

"Table stakes, I believe," he announced.

"Yes, indeed," Willoughby said amiably, "table stakes it is. But I think I will be just able to match you. If, that is," he added, pausing dramatically, "you will allow me to include this excellent watch and these gold cufflinks, in order for me to make the final hundred dollars."

Aware that he had stripped the man completely, that there was no more milk in the cow, Charles nodded courteously—and just for a moment, Longarm wondered if perhaps it was the younger man who was the professional gambler. Surely, no one could be this certain he had won in a game of poker he was playing with a perfect stranger. Then he remembered the fellow's confident assertion that he had finally found a square game.

The cufflinks and the watch joined the pile of treasure—a glittering mound of gold and silver coins, chips, and crisp bills. "Looks like I'm calling you, young man," Willoughby said, his tone of voice almost gentle.

A triumphant smile on his features, young Richter spread four kings and a joker in front of him. A gasp went up from the spectators; it had already been established that the joker—the imperial trump—was wild. But what everyone except Richter realized was that its resemblance to the ace of spades had misled the man. He did not have the fourth ace, as he mistakenly thought. They were still out. Silently, all heads turned to Willoughby.

The man spread his hand out before them. Sure enough, there were the four aces. A groan broke from the mouth of Charles Richter. He had been in the act of coiling his arm around the sparkling treasure. Leaning forward swiftly, he peered at Willoughby's discarded hand. Then he reached back to his own exposed cards and lifted the treacherous joker—the counterfeit ace. He slapped it back down onto the table.

"My God," he groaned, pulling his arm back from the pot.

"Sorry," said Willoughby, his drawl quietly resonant in the hushed room. Without any particular eagerness, he slowly, carefully drew in his winnings. Seemingly without regard for those still encircling the table, he began to stack the chips and coins neatly to one side.

His jaw slack, his mouth downcast, Charlie watched Willoughby. Longarm saw the young man's mouth tremble. He thought the fellow was going to burst into tears. But Richter managed to get a grip on himself. He looked away and rose to his feet, moving like an old man. As Longarm followed his progress, it seemed to the lawman that Charlie Richter had balls of lead chained to his feet.

He was obviously in no hurry to face Lydia.

"If you don't mind," said Willoughby, addressing

Longarm, "I believe I'll just call it a night. It *is* rather late, and I had not intended to stay up this long."

Longarm smiled warmly at the man. "At your age, you need your sleep, is that it?"

"Indeed, sir, you struck the nail right on its head," Willoughby responded, obviously determined to take no offense. "And now, gentlemen," he said to those still clustering about the table, "if you'll let me by."

Hastily, the awed spectators backed up to make way for Willoughby. He moved past them with his frock coat's pockets bulging with coins, his billfold too thick with bills to fold, forcing him to hold it in his right hand. He might have been tired, but he sure as hell moved energetically enough. Longarm reflected that money has a way of invigorating a man.

Longarm got up and stretched his long frame. He had played in shirtsleeves and vest, his brown tweed frock coat and snuff-brown Stetson hung on a coat tree in the corner. He strode across the room, slipped into his coat, and placed the Stetson carefully on his head, positioning it dead center and tilted slightly forward, cavalry-style. The hat's crown was telescoped in the Colorado rider's fashion. For Longarm, however, it was simply a legacy from his youth, when he had lit out to ride in the War. Whether he rode for the North or for the South, he tended to disremember. It never did pay a man to talk too much about his past this far West, anyway.

Clamping his teeth down on his cheroot, Longarm left the small, semiprivate gambling parlor and threaded his way along the thickly carpeted halls until he came out into the main saloon, where he had left his crossdraw rig and Colt. He had considered the double-barreled .44 derringer riding in the right-hand pocket of his vest sufficient insurance in case of trouble; the derringer was clipped to a gold-washed chain attached to the Ingersoll watch riding in his lefthand pocket.

Longarm asked the barkeep for his rig. The man knew Longarm and his gunbelt well. Longarm took it and, slipping quickly out of his coat, casually belted the supple cordovan leather belt around his waist, adjusting it to ride just above his hipbones. The waxed and heat-hardened holster held a double-action Colt Model T .44-40, with a five-inch barrel and the front sight filed off. Its solid heft comforted him as he shrugged back into his coat, nodded to the barkeep, and left to find the desk clerk.

"Why, yes, Mr. Long," the bespectacled desk clerk replied cheerfully to Longarm's pleasant inquiry, "I do believe I remember that gentleman. Mr. Willoughby *is* a real gentleman, I might add. He's a great favorite with the bellhops."

"Generous, is he?"

"Most decidedly so."

"How long has he been staying here?"

"Almost a week now."

"I think he might be expecting me for a drink in his room about now. Did you see him go up recently?"

"As a matter of fact, I did."

Longarm smiled. "He forgot to tell me his room."

"Room 409."

Longarm smiled a second time. "And the Richters, Charles and Lydia. They were supposed to join us later. I disremember their room numbers, as well."

"The Richters?" He frowned, then brightened. "Oh, yes! That fine couple! That would be room 506, Mr. Long."

Longarm thanked the desk clerk, left him, and started up the broad, carpeted stairs.

A moment later, Longarm rapped softly on Rufus Willoughby's door. The sound of purposeful activity coming from the other side of the door halted abruptly. Longarm could almost see the fellow pausing in sudden alarm. After all, who could be knocking on his door at this hour—if not the distraught young worthy he had just fleeced?

"Who is it?" Willoughby called warily.

"Why, it's just old Custis Long, friend. You remember me."

There was a significant pause. Willoughby was obviously trying to decide whether he had any reason for being wary of Custis Long. Apparently, he concluded that he had not, and approached the door with confident, unhurried steps.

When he pulled the door open, he found himself staring into the bore of Longarm's .44.

The man backed hastily into his suite, both hands held prudently over his head. Longarm followed him inside, kicked the door shut behind him, and smiled. Willoughby had been in the act of packing when Longarm had knocked. Two valises were sitting on the bed's coverlet; one was already packed and buckled shut. The man was obviously satisfied with his take this evening, and had decided to seek newer, perhaps even greener, pastures.

"You can put your hands down, Willoughby."

The man did as Longarm suggested. "I would never have taken you for a footpad, Long."

"And I never would have figured *you* for a professional gambler, until I began noticing a few things."

"A few things?" Willoughby backed up until he was sitting on the edge of his bed.

"I admit it was the last thing I was looking for—until the end there, when you suckered young Richter. It was purely a thing of beauty, the way you handled those cards. And then those fingers of yours."

The man glanced quickly down at his hands, then back up at Longarm.

"They're uncalloused, softer than a woman's," Longarm told him.

The man's shoulders slumped. "Go ahead," he said. "Rob me of my winnings. But I warn you, as soon as you leave this suite, I'll call the local constabulary. You're well-known in this town. They'll have you good and proper, and I *will* press charges. After all, you have no real proof that I cheated. Soft hands and dexterity with cards are hardly evidence enough."

Longarm took out his wallet and showed Willoughby his badge. The man paled, but remained unyielding. "You have no proof, Marshal. And you *are* in my room without a warrant."

"Now that has me real worried, Willoughby," Longarm said, walking over to the bed and reaching out for the valise the gambler had already packed.

"The money's over there!" Willoughby cried quickly, pointing to the top of the dresser. "There's no sense in unpacking that suitcase."

"Get things all messed up again, wouldn't it?" Longarm agreed reasonably.

Willoughby took a deep breath and nodded. "Yes." He took out a handkerchief and mopped his brow. "It would."

"Too bad," Longarm said, holstering his Colt and unstrapping the valise.

When he threw back the cover, he found what he was after at once. It was sitting on top of a neatly folded vest. Smiling at Willoughby, Longarm pulled forth the object.

"No proof, Willoughby? What would you call this ingenious device? I've got to give you credit, though, you didn't overuse it."

"Never do," the gambler replied glumly. "I never use the machine too much. Even in a big game, three or four times in a night are enough. I wasn't even going to use it tonight, but that kid was so green." He shrugged unhappily.

The "machine" Willoughby referred to was a sleeve holdout. Longarm examined it carefully. A metal clamp fastened to a scissor-extension was in turn attached to a half-collar that was capable of being buckled to Willoughby's arm. This was not the first holdout Longarm had examined, and he knew how it worked. All the gambler had to do was bend his elbow and the needed card would be extended into his palm. When his arm was straightened, the device retracted the clamp holding the card.

"You going to confiscate that?" Willoughby asked. He seemed a mite desperate. What Longarm held in his hand was, after all, his source of livelihood.

"Well, I was just giving that some thought."

With a snarl, the gambler dug swiftly into his belt and pulled out another machine, somewhat more lethal than the one Longarm was holding in his hand. It was a mean-looking belly gun, a sawed-off .44 caliber Remington revolver. Longarm did not hesitate; he swiped at Willoughby's gun with the holdout. The scissor-spring caught the hammer of the belly gun and ripped it from the gambler's hand.

As the gun thumped to the floor, Willoughby lunged. Longarm waited almost casually, parried the man's first clumsy right cross with his forearm, then stepped in close and hit him with his open palm across the mouth. It staggered Willoughby, but he seemed about to charge again, so Longarm stepped closer and slapped the man a second time, harder. Willoughby's head snapped around. Holding his cheek, he sank, utterly defeated, to the floor.

Longarm picked up the belly gun and tossed it onto the coverlet.

"Come on," he said to Willoughby. "You're going to give that money back to Richter."

"It isn't all his," the gambler said, looking up at Longarm in astonishment.

"I know that. But I know the fellow who sat opposite me, and I know how much I lost. And I am sure Richter knows how much you took from him. Let's go."

"You're not going to turn me in?" There was a flicking of hope in the man's eyes.

"You return that money first off, then take yourself and that machine of yours out of Denver on the first train. I don't care if it's going north, south, east, or west. You hear me?"

The fellow scrambled to his feet. His cheeks were swollen slightly, but he was recovering from his ill-usage with remarkable speed. "Yes, sir, Mr. Long. I hear you!"

Longarm was standing in the lobby about a half-hour later, watching Rufus Willoughby leave the hotel, when he was aware of a warm presence moving up behind him. From the perfume she wore, he knew who it was. Turning, he found Lydia's face inches from his own.

"I was hoping you'd still be here," she said, smiling. "I wanted to thank you personally."

"Charles already thanked me, Lydia. No need for you to put yourself out."

"I know. But *I* wanted to thank you. Do you realize that those losses in that poker game had left us—my brother and me—destitute?"

"I suspicioned as much. From your attitude during the game, I figured you'd be in some trouble if your brother lost what he had. If you'll excuse me for being blunt, he's playing the fool and you better watch him real carefully."

"I know, Mr. Long. That's why I wanted to thank you . . . to *really* thank you."

"Miss Lydia," Longarm said, taking her gently by the elbow and escorting her toward the stairway. "You ain't really Charles's sister, are you?"

She blushed. "Why, of course! Whatever do you mean?"

Then she saw the slight smile on Longarm's face and took a deep breath.

"All right," she said resignedly. "We are not brother and sister, Charles and I. But we do plan to get married, just as soon as this inheritance of his is settled. We thought it would cause less of a stir if we traveled together as brother and sister."

They moved over to an upholstered sofa against one wall and sat down. "Inheritance?" Longarm asked.

"A valley, Mr. Long! I've been there! I've seen it. And there's treasure, a whole roomful of it. It reminded me of that story of Hawthorne's, where king Midas visits his gold-filled storeroom."

"And this, you say, is Charlie's inheritance?"

"I know it sounds like—like something out of *The Arabian Nights,* Mr. Long, but there really is such a place."

"And where is it?"

"In Arizona Territory, near the Superstition Mountains. The Indians own the valley now, but it really belongs to Charles."

"That's hard to believe, ma'am."

She frowned. "I know it is, but it's true. And Charlie has powerful friends. His claim has already been examined, and it's all legal and proper." She smiled suddenly, and moved herself closer to Longarm. "But that's not why I came downstairs to find you. My God, Mr. Long, do you know what a delight it is for me to sit next to a real *man* for a change? I was watching you all during the game! Why do you think I stayed in that close, fetid room for so long, sipping on that poisonous drink?"

Longarm smiled and got up, pulling Lydia gently to her feet also. The lobby was deserted except for a few dozing bellboys. The desk clerk was in his office. Longarm drew Lydia gently toward him, kissed her fully on the lips, and let his lips move back along the line of her jaw. Then he kissed the softness under her ear, after which he moved back and kissed her again on the lips.

When he released her, she was standing with her eyes nearly shut, her face flushed. "Please," she said, opening her eyes and smiling. "Let's hurry. You must have a place!"

Longarm shook his head. "No, Lydia. You belong with Charles, and with all that money and land. You can have all the baubles that a woman like you craves. I'm just a policeman." He slapped her playfully on the backside and led her gently toward the stairway. "Don't tempt me—or I'll give you a *real* spanking."

"I wish you would!" she cried fiercely, her eyes looking at him pleadingly. "Oh, Custis, I wish you would!"

Longarm laughed. "Upstairs now, Lydia."

She saw that it was useless for her to plead, that his kiss was all she was going to get. She smiled suddenly, and it was dazzling. "Perhaps we will meet again—under different circumstances."

"Maybe. I certainly hope so, Lydia."

She looked at him for a long moment, as if she were storing in her mind's eye everything about him she favored. Then, with a brief smile, she turned and moved with exquisite grace across the lobby and up the stairs.